THE CINNAMON COLT
AND OTHER STORIES

J·P·S BROWN

The Cinnamon Colt

AND OTHER STORIES

A DOUBLE D WESTERN

DOUBLEDAY

New York London Toronto Sydney Auckland

A DOUBLE D WESTERN
PUBLISHED BY DOUBLEDAY
a division of Bantam Doubleday Dell Publishing Group, Inc.
666 Fifth Avenue, New York, New York 10103

DOUBLE D WESTERN, DOUBLEDAY,
and the portrayal of the letters DD
are trademarks of Doubleday, a division of
Bantam Doubleday Dell Publishing Group, Inc.

Library of Congress Cataloging-in-Publication Data

Brown, J. P. S.
The cinnamon colt and other stories/by J.P.S. Brown.—1st ed.
p. cm.
Contents: The cinnamon colt—Butterfly dog—The comet—
Plácido—The widow's gift—The Mulatos River journal.
1. Mexico—Fiction. I. Title.
PS3552.R6856C56   1991
813'.54—dc20   91-25689
CIP

ISBN 0-385-41499-4
Copyright © 1991 by J. P. S. Brown
All Rights Reserved
Printed in the United States of America
February 1992
First Edition

10   9   8   7   6   5   4   3   2   1

For my son Billy and his *canelito*

Contents

Introduction   ix

The Cinnamon Colt   1

Butterfly Dog   13

The Comet   20

Plácido   35

The Widow's Gift   59

The Mulatos River Journal   79

Introduction

These were the first stories I wrote in quiet times as a cowboy on ranches and cow camps and also in hotels and airplanes in a rush to do business trading cattle. They were so heartfelt that they were worked on when nobody was looking. I was seldom caught working at them, because early on I found that I could not show them to anyone without being shamed. "Now you think you're a writer?" would be the comment, or at least the expression on the face of the reader. Others knew better how to write my stories and soon they were suggesting I change them, or suggesting better stories for me to write.

Then, after a long time, I contracted hepatitis and was too weak to do anything but push a pen across paper for about two hours a day and two people, Tad and Rachel Pfister, liked my stories unconditionally, and gave me the encouragement I needed to keep working. These, and the stories that became the novel *Jim Kane*, are the best that I wrote before anybody else was interested in my writing. I was sure they would help feed my family during my recuperation, but *Jim Kane*, the first of them that were ever published, was not sold until seven years later.

They are the stories from my heart as a cowboy. I have always been a cowboy first. I became a writer from necessity, because cowboying did not pay enough. Writing has never paid enough, either, but that's all right. That is where my talents seemed to lie, so I dedicated myself to it.

These stories were garnered in my first years in Mexico, where I first tried my hand as a writer. They could have been about Idaho, or Arizona, or New Mexico, other places that I cowboyed, packed and traded cattle and horses, but they are about Mexico because the people in Mexico are as worthy as anyone else and not many cowboys got to know them and write about them. The men, women, and animals I met who people the Mexico I know are the best I have ever known, and the worst. The finest man I have ever known is a Mexican, and the very most evil man I have ever known is a Mexican.

I was a full-time cowboy when I wrote about these men and animals and tried to tell the truth about them the same as I tried to clean a pasture when I went out to do it horseback. I was in love with the way I made a living, in love with the animals and the situations. Nothing made me feel better than to see an old cow baling off a hill trying to get away and me all ready to stop her. Nothing made my heart beat more pleasurably in my breast than that moment when I turned my horse toward home in the evening. Nothing has ever been more pleasurable to me than cowboying and writing about it.

Writing, like cowboying, ranching, and trading cattle, is an awful gamble. We put everything on the line and hope to keep on living after that. Everything I believe and love about horses and cattle and people were gambled in these stories. Now they are in a book for other people to read. Thank God for life.

I hope when people read these stories they will be as happy and sad about Mexico as I, and can *live* it with me. I hope they will learn to love my people with all their heart, but be careful of evil when they go to Mexico themselves. There is probably no more beauty in Mexico than there is in any other place, but if that is true, there is no more evil, either. Life is so good, it gives us to find out all the good and all the evil we dare to look for.

These stories are about a life. They're not good and they're not bad, as most lives must be. They are about beauty and goodness when they hurt. They are about the short lives of animals and the long, long lives of people. I hope people can throw their hearts to the winds when they read them, as I did when I wrote them.

THE CINNAMON COLT
AND OTHER STORIES

The Cinnamon Colt

In Mexico a favorite loved one is called el consentido. *A* consentido *is someone I appreciate with all my heart. The word is usually applied as an endearment to some person, like a favorite son, but it is often applied to a special charge, such as a favorite horse or dog or even a mule or an ox.*

Literally, the word carries an implication that the consentido *is spoiled, as he has the consent of his master in anything he does and his wishes are indulged because of his master's affection. However, a good master knows that if he is to be a good husbandman of his* consentidos, *he will see that they perform their certain duties.*

Bill and Cruz could see their boy was becoming a man. He was such a good boy and gave them so much pleasure they were afraid he might not endure. He was called Billy and he was doing the work of a man on the ranch they had cleared out of the brush along the Mayo River in southern Sonora. He was a good hand with horses and cattle. Bill never had to give him orders. He did his work with a gentle instinct for the needs of the animals that was a wonder to Bill.

On the boy's twelfth birthday, Bill put on a fiesta for him. Friends came and brought their horses and their families. Bill corralled some steers and held a *jineteo*, a steer riding competition, among the boys. Bill's corrals were under giant *álamo* trees beside the Mayo River. The mothers and their pretty daughters prepared *carne asada*, broiled beef, over mesquite coals in the grassy shade under the trees. They warmed great sheets of tortilla and pots of frijoles *charros*, whole beans served in their soup with onions and garlic and salt with salsa of tomato and green chili. The men drank bottled beer that had been chilled in washtubs filled with ice.

Billy drew a four-year-old brindle steer with high, white horns in the *jineteo*. Bill was at the chute helping him mount the steer and Juan Zaragoza's son, an overgrown thirteen year-old, romped by blowing a police whistle. Juan walked up to the chute.

"Bill, no, *hombre!*" he said. "What are you doing? That steer is too big for your son."

Bill ignored Juan. He did not want the boy to be influenced by his caution and he did not have time to answer, or to argue with him. Juan was always absolutely, unswervingly self-righteous. Bill concentrated on tightening a rope and surcingle around the steer. He then wrapped the running end of the rope around the boy's hands to give him a better hold.

"No, no, hombre!" said Juan. "Don't tie him that way. It's dangerous." Juan grabbed the end of the rope and tried to unwind it.

"Move out of the way, Juan," Bill said quietly. "This is not the first time I've helped my boy onto an animal's back. Move to one side, please."

Juan was offended. "All right. I'll get out of the way, but I'm telling you, you are endangering your son's life," he said.

Bill stepped down off the chute, waited for the boy's nod, and opened the gate. The boy leaned back and spurred the brindle on the neck to start him into the arena, as he would spur a horse. The steer burst forth with his tongue out and his eyes bulging. He bucked in a tight circle, kicking high behind. Every time he returned to the ground, the boy's spurs hit him in the shoulders and sent him aloft again. The brindle had a trick of shaking his body sideways and kicking his hind end the opposite way. His hide slipped and rolled and quivered under the boy. The boy kept a tight seat, his legs swinging forward, his spurs ringing off the steer's neck and shoulders. He rode the brindle through the meanest part of the bucking, until the steer began to tire and buck straight ahead.

Then the boy's surcingle loosened and he lost his seat over the loose hide. The steer began to spin and hook a big horn at the boy's head as he hung behind his shoulder. The boy lost his hold and went off into a small pile of supple arms and legs and buttocks, barely stirring the dust in the deep sand beside the river. He bounced up and doffed his big *charro* hat for the applause of the people. The band of mariachis Bill had hired for the fiesta saluted him with a *diana*, the short tune of accolade. The boy had made his ride, had contested the steer, and now was safe.

"Someday you will hurt that boy if you keep tying his hands like that," Juan Zaragoza said. "Also, he would stand a better chance of staying on if he gripped the steer's sides with his spurs. Nobody can ride a steer if he tries to spur him in the shoulders like that."

"He would get hurt if I didn't help him secure his grip on the rope," Bill said. "I won't let him grip the steer with his spurs yet. I don't want him to be thrown forward over the horns. He can learn that later if he decides to ride bulls when he grows up. I want him to always buck off cleanly."

"You should not make the boy ride."

Bill laughed. "I don't make him ride, Juan. He rides because he wants to stay on. He does not like to fall. The only contribution I make is my encouragement. Please try to enjoy the fiesta, Juan. The boy made a nice picture for you."

Juan Zaragoza walked away. Bill smiled to himself, thinking how hard it was for Juan to enjoy himself when he wanted to be right all the time.

That evening, during supper, Bill gave his son the cinnamon colt. The colt was a chunky red roan, the color of cinnamon. His sire had been a Texas stud Bill sold after he bred Cinnamon's mother. The dam was a well-built, small, common mare Bill had raised. The colt was gentle and noble. He had been easily broken to ride. He was a two-year-old and ready to go to work for a boy who would give him special care and splendid duties to learn.

On the day after the boy's birthday, the family went out to the pasture in the pickup to bring in the colt. Two visiting ladies from the United States accompanied them. The colt had been running free and alone for a month on fifty acres of alfalfa pasture. When the people walked out into the field, he threw up his head and swung his body in a prancing circle. He preened his tail, flared open his nostrils and blew like a bellows to rid himself of the smell of the people. He strained his ears toward the humans' raucous sounds. He relieved his hearing often by flicking his ears backwards, away from the humans.

Bill handed a halter and a *morral*, a feed bag, full of grain, to his son. "He's yours," he said. "Catch him."

The boy took the halter and morral and walked into the field. He walked with a broken grace his ride on the brindle steer had caused.

He is already a horseman, thought Bill. He must have pulled something riding the brindle. He has not complained about it, though.
The colt and the boy confronted one another. Bill could see that
the boy, unreasonably, as in his boy dreams, wanted the colt to love
him immediately. He was also wanting to be master from the first
moment he laid his hand on the colt. What a great stroke of luck it
would be for the boy if the colt let him walk up to him and catch
him as he was, full of a month's freedom.

The boy was walking too cautiously, too slowly, though. He was
too anxious to get familiar with the colt. He offered his hand in a
futile overture of friendship. The colt wheeled away, his dark eye
exaggerating, pretending he saw a sudden hellishness in the boy.
The boy followed as the colt raced around the pasture and showed
off while he eluded the boy.

Bill, Cruz, their little daughter Patsy, and the vaquero, Plácido,
helped drive the colt into a corner of the pasture fence and the boy
caught him. Bill saddled him at the pickup and the boy mounted
and rode away along the top of a canal bank toward the house.

As the boy rode, he occasionally, shyly, sneaked glances at the
shadow he and his colt were making on the ground, discovering
being one with his own horse for the first time.

He sits a horse exactly as my father did, thought Bill. So straight
and proudly centaur. What a fine moment for him, riding away on
that good colt and riding so well.

"What a little man," said one of the ladies from the United
States.

"A beautiful horse, too," said the other lady. "Billy is sure a good
rider."

Bill drove everybody back toward the house in the pickup, keeping his son in sight. He could not keep his eyes off the boy and the
colt, but they paid no attention to the pickup as Bill drove by them.

Don Filiberto Rivas was waiting by the front gate at the house.
He was a *castrador,* an expert castrator of horses. Bill stopped the
pickup at the gate. "Don Filiberto, how are you?" he asked.

"I am well, thank God," Don Filiberto said. He was an old man,
thin and wrinkled from working without enough to eat or drink on
long, hot days.

"What brings you, Don Filiberto?"

"Maybe it is time to geld those colts you were telling me about."

"I haven't caught them up. Why now?"

"The moon is right. The weather is right."

"Isn't it too hot?"

"Not late in the day, like now."

"When will the time be right again?"

"Not for another month."

"Let's wait until next month, then."

The boy rode up on the cinnamon colt.

"Good afternoon, Don Filiberto," the boy said.

"Good afternoon, young man."

Bill watched the old man make a quiet, Indian appraisal of the amount of growth the boy and the horse had put on since he had last seen them. His eyes showed pleasure in the latest development, the joining of the two.

He turned to Bill. "How much for the cinnamon?" he asked, keeping all expression from his face.

"I don't own him anymore," Bill said, inclining his head toward the boy.

Don Filiberto looked up at Billy. The boy gathered his reins quickly, causing the colt to toss his head.

"Ah, he belongs to the youth, does he? Sell me the cinnamon, boy," Don Filiberto said.

"He's not for sale, Don Filiberto," the boy said.

"Then, if you won't sell him to me, I know another man who will give one hundred thousand pesos for a beast like that," the old man said.

The boy smiled and colored. He was embarrassed at having to refuse the old man, but he was delighted to believe anyone who would tell him his horse was worth a great price.

"I will never sell my horse," he said.

"Well, this man might want to harness him to a plow. He looks strong. Does he know the plow?"

"No, señor, this horse is my saddle horse."

"Why not sell him, then? Your father will always have saddle horses available for you and you can buy five or six saddle horses with the money you can make from one plow horse."

"No, hombre! Good saddle horses are scarce. Besides, I couldn't sell this horse. My father just made a gift of him to me."

"Ah, that's it. Those gifts are rare. You are married to the colt, then. Until death."

"I don't want to sell him."

"Then you must loan him to me on Independence Day so I can ride him in the parade."

The boy looked to his father for help.

"What do you say? Will you loan your horse to Don Filiberto?" asked Bill.

"Maybe my father will loan you a horse, Don Filiberto," the boy said. "I'm planning to ride in the parade myself."

"I was hoping you would loan me your cinnamon," said the old man.

"I would, Don Filiberto, but my father says a man does not loan his pistol, his woman, or his horse."

"Ah, that is true with *charros* like your father. Charros are also allowed to marry their horses. I had forgotten. Please forgive me."

The boy relaxed. He was sure now that Don Filiberto had been joking. He looked away and sighed.

"Do you have time to geld the cinnamon before dark?" Bill asked Don Filiberto.

"Yes, I think so," Don Filiberto said.

"Don't you think we ought to geld your horse while Don Filiberto is here, son?"

"Yes . . . I guess so," the boy said, softly.

"Go and unsaddle him, then, and lead him over to the round corral. That one is probably the cleanest."

The boy rode away on the horse. Don Filiberto climbed into the back of the truck and Bill drove to the house. In the kitchen, Bill filled a bucket with cold water. He handed his whetstone to Don Filiberto. The old man unwrapped a clean handkerchief from a long, narrow, much-used blade. He began honing it as he walked to the corral with Bill. Cruz followed with the guests. The boy was holding the colt in the corral. He patted his colt on the shoulder, waiting.

Bill thought, the horse is full of green alfalfa and the weather is dangerously hot. If I was doing it I would certainly lose him, but Don Filiberto is the best in the country and his judgment is good.

Bill put the loop of a long cotton rope around the colt's front feet and he and Plácido threw him down on his side. Bill held him there with his knee on the colt's neck while Plácido tied the front feet to the lower hind foot. Then they put a collar around the colt's neck and tied the top hind foot high on the colt's shoulder, baring his genitals.

The colt was now as nearly completely incapacitated as the men could make him, with all four legs firmly tied and a grown man kneeling on his neck and twisting his muzzle back toward his shoulder. The colt was already hot. Bill's trouser leg on his neck was soaked with sweat. The sweat ran on the colt's nose beneath Bill's hands. He brushed mud of sweat and corral dirt from the colt's muzzle and eyes.

"Do you want to do it, Bill?" Don Filiberto asked.

"God, no," Bill said. "I would lose a horse I care this much about. Please do it quickly. The colt is hot."

Don Filiberto began his business and the colt began to fight. He found an inch of play between his top hoof and the collar and fought with that inch, lunging against it until he frayed it and loosened it and kicked the foot free. With the operation only half finished, the men had to wrestle with him to tie him again with the incisions made and an organ bare and hanging out by a stripped cord. Cinnamon was no longer the docile pet. The unexpected, undeserved violence had turned him into a half-ton of desperate, suffering muscle and nerve that the men could not handle gently.

When Don Filiberto resumed the operation, one testicle that had been flopping on the ground during the struggle was covered with dust and manure. The colt's sides were heaving and his breath was tearing through his throat. He had also been down on the ground in shock too long.

"For God's sake, hurry, Filiberto," Bill said.

Don Filiberto made a slice and held up the dusty testicle. He bent to his business again. "I haven't been able to get hold of the other one," he said. "He's drawn it up into his belly. Ah, I have it. Hold him. Please be nice, little Cinnamon. ¡Ah, caray! I lost it again. I've never seen a colt so strong. He is a *tigre.*"

Don Filiberto straightened. His hands were bloody to the wrists. He was tired. His fingers were stiff and weak from groping in the hot blood. He stooped to his job again. The blood on his fingers had dried and he got another hold on the organ, forced it down the belly into the open, sliced, peeled, separated veins, and finally cut it free of the colt. Then he washed the empty cods and the insides of the bloody thighs with cold water, and he was finished.

Bill untied the cinnamon colt and he stood up shakily, his eyes desperate, his head outstretched, his sides caving in behind his ribs with every breath. The blood ran in steady rivulets between his hind legs, over the hooves, into the sand. The boy was pale, looking into his horse's eye. The eye no longer paid him any mind.

Bill made the colt walk a few steps and handed the lead rope to the boy. "Stay with him, son," he said. "Lead him around slowly. Don't let him lie down and stiffen. Keep him moving."

Bill was relieved the business was over. He was afraid for the colt. Shock was the enemy. Maybe the colt would become aware of the boy again. Could horses love boys? He doubted it. Why love any kind of man? Not on the first day, or on the thousandth. Colts had heart for other than pumping blood, though. Maybe this one would respond to the boy if only to help himself.

That night at supper with the ladies from the United States, the boy forgot his worry for the colt because he was so proud of him. The ladies were green and the boy was veteran. The ladies were impressed, but not quietly. They could not admire with their mouths closed. The boy was a prize the ladies had discovered in Mexico. They had never dreamed such a stalwart boy existed. He was doubly a prize, better than a curio, because he could answer questions and was at their disposal because of his good manners.

"What did you think of that old man and your father doing those things to your horse? I couldn't believe they were doing such bad things," one lady said.

"I don't know," the boy said.

"Doesn't it hurt the horse?"

"Yes." He was sure of that.

"Aren't you mad at your father for doing that to your horse?"

"No."

"I think your father is mean, don't you?"

The boy looked at the lady. He had already answered.

"Don't you, young man?"

"No."

"What if the colt dies from all that?"

The boy stared at the lady.

The other lady tittered. "He's not going to die, is he, little man?" she said.

The boy smiled. "No."

"The colt could die, couldn't he, son?" Bill wanted to be sure the women were not distracting the boy.

"Couldn't he, son?"

The boy stopped smiling. The tittering lady chattered on about

Cruz's dessert to change the subject. Bill watched his son. The boy finished his supper, excused himself and went outside.

Later, Bill lit a cigar and took it outside. He found the boy with the cinnamon colt. The colt had cooled and was eating hay out of the boy's hand. He rummaged over the hand softly with his lips and picked up the alfalfa leaves and chewed, then dipped his head for a flake of hay on the ground and was brought back by another small handful. Bill took the boy back to the house.

Bill went out to the corral before sunup the next day to look at the colt. He had eaten well. His bleeding had stopped. There was no shade in the corral so Bill turned him out where he could find shade in the pasture that surrounded the house. Later in the morning, Bill saw him dozing under a mesquite tree. His head was low, bowed close to the ground, and Bill figured he was bound to be suffering. He should recoup noticeably tomorrow.

At mid-morning, Bill drove the five miles into town to do some telephoning. He was standing in the lobby of a hotel on the edge of town, waiting for the answer to a call, when he saw the boy riding fast toward the hotel on Pajaro, Bill's top horse. Pajaro was lathered. The boy had galloped him all the way from the ranch. Bill was furious.

The boy slid the horse to a stop and scattered gravel all over the panes of the hotel's front door. He dismounted, running, and collided with Bill as he stepped outside.

"Papá," he said. "The little cinnamon is down." All the color was gone from his face. When he saw his father was angry, his face began to break. He could not stand one ounce of Bill's disapproval. Bill had never known what to do about that.

"Don't start crying, now," Bill said, still angry. "When did he go down?"

"Just a little while ago."

"Did you try to get him up?"

"Yes. I couldn't," the boy said, and he started to cry.

Bill put his arm around the boy's shoulders. "Well," he said. "He's probably all right. He's just sore and tired. Let's go look at him. Go tie your horse."

Bill went back in the lobby and asked the clerk to save him a report on his telephone calls while the boy tied Pajaro to a tree on the hotel's front lawn. They drove back to the ranch. When they arrived at the house they could see a small crowd of Indians standing by a trough that watered the stock in the pasture.

"Where's the colt?" Bill asked his son.

"By the trough."

The man and his son started walking toward the crowd of Indians. Then Bill saw the colt lying up against the trough.

"He's lying awfully flat, son," he said.

One of the Indians left the crowd and walked to meet Bill. He was swinging his machete at the top of the grass at his feet.

"*¡Se murio, Beel!* He died," the Indian called to Bill. "*Se acaba de morir el canelito.* The little cinnamon just finished dying."

Bill walked on until they were standing over the colt. The dark eyes were still clear and had not begun to glaze, or catch the dust. Plácido was standing at the trough.

"He was all right," Plácido said. "He was standing over there under that mesquite. I saw him. He walked over and joined the bunch, then walked across the open to the trough with the rest of the horses. I noticed then that he was blowing badly. I went and got a halter so I could lead him to the shade. He drank a few swallows and went down. I ran back and bathed his head with water from the trough, but he died."

Bill looked around and saw the boy was walking away. He caught up and put his arm around his shoulders and walked with him away from the Indians. The boy had not shown his fear or his sorrow to the Indians. He was succeeding in hiding it from himself, too. He was taking no chances, though, he was getting away from there. They met Don Filiberto Rivas walking toward the crowd.

Don Filiberto asked, "What happened to the little cinnamon?" The boy turned his face away from him.

"He died," Bill said.

"*Lástima.* A shame. It weighs on me. Did he get out in the sun?"

"Yes."

"He should not have been allowed in the sun."

"It's my fault," Bill said. "*Ni modo.* No way to remedy it now. It is done. He can't be made to live again."

Bill caught up with the boy again.

"Son," he said. "We all have to die. Every living thing has to die someday. You'll have other horses you'll love and they will die. I will die and so will Cruz. So will your sister. You had bad luck that you only had your colt one day. I'm awfully sorry."

The boy nodded.

Bill and his son got in the truck and he started it and turned it around. Plácido caught up to them horseback.

"And the meat and the hide?" he asked.

Bill turned off the ignition. He drew a deep breath.

"What do you want done with the horse, son?" he asked.

The boy did not answer. He had only just begun to work on his grief.

"Do you want to drag him away for the buzzards? Do you want to bury him? Or can the Indians bone him out for the meat?"

The boy was silent.

"There is no reason for losing the meat and the hide," Plácido said. "The Indians want the meat and the hide is very good. The colt had a lot of meat."

"Son?" Bill asked. "The colt can still do someone some good."

"Bone him, then," the boy said. "I guess. Butcher him."

"Tell the Indians they can have the meat and I'll take the hide to the tanner. You bone him, Plácido."

"What, man? The Indians already have him skinned."

A week later, at a charro festival, Bill was standing under a fly of a tent drinking beer, when Juan Zaragoza walked up to him again.

"What happened to the little cinnamon?" Juan asked.

"He died," Bill said.

"Why? What from?"

"Castration, blood poisoning, a thousand stupidities."

"He was beautiful. I would have given you two hundred thousand pesos for him, but only before you let a kid ride him."

"The boy rode him ten minutes."

"I heard all about it. I hear you let Filiberto Rivas castrate him. He knows nothing about castration. I wouldn't let him castrate my cat. You should have procured an expert. An expert would not have done it during that time of the month. The moon was bad. The weather was hot. I hear the colt was full as a tick. It was an awfully stupid thing you did."

"Oh, for God's sake, Juan," Bill said. "Ever since the colt died I have been surrounded by experts like you. Do you know what, Juan, I don't want to hear about how much of an expert you are."

Just then Juan's overgrown son ran full speed into his father, blowing his whistle. He did not slacken. He rebounded, ran between Bill and Juan, ran away with his head thrown back, and did not spare his wind on the whistle.

Juan laughed indulgently. "He sure likes that whistle. He never stops running and blowing that whistle. He never rests. I don't know what to do with him."

"Give him something to do," Bill said. "He would make a good steer rider. Bring him around to the chutes and we'll let him ride with the rest of the boys. He'll forget all about that whistle."

Juan Zaragoza swelled with anger. "I'm not crazy. I think more of my son than to risk hurting him in an arena."

"Raise him with fear, then," Bill said. "He'll need it to grow up and be sane like you."

Butterfly Dog

Mariposa *means butterfly in Spanish. A child once told me a butterfly is a stick that flies on beautifully colored wings. She would catch them, press them in a book, and forget about them.*

Tom Coyle was receiving cattle at El Limon in the Sierra Madre of Chihuahua the first time he saw the bitch dog Mariposa. She was keeping herself delicately aloof from a pack of hungry mongrels Manuel Anaya had brought to help with the roundup. Her thin shell of a carcass did not make much track on the campground. She could not have weighed twenty pounds. Her ribs and backbone were so visible she looked like a black and tan harp.

She watched Manuel all the time. Tom could see she loved only Manuel, although he gave her little attention. He certainly never fed her much, but then Tom figured he did not have much to give away. Manuel was skinny, too.

Mariposa lay against the cool mortar of the main building of the old, crumbling hacienda at mealtime. She watched the other dogs fight over scraps the vaqueros dropped indiscriminately on the ground around their table. She rested and licked her sore places and waited. She seemed to know when Manuel was about to give her something and she stood up and looked at him and made ready to catch it. He tossed her the remnant of a tortilla without looking at her. That was all she ever seemed to get from the man, that and the odor of the food.

Later, when Tom had a chance, he took some food to her. She took it distrustfully and made Tom feel guilty. He did not like feeding another man's dog and he did not like anyone feeding his dog. He would not want Manuel to think he was trying to make Mariposa switch loyalties. He quit worrying about it when he saw she did not think any more of him because he gave her food. She ate the scraps Tom gave her, but she looked him over carefully before she allowed herself to pick them up. She would not take them from his hand.

Tom was buying the cattle from Juan Vogel. The Vogel vaqueros were bringing cattle from a holding pasture into the corrals at El Limon, a camp located in rough mountain and canyon country. The cattle were being branded, castrated, and vaccinated for Tom. They were *corriente*, native, bulls over three years old. At the end of that summer, Tom planned to drive them to the railroad and export them to the States.

Manuel and his dogs had been working outside this pasture on a general roundup of the Vogel ranch. He was finished out there now and he brought his dogs to El Limon to help bring in a remnant of cattle that had been getting away each time a drive was made. These remaining cattle were the craftiest of all the *partida* that Tom wanted to brand. They had been successfully resisting the change of ownership. They had been started toward the corrals and the knives and the branding fires with other cattle every morning, but managed to disappear before they got to the corrals.

The vaqueros worked afoot in that steep, rocky, brushy country. They wore huaraches made of strips of tire tread tied to their feet with leather thongs. Their bare, stubby feet were tough as horse's hooves. A man on horseback could not keep the wily cattle together in that rough country. The bulls could go too many places that a horseman could not go. All they had to do to escape being gathered was take a path where a horse would not have good footing, or slip into brush where a man on a horse could not follow.

The serranos, the men who lived and worked in the Sierra Madre, could go anyplace afoot a bull could go, and many places he could not go. They did a good job of keeping cattle once they found them, but the wiliest bulls often escaped by hiding quietly a few steps away, or by running over steep ground where they could use their strength and speed and momentum to get away.

The cattle the vaqueros were gathering at El Limon were practiced at getting away. They never made any mad downhill rushes on their own. They just watched for a place where two or three steps would get them out of the jurisdiction of the vaqueros.

Down in the camp, Tom and Manuel were waiting for the first bunch of cattle the vaqueros were to drive in that morning. The sun was hitting the top of the hill where the cattle would first appear. The descent to the corrals from the top of the hill was steep. The vaqueros had to stay above the cattle and drive them down off the hill into a canyon below the corrals and then uphill again to the corrals. The drive from the top of the hill to camp was over half a mile because the cattle had to cross the canyon. The line of sight that Tom and Manuel had from the camp to the top of the hill was only half that far.

Two, big, spotted bulls, the first to show on the drive, appeared in the sun at the top of the hill. They walked over the crest and started down. They ambled, rocking back and forth slowly on their front feet, barely gaining ground down the hill. They stopped before entering the shade that the light of the morning sun had not reached. They sunned themselves and waited. They listened for the other cattle on the drive behind them. Then, they turned and walked calmly together into the brush. From camp, Tom could see only the fine, white brushes at the ends of their tails with the sun glowing through them. They did not move.

More cattle came over the hill, walking almost as lazily as the first two. The vaqueros came behind them at a trot, working hard to keep them together. A vaquero would drive a bull a few steps and then have to leave him to go move another. The bull would stop and wait to be driven again, hoping the vaquero would go far enough away and become so busy that the bull could slip away and hide. He did not have to go far to escape in that brush, just a few steps into a thicket, like the two spotted bulls had done.

The spotted bulls stood quietly together in the brush waiting for the drive to pass them by. They stood still and shaded themselves under cover. They were making an indolent, leisurely escape.

The vaqueros pushed the last of the cattle off the crest and into the shade of the descent. They passed the two spotted bulls. Manuel Anaya shouted to them and told them where they were leaving the two bulls. One man went back to them. The bulls moved deeper into the brush and disappeared. The cattle the vaquero had been driving turned back toward the sunny crest of the hill. They did not want to go to the corrals. The vaquero had to leave the two spotted bulls in the brush to head the cattle back off the crest.

"¡Oocha, oocha, Mariposa!" Manuel commanded. The dog sailed

to the attack, her pack of lesser dogs following. She fell into the canyon below camp out of sight. The noise of the pack fell with her, echoing, decreasing. Then she rose like an arrow through the brush on the other side of the canyon, leaving the pack behind. She went to the vaqueros on the hill. The two bulls had come back in sight and were moving fast toward the top of the hill. Mariposa overtook them just as they reached the crest. She rushed to the front of them, but they charged around her, hooking their big horns at her. She got back in front of them and was snapping at their noses when they forced her over the crest and out of sight. The pack went yapping after her.

The vaqueros drove the rest of the cattle into the canyon and started pressing them to climb up to the corrals. The leaders lined up the narrow trail until they could see the gate and then balked, turned back, faced downhill, and hooked at the cattle that were still trying to climb out.

The Mariposa dog and her pack came back over the top of the hill with the two spotted bulls. The bulls were now completely intimidated. They flew down the hill and dove pell-mell into the herd in the canyon, hunting friends. They were in need of consolation. The Mariposa dog had made them want to be back in the fold. They stood and looked back at her from the safety and anonymity of the herd and heaved with the excitement she had caused in singling them out.

Mariposa and her pack got behind the herd and put it quickly up the hill and into the corrals. She nipped heels right up to the gate. The cattle were glad to make it into the corrals and be rid of her. They turned and looked at her when she stopped at the gate. She turned away from them and walked slowly to her shade by the building to lie down, pant, and rest.

The Mariposa helped finish the work at El Limon and Manuel took her home. Tom Coyle saw her now and then at Trigo, the headquarters of the ranch where Manuel and his family lived. Tom always looked for her at Manuel's and if he did not see her he asked about her.

Once he rode up to Manuel's house and found him scraping an ocelot hide on a table. The dog was standing under the table watching Manuel work. Now and then she moved up to smell the edge of the hide. She would sniff it and look straight into Tom's eyes. The color, markings, and texture of the fur were unblemished. The hide had belonged to a *gato tigrillo* in his prime and would bring a good payday to Manuel. The cat was a foot and a half longer from nose to tail than the Mariposa.

Manuel told Tom the Mariposa had caught the ocelot for him and suffered no injury in the fight. Manuel had been crossing the stream at Teguaraco when the dog jumped the cat in the brush. She ran him through the water toward Manuel and he almost collided with Manuel. She cornered him under a cliff on fine scree. He lost his footing in the scree, a phenomenon that seldoms happens with any cat, and the dog caught him against the wall of the cliff and broke his back. Manuel killed him with a rock.

Mariposa watched the faces of Tom and Manuel as they talked. Then, when she did not hear her name mentioned for a while, she lay down under the table to rest.

A year later Tom rode into José Anaya's camp at Tecoyagui with a party of hunters. José was Manuel's son. Tom had been leading the hunters through the brush in twilight for the past half hour. He had taken them on too big a circle that day, their last day of hunting, and they had tired on him. The lamplight of the house at Tecoyagui was not a welcome sight to Tom. The lamplight meant it was too late to be arriving at Tecoyagui. José's camp was at the foot of a high trail Tom's hunters would have to ride before they could make their own camp. Tom had sent their beds and provision too far up the trail that morning. They would never catch up to them now. They would have to camp somewhere without beds and provision and Tom did not want to impose on José. Tom would not miss the provision. The hunters had packed too much belly comfort on the mules to suit him, but he was sorry he had exhausted them so they were stopping at Tecoyagui.

When he dismounted to open the gate into the yard at José's, Tom saw the shape of an animal hanging in the darkness from a limb of a mesquite over his head. It hung absolutely still, straight down from the limb.

The hunters rode past him through the gate. Not one of them noticed the figure hanging there. Tom noticed it because it was ominously familiar, but its stillness was so absolute and it was so close by the place a man had to stand to open the gate, that he could not believe what he was seeing.

Tom ducked under it and closed the gate and then walked around it, leading his horse, so he could see it better on the side the lamplight touched it. He saw it was a little black-and-tan dog hanging rigidly by a wire around its neck. The nose pointed sharply straight up the wire. The tail pointed straight down in line with the wire. All that was left of the dog now depended on a wire stretched tight in the dark, touched by lamplight, at the bottom of a canyon in the Sierra Madre. Not a breeze stirred it.

Tom led his horse to the house. The hunters were lowering themselves stiffly from their saddles. Tom decided they would have to stay the night there.

José Anaya came smiling to him.

"Come in to the coffee, Tomás," José said. "Tell your friends."

"How is it with you, José?" Tom asked.

"*Mucho piojo.* Much lice. Much ruin," said José, smiling, and he made the gesture of cracking a louse between his thumbnails that meant he was suffering hard times. "But we'll make it unless the rains come too late again. We've lost many cattle from hunger and drought, though."

"We saw no game, either. Not even a track. *Menos mal.* Let the poor things live, if they can."

José handed Tom a cup of black coffee. Tom wondered how many times José's woman had reboiled the grounds. It was a big sacrifice for this family to give away its coffee. Tom would be leading the hunters out of the Sierra the next day. The grouchy hunters were headed back to their land of plenty without having killed anything in the Sierra Madre. He would lighten the packs on the mules and send some famously advertised canned goods back to José. José would appreciate them more than anyone in North America, even though he had certainly never heard their famous names.

Tom squatted on his heels and sipped his coffee. José began unsaddling his horse for him. "You will stay the night, won't you?" José asked gently. "You have to. These men can't ride that bad trail. The night is too dark for anyone to travel now."

José laid Tom's saddle down on its side, slipped the bridle onto his horse's neck so he could eat, and poured him a measure of corn on the ground.

"What happened to the dog?" Tom asked.

"We caught her in the provisions."

Tom said nothing.

"She was a good dog," José said.

Tom sipped his coffee.

"You remember my father's dog, the Mariposa?"

Tom could not answer. Be careful, he thought. Keep your gringo mouth shut. He knows how much you liked her. Still, why in the hell? That good little dog.

"She alighted on the wrong flower," José said. He tried to smile, as if to share the pleasure of a small joke with a friend.

The Comet

Jim Kane had asked Chapo Almada to meet him at Satebo in the
Sierra Madre of Chihuahua on the fifteenth of November. He drove
to San Bernardo early on the fifteenth and unloaded his horse from
the back of his pickup at Poncho Velderrain's store. He put on his
chaps, tied his blanket and *morral* on his saddle, mounted the horse
Pajaro and rode toward the Sierra Madre. His red dog coursed in
circles around him.

Kane had not been to the Sierra in two years. He rode up the
road to Puerto de Bacajaqui, the pass that overlooked San Bernardo,
and stopped to let Pajaro breathe. For a year the big sorrel had only
been worked in the corral. He was short of breath and sweating
heavily. He was loaded with a sixty-pound stock saddle, forty feet of
nylon lariat rope, a heavy wool Mayo blanket, a morral full of lunch,
a pistol belt with .45 cartridges and Kane's sixshooter. Kane was
twenty pounds overweight. In chaps, leather brush jacket, boots,
and spurs, he weighed at least two hundred ten pounds. Man and
horse were winded and sweating, most of the morning was gone,
and they still had thirty miles to go before dark.

"Pajaro, we are quite a pair," Kane said, and started down the
other side of the pass.

Three hours later Pajaro threw a shoe and Kane was forced to
turn back to San Bernardo. He cussed the horse for the way he
tracked, overstepping with his hind feet. He was sure the horse had
overreached and stepped on the heel of a front shoe and stamped it
off.

In San Bernardo Kane and Pajaro were considerably leaner. Kane rode up to the back of Poncho's store and dismounted. Poncho came out.

"I thought it must be you by the sound of the horse," he said.

"It's me all right," Kane said.

"What happened?"

"Pajaro threw a shoe. I shod him carefully and well too. I couldn't find the shoe on the way back so I had to come all the way back."

"Unsaddle him and we'll have Benjamin make you some extras."

Poncho brought a piece of cardboard and Kane planted the horse's feet on it and drew the outline of each hoof, then sent a boy with the cardboard to the blacksmith's.

"And now?" Poncho asked.

"I'll have to go tomorrow. There's no moon. I don't like riding up those bad *cuestas*, grades of Las Parbas and Arroyo Hondo in the dark," Kane said.

"I was going to say that. You'll have to stay here and leave early in the morning."

"That's it. That's all."

Poncho came out of a bin with an armful of milo maize stalks.

"This not the best feed," he said. "Will your horse eat it?"

"Of course. He has no preferences."

In the afternoon the blacksmith sent the shoes and Kane tacked on the one the horse needed and put the extra shoes in the morral.

In the evening they ate flour tortillas and cheese with coffee for supper. They sat on the front porch of the store after Poncho closed. Poncho was trying to quit smoking and gazed longingly at Kane's pipe. He had not smoked a cigarette all day. Kane told him he had it whipped now, having held off through the first day. He continued puffing on his pipe. The stars were very clear.

"I guess the comet is gone now," Poncho said. "During the warm weather I slept out here and I saw it every morning. Beautiful."

Kane had never seen so many stars fall in one evening. One big star fell and the whole sky brightened.

"The woman in Argentina prophesied flying saucers for next month," Poncho said.

"What woman?" Kane asked.

"The one who prophesied President Kennedy's death. She says the world will be invaded by flying saucers during the month of

December this year. They've started, I guess. A farmer at Mocuzari was picking his corn and pumpkins the other day when he heard a humming noise coming closer. He looked up and saw a small cigar-shaped thing with wings streak in and blow up against a hill. He kept on picking his corn and when he was through in the evening he went to see the thing. He found it crushed and melted together. A curious paperlike insulation was scattered around it. He left it there. It is still there."

"Probably it was some weather apparatus the United States sent up," Kane said.

"Probably," Poncho said. "Anyway, no one will ever be interested in invading San Bernardo."

In the morning Kane drank a cup of coffee and left early.

Pajaro was not blowing badly at the Puerto this time. Kane turned up the arroyo he thought was Los Mezcales. It seemed narrower than he remembered. Then he came to a narrow place with a gate barring the way and began to suspect he was on the wrong trail. He had suspected so the day before but questions he put to Poncho made him believe he had been on the right trail. He rode on watching for the lost shoe and found it where he thought he would find it in a rocky place where Pajaro had stumbled the day before. He rode on, his suspicions increasing, uncomfortably riding, impatient, and when the trail began to lead him away from the direction his instinct told him he should be going, he stopped being uncomfortable and began to watch for ways to leave the arroyo.

He met a woman driving some cows and asked for the way to the Arroyo de los Mezcales. The woman said to watch for some *sembradores,* farmers, and ask them. Kane rode on and came to a place where the arroyo ran between two fields of corn. The cornstalks and leaves were bleached and dry. Kane could hear a loud rustling and crackling where something moved inside them. A brown dog came out barking, hazing Kane away from the place where the corn was rustling. Thick clumps of *vainoro,* graythorn brush, on the edge of the field, hid the rustling place from Kane. He rode around a *trinchera,* a fence made of rocks stacked tightly together with no mortar, a wide square fence with the rocks leveled on top. He saw a trail through the field that led the way he wanted to go. The dog pressed his horse closely, snarling and sucking his breath savagely, hackles bristling. Kane tired of it, whirled and spurred his horse in a lunge at the dog. The dog tucked his tail and moved away with a

fearful, evil eye on Kane. Kane rode over a little rise and saw the
men gathering corn in the glaring November sun. He reined Pajaro
through the field toward the men carefully to keep him from stepping on the pumpkins.

The men stopped work and watched as he approached them.
Kane called good morning. The men carefully, politely, answered
him. Kane stopped his horse a good distance from them.

"Pardon, is this the road to Arroyo de los Mezcales?"

The men closed until they stood side by side. "Yes, it is," the
younger man said. "Keep going this way and you will find the gap
to Puerto de los Mezcales, then a *bajada*, a long going down on the
other side of the gap, and you will come out at Rancho de los
Mezcales."

"Thank you. Where did I miss the Arroyo de Los Mezcales?"

"You turned up the Arroyo de Bacajaqui before you reached it,"
the young man said.

"Thank you," Kane said.

Kane rode up a dry steep draw toward Puerto de los Mezcales.
Leaves fell dry on the trail. He was concerned the draw would be an
extra climb in a long, all-day trail, but Pajaro easily topped the gap.
Kane recognized and remembered the red earth on a ridge above
Rancho de los Mezcales.

He rode down through sloping fields where piles of husked corn
dried. Pumpkins lay in heaps beside the trail. A young boy bundling
dry cornstalks did not see or hear Kane ride by.

Pajaro walked into forest again where light off November
bleached leaves cut the shade and made cool leafy light on the trail.
Kane rode by the ranch and saw no one. He was happy to be on the
right trail. At Jecopaco he caught up to Manuelito Valenzuela who
was going afoot to Avena.

"Do you want *naranjita*, little orange?" asked Kane's friend as he
staggered beneath an old hat that thatched his curly hair.

"No thank you, Manuelito." Kane reined up. "I'll just visit with
you awhile as we go."

Kane walked his horse beside Mauelito. The spare, frail little
man's expression was vacant as he wiped his pug nose with orange
sticky fingers. Hise tire-soled huaraches did not match.

"I'm *tiernito de la vista*," Manuelito said. "Tender of sight. But
I'll get there *poco a poquito*, little by little."

"Andando, andando," he chanted. "Going on walking. Even if it is only by burro I can always *andar*. You go on."

He sat under a mesquite by the trail, unslung his oranges from a bandana over his shoulder, and rested.

"I'll continue as soon as I operate my orange," he said, and opened an old rusty knife. Kane hesitated, agreed, rode on. He did not want to leave the little man there, but he had two long tired-horse climbs ahead before dark. Night would catch him on the last.

He rode in shade now. He watched the shade climb on the hills above him. He saw an *arriero*, a packer, with his burros gain the top of the trail and the sunshine. Kane raced the sun to the top and Pajaro beat the evening to the pass called Puerto Las Parbas, port of the flocks. Kane let him stop to blow and rest.

The horse revived going down the next *cuesta* as he entered the shade and pines of Chihuahua. Arrieros had made an early camp by Arroyo Hondo in the bottom and were already enjoying their fire. A woman was preparing a meal. The fire was bright. Arroyo Hondo was deep inside the breast of the mountains and the camp was darkening quickly. Kane started up the last steep grade in twilight.

At the top Kane caught Che Che the arriero afoot with his burros. He had been ahead of Kane on Las Parbas. Che Che, with his white smile in the dark boy's face was driving his burros to Avena. They came in the dark to the hacienda and slid back the *trancas*, the poles, to open the gate in the night.

Don Juanito, the caretaker, walked out on the porch. The old man guarded the hacienda keys for doors he could no longer lock. He gave Kane the *abrazo*, embrace, of welcome, of happiness at seeing a man too long absent.

Kane unsaddled his horse and laid his saddle beside *aparejos*, packsaddles, stacked on the porch. Another visitor was there before him.

"Fausto is here," Don Juanito said, and Fausto Willis walked out of the darkness tiredly dragging his spurs on the cobblestones. Don Juanito carefully began putting away all the saddles and gear of his visitors while Kane and Fausto visited.

"Don Juanito, do you have a *trago?*" Kane called. "A swallow of mescal?" The old man went into his *bodega*, his stores, and filled Kane's flask.

Fausto walked through the old dining room where no one dined anymore and passed on to finish his supper in the lamplit kitchen.

Kane turned back to see to his horse. Pajaro was still tied to the fence and Kane thought he was unattended, but the Avena custodian had already gone to him.

"Ah, there you are Pajaro, *Carajo*," Don Juanito said. "How good to see you." He thought no one heard him. "In a moment you will have corn, Carajo. Everyone eats at Avena." Kane stopped in the darkness.

As Kane and Fausto ate supper in the smoke-blackened kitchen by an open fire Don Juanito prepared corn for Pajaro. His hard dark hands rubbed a cob against ears of dried corn. The kernels fell into a basket on his lap. He took the full basket of corn to the nickering horse and poured it into a heavy cast iron bowl on the ground. He puffed on a cigarette of homegrown tobacco wrapped in a cornuhusk and watched the horse eat.

Later, in the master bedroom of the house, the one room that was kept locked, the old man unlocked a large trunk, removed heavy blankets, and spread a bed for Kane. Kane and Fausto smoked, passed the flask, talked about the husbandry of livestock, and slept.

In the morning Kane heard Don Juanito calling Pajaro early to his corn. Kane and Fausto walked out under cold stars, took short swallows of mescal, and went inside to the hot, black, syrupy coffee. When he was ready to leave, Kane looked for Don Juanito to thank him for his hospitality. He found him opening ripe pumpkins for Che Che's hungry burros. The burros followed him and searched him for bites of the hard *calabazas*. "Eat burros, eat," he ordered as he broke up the pumpkins and scattered the pieces.

Kane mounted his horse and left Avena with Fausto. Fausto was a big man, a fat man riding a small bay horse. They stopped in the Avena orchard of *membrillos*, quince trees, and filled their morrals with the heavy, yellow, sour fruit.

They struck a trail through the pines toward San Agustín and Satebo. Fausto was taking a herd of purebred piglets to San Agustín. The pigs were new stock, new hope, for his ranch. Che Che and Daniél were his drovers. They stopped often to urge the animals along softly with the palms of their hands. "Carefully, slowly," Fausto cautioned the herders as he passed. "These are *finos*, aristocrats. Ease them along."

At the top of a grade ahead of the herd, Kane and Fausto encountered René driving burros laden with feed. René was very small, maybe ten years old, with tiny chapped hands that gripped a big switch. He kept his little feet busy moving the burros and only looked his greeting at Kane and Fausto.

Kane and Fausto rode across the sunny, grassy, open tables of high ground called Las Mesas where a man called to them from across a ravine. They stopped and listened in the sudden quiet. Their horses searched the ravine. The caller listened too. *"¡Hua!"* he called again. *"¡Hua!"* Kane and Fausto answered and they dismounted to wait. They heard the caller's horse coming long before they saw him round the last bend in the trail.

Chapo Almada, a small man perched like a boy atop a small horse, riding easily, smiled when he came in sight. His horse strode up at a running walk and shied at the strangers. Chapo spurred him with mean heals to turn him back toward the visitors. He had found an audience for his horsemanship.

"Meestair Gringo," Chapo greeted. "Wait until you see the *llavúdos,* the big keys, I've gathered. Their keys will open any lock."

"How many?" Kane asked.

"Fifty young bulls with horns well matched and perfect for Gringo rodeo."

"Let's go, then, Chapito."

The three men rode around the ravine and down off the mesas into warm brush country. The trail passed through fields of wild *amól,* good for making soap, and *diabóli,* good for making wine. The men stopped at the grotto of Los Bitáches, the wasps, tied their horses in the shade of a mesquite, loosened their cinches, and unrolled a spare lunch of tortillas, beans, and cheese. They climbed with saddle stiffened legs down to smooth warm rocks by a spring and drank from a deep pool of water. After the rest, Fausto, the sun on his face, his hat *a media cabeza,* on the back of his head, left for San Agustín.

Chapo and Kane, glad to begin their work, rode across a brushy high mountain to the hacienda in its basin, Satebo. Kane left Chapo at the main house and rode down the hill to the home of Don Victor, Chapo's *mayordomo.* The women of Don Victor were grinding their corn. The mayordomo, aged now, slower, came forward to greet him.

"Get down, *joven,* young man," Don Victor said. "Have coffee or a trago. We'll eat soon. The road is long from Avena." Kane sipped sweet black coffee in small heavy cups served on a clean linen tablecloth. The three women of Don Victor served the men on bare feet on the swept and washed earth floor. Chapo came down leading a brown mule for Kane to saddle. The beast had been long in service.

Chapo and Kane rode straight up a mountain above Satebo, then straight down toward El Potrero. They skirted a deep gorge of deadly white rock that was swept with white water.

They jumped a black, a spotted, and a red steer and drove them to the top of the gorge where they scattered in the brush. Kane roped the black, tied him to a tree, and joined Chapo after the red. He spurred the mule for high ground ahead of the steer and lost a spur. He made it *a golpes,* by weight of heavy blows, took down his rope, and waited behind a knoll. He heard Chapo whooping below. He backed the mule until he could see over the knoll, and the red steer came in sight around it. He jobbed the mule with one spur and got ahead of the steer. The steer whirled and trotted back down the draw. The brown mule was as responsive to Kane's urging as a dead carcass. The red steer took his time. He knew by the sounds of Kane's whipping and spurring, pounding and cussing, that he was in no great danger. He saw Chapo, fell into a wash, and went through a fence into the pasture where the men had wanted him in the first place.

Several cattle were penned in a rock corral off the pasture and Kane dismounted, rested his arms on top the wall, and examined them.

"You don't have to take the ones you don't want," Chapo said, watching Kane, already knowing he would approve of the stock. The cattle were wide-horned *corrientes,* natives. Twenty head of them milled gently among Chapo's cows and heifers. Kane hoped Chapo had thirty more like them.

The steers were all colors. Their smooth coats shone, their eyes were clear, their muzzles moist with clear beads of health. The red, brown, and roan coats looked velvet and were outlined with streaks and spots of clean white. Their glistening eyes were sensitive, vulnerable, true, the eyes of free servants. Chapo and Kane rode out of El Potrero, their work done for the day.

At a gate on the mountain above Satebo, they came upon the

spotted steer that had escaped. Bartolo the vaquero was with them, afoot. The men uncoiled their ropes, built loops, and hemmed the steer against the fence. Chapo missed his loop. The steer ran toward Kane and he missed also.

Bartolo, the last in line, turned the steer downhill and ran in pursuit. He swung a big loop over his head, the loop sang, cleared the brush and sailed, open stretching and hungry ahead of the steer. Spotted steer, making escape, all downhill, ran away from the men, away from the ropes, back toward his solitude. Then, unbelievably, Bartolo's rawhide snaked over one horn, past one wild eye, and around his neck. He was caught *a media cabeza*, but he still had a chance to get away. He enjoyed the momentum of two hundred kilos falling off a steep rocky hill. Bartolo was barefoot in *huaraches*. The man ran with one hand on the rope and one hand free to protect his face from the brush.

Bartolo flashed through the brush like a rag tied to a plummeting rock. The spotted steer slowed to change course and Bartolo jumped into a mesquite and took a wrap of his reata on the hardwood. The coil smoked the imprint of the braided rawhide on a limb.

Spotted bucked in a circle against the reata, heedless of the brush, cactus, and trees in his way. When he finally stopped, he stuck his head in a bush.

The sun had gone down and the men wanted to reach Satebo before dark. They tied Spotted to the tree and left him to pass the long night wringing his horns against his bonds.

Chapo and Kane went down to a supper of potatoes and coffee at Don Victor's. Afterward, they sat by the fire and talked about the work while Kane smoked his pipe. At bedtime they swallowed a trago, dressed in all their clothes, and rolled in their blankets on the floor.

Kane slept an undreaming, unmoving sleep with spurs on. In the morning when he awoke he found that Chapo had risen and gone after spreading his blanket over him.

He walked in the chill to Don Victor's where he ate potatoes, tortillas, and coffee by the fire again.

He walked down the hill and found Pajaro, resting shot-hipped, and sunning himself. He swung up on his bare back and rode him to Don Victor's to give him corn.

Chapo and Kane rode back to El Potrero and Kane untied the steer to lead him back to the rock corral. Spotted dragged his feet, blindly angry, as he was led doggedly by the cow horse. The sweat of hard work frothed on Pajaro. The drag of the steer marked his back for life. In the corral with the other steers already gathered, the vaqueros tied a bell to Spotted's horns and hung a club under his neck that would knock his legs if he ran.

The trancas were lowered and the cattle were driven away from their lifelong *querencia,* their haunt. They streamed down the arroyo of El Potrero, by the ugly white gorge. They were contained by fear on the narrow trail as they passed La Rodada, the rolling place, where cattle had fallen before. They surged to get past the edge of the sheer gorge, carefully crowding each other to get by, a train of life passing an occasion of death.

Kane rode behind the herd as it snaked past the gorge. Chapo and his vaqueros were in front, holding, slowing, and husbanding it. A portion of the herd was around a switchback out of sight of Kane and out of sight of Chapo above the sheerest, smoothest, steepest precipice when Kane heard a sudden rolling, brush crashing plunge of something that was swallowed in the gorge.

Pajaro slipped on a band of smooth rock, scrambled, slipped again, and went down on his knees. Kane stepped clear and hurried ahead to help him. Pajaro lunged to his feet and rang his hooves clear of the rock. Kane caught up to the herd as it topped out above a *cajón,* box canyon. The occasion of death was behind them.

The bottom of the canyon, always in shade, was dammed by a dike of solid white rock that held pure, rock-bedded spring water. Brush and maguey that grew tanaciously to the cajón's steep sides brushed Kane's hat as he rode through to the bed of a warm sandy arroyo.

He counted the cattle into a field of cornstalks fenced with rock and found that one steer was missing. Nabor, the vaquero who always smiled, smiling took a knife and a stone up the trail to save any meat that might have fallen in the gorge. At Satebo at dark during a supper of garbanzo and coffee, Nabor came in, still smiling, and assured Chapo he had found no meat in the gorge.

Chapo and Kane morninged and saddled and returned to El Potrero. Kane was on the brown mule again. He rode to the top of a small peak above Potrero's basin, heard a voice, and searched the cliffs over his head. Nabor was perched on a high cliff above him.

He sprang along the rim of the cliff to a spot closer to Kane, cupped his hands around his mouth and called again. Kane did not understand a word. He was not even sure the calls were for him. He left his spot to search below Nabor. He followed a draw back to the corral where Chapo waited for him.

Chapo was heating branding irons. They lay in smoldering cow manure coals, softly red under light ash. Kane rode the mule into the corral and roped the Satebo heifers by the heels and Chapo branded them. When the job was finished, the two men smoked and waited with their backs to the sun-warmed rock for the vaqueros to come with the drive of steers they would move that day.

Later, Kane was waiting alone when he looked up and saw Bartolo chasing the red steer that had caused Kane to lose a spur. Bartolo had caught him and tied a bell on him to drive him in. The steer was climbing high and getting away. Bartolo turned him but was unable to follow him toward the corral because of the steepness and rockiness of the slope. Kane ran afoot up the trail above the corral, listening to the bell, not looking up, carefully running on his bad, loose knee, but making it in time to head the steer into the corral. The steer stopped outside the corral, peered over a rise at Kane, ears forward, dark face alert, horns still, their points bracketing Kane. Then he gave up and trotted into the corral.

Kane roped the steer and they had him at last and Kane stopped being angry about losing the spur. The vaqueros tied a green log to bang his knees and fastened the bell by a strap over one ear.

Kane went back to Satebo with the vaqueros, ate once more with them, swallowed a trago, and said goodbye. Don Victor rode with him as far as Los Bitaches, the old man insisting the trail was too long for a man to start alone.

They talked about someday hunting wild pigs together. In his youth Don Victor had run them into their caves, smoked them out, and clubbed them. He rode ahead of Kane on the slow brown mule. His gray hair curled out from under a peak-crowned, sweat-muddied, homemade palm hat. His thin neck was weathered under the hat. His thin face turned to speak to Kane and showed sharp cheekbones, gray mustache, Spaniard's chin whiskers. He wore a Mexican denim brush jacket sometime bought with God only knows what and khaki trousers on thin legs under the thick, billowing bullhide *armas,* saddle armor. His bare, crusted, deeply cracked heels in hua-

raches punched the mule and flapped the long armas to coax him up
the trail.

At Los Bitaches, Kane and Don Victor drank the *estribo,* the drink
for the stirrup, of *lechuguilla,* and Don Victor turned back.

Kane rode up the long steep climb to Puerto Los Sauces and onto
Las Mesas where Kane's red dog jumped a hare and got outrun,
then up to the top of a ridge where he could see the Río Mayo slash
through the Sierra by Guasaremos twenty miles to the north, and
the Chinipas airstrip twenty miles to the south. At Avena, he
stopped for membrillo again and watered Pajaro under the pines in
a cold, chalky, rocky creek bottom. Che Che said Don Juanito was
out picking corn. Kane ate a quince and rode on but Pajaro lagged,
wanting a break and Don Juanito's corn.

Kane soon regretted he had not rested the horse near Don
Juanito's kitchen. He was bothered by the horse's labor until finally
he was too tired himself to push on. He stopped at the Rancho
Quemado airfield, unsaddled, ate a burro of beans and tortilla,
drank a swallow of mescal, and snapped his pistol while he watched
Pajaro's breathing subside.

He left the airfield fresher, but he was still on top the sierra and
the sun was closing toward the horizon. He dismounted and led
Pajaro most of the way down the grade to Arroyo Hondo to stretch
his legs and revive himself.

He kicked a rock free, watched it roll and tumble, then spring and
twist and spin, buzz, strike and bound out of sight, then heard it
tear through the brush and stop dead on the bottom. Soon he was
at the bottom watering in the arroyo's spring.

Pajaro climbed the last bad grade to the mighty edge of the sierra
at Las Parbas. Kane let him blow and graze on thick grass, then
headed into the sun. Shade climbed the mountains above him as he
reached the smoother trail at the bottom of the grade and Pajaro
found ground for his foxtrot.

Kane saw smoke, then smelled it, then rode by a man who had
built his fire and quit the trail for the night. He saw no pack animals,
no saddles, no provision, only a man sitting alone who guardedly
returned Kane's greeting.

He rode through bunches of cattle, remudas of horses, struck
Arroyo de los Mezcales again and felt and smelled a warm salt
breeze from the Sea of Cortez. Pajaro trotted out but could not

catch up to the sun again as the light topped the side of the arroyo ahead.

He rounded a bend of sheer rock and a five-foot, bluish-black, ugly-headed *curua* snake lay insolently across the trail. He stopped and the snake moved unhurriedly away. She was thick-blooded, torpid, in the November cold. The sun was all gone for the day.

Abruptly Kane met a rider on a small, neat mule. A man afoot hurried to the other side of the mule. The rider, up close now, was gotch-eyed, leather-jacketed, an armed *pistolero*. A blanket was tied behind his saddle, a big automatic stuck in his belt.

"O.K.," the man on foot said and Kane saw he was Nito Vega. Nito always said "O.K." as a greeting to Kane. "O.K." was the only English he knew. He was dressed in a light, white, filthy, dress shirt with no undershirt, no coat. He hurried in his huaraches beside the pistolero and Kane knew gotch-eye was bodyguarding and Nito was carrying cash for his store in Guadalupe Victoria.

Kane asked where they would sleep that night. They were as far from anywhere as he was. Nito said, "Anywhere." Nito Vega, for all his money, would sleep under an old rock, away from people. Kane and Nito were good friends, but they passed on the trail without halting, saying, "until later." They both had to be somewhere before *"muy noche,* late night."

Kane went on without looking back and later met two small boy arrieros singing in the canyon to hear their voices rebound. They stopped singing when they saw Kane and stared, Indian-faced, at him as they passed. They kept quiet and did not look back while Kane was still in sight and earshot.

Later he met another arriero who stopped, wanting to talk. He said, "You'll never make San Bernardo. Too far to San Bernardo. You might make Rancho de los Mezcales. You go in deep evening shade now."

Kane needed to go all the way. He was shipping cattle in the morning. He vowed to go all the way. Pajaro used a ground-covering foxtrot, no good on the grades, no good on rock, but smooth and efficient on the level. Passing Rancho de los Mezcales, he told himself he could still see, and if he could see, his horse could. The sky still held a glow on the horizon.

Around a bend in the trail, Kane came upon a campfire, but no one was in sight. He turned his head away as he rode around the circle of light so as not to get it deep in his eyes and be unable to see the trail. A half hour later he reined Pajaro into the completely unyielding, hard thorny branches of a vainoro. He promised his horse he would not guide him anymore as he backed out with a hole in his hat and a scratch on his face. "Son of a bitch," he said.

He realized how little he could see with no moon and the evening star big as a light bulb and so bright that looking at it ruined his night vision. He slowed to a walk and lay over Pajaro's withers each time he sensed something in front of his face, trusting completely in his horse.

He was unable to see the trail at all now, barely able to see the brush silhouetted against the stars. When he saw the outline of brush, he could not tell how near or far away it was. His horse was following the dog. He bet his dog with those yellow eyes could see.

Kane stopped to drink and eat cold tortilla, not wanting to light a fire to warm it. He tossed pieces for his dog to snatch in the dark.

Remounting and going on refreshed, he passed through the black rock of the *Cajón de la Virgen*. The canyon was too dark for him to see the niche where someone had seen the Virgin, it was said. He knew most of the brush was behind him now. Then the arroyo dwindled where he remembered it should and he was out.

On a wide, white, ranch road, plain in the darkness, Pajaro could foxtrot again. Kane lit his pipe for companionship, but the light bothered him until the coals burned down in the bowl.

Passing by a ranch house with its dogs snarling and its bothersome lights, he was shifting his weight on his stirrups, weaving, bone-tired. He kicked both feet out of the stirrups, struck a rocky place, got topheavy, lost his balance, and pulled leather.

Pajaro topped the Puerto de Bacajaqui. Kane was stiff but his custom made him turn back for a last look at the Sierra.

Seeing the lights of San Bernardo and hearing music, he remembered the town was celebrating a holiday. A strong ocean breeze from a hundred miles away over the desert flat of the coast warmed him as he rode down from the pass.

He watered his horse in the stream below the town, then trotted up to the store and shouted a greeting. No one seemed to be in the store, everyone should be at the dance. He might have to ride over to the music. He hollered again, dismounted, tied Pajaro to a fence, loosened his cinches. A door opened and Poncho's brother Manuel came out to shake hands. Kane told him he had left Satebo late. Manuel said the fiesta had only just begun.

"You and Pajaro are barbarous to come over that trail in the dark," he said.

Kane asked him if he had seen the comet.

"No, it didn't come back, it must have burnt out," he said. "Why must you go on tonight? Stay for the fiesta."

Plácido

I, Plácido Ruiz, was born in Camoa, municipality of Navojoa, State of Sonora on the twenty-sixth of April, 1936. I was the son of Jesús María Ruiz Borbón and María Elena Valenzuela Cantú. We were thirteen males. All died in their childhood except my oldest brother Ramón, my younger brother Enrique, and I.

I was three when my mother died. My mother's spinster sister Concepción came to live with us then. My father died in 1944 at the age of thirty-three of the *sarampión*. We lived in a very clean place called El Sabino and he had never been sick, but one day he was summoned to work away from home, I don't know where, and he was gone a week. He brought the disease back with him and died of it. We all got it then, but we never even went to bed. We were told that the best way to cure it was not to pay attention to it. We were children and the measles only made us uncomfortable for a short time.

After my mother died I suffered for affection until I married. I was treated like a feather, blown from one side to another, and ordered to keep my distance. Ramón was my aunt's favorite and Enrique was her godson. I did not have anyone.

After my father died we moved to El Datil, on the Mayo River, closer to Navojoa. I started school, went three days, and was taken out to work for José López, a rancher. I earned fifty centavos a day herding his cows at pasture. He was a good man and advised me never to be a thief or an idler. I worked and lived with his family at Colonia Rosales for three years. I went out with the cows at dawn and brought them back at night through the *datilera,* a long, long lane lined with date palms.

Those date palms were planted in the time of Don Porfirio Díaz, before the war of Alvaro Obregón, and are still standing. Families planted them first in their yards and then, when they grew large enough to defend themselves, transplanted them in the lane. The same families are still harvesting the dates every year.

For years my official duty was to climb the trees and do the picking. I used a rope around my waist and around the tree and climbed barefoot. I competed for the dates with the thorns, the *cachoronas*, and the little black ants.

In order to reach the dates, I had to clear the thorns away with a machete all the way to the top of the tree. The thorns of the date palm are like knives four inches long with points an inch long. Once, as I was shaving the trunk ahead of me, a thorn sprang off the machete and pierced my hand between the knuckles of the first and middle fingers, through the palm to the back of my hand.

The ants were small but their sting was bothersome and made a man itch. The lizards panicked when they were discovered and sometimes the first refuge they found was inside my clothes. In there, they became rough and lively. Once, one got inside my sweatshirt under my armpit. For two hours I was forced to endure her presence, or fall. The ordeal was awful. Most of the time I am so ticklish I'm dangerous to myself.

Cruz and I had only been married a short time and she was standing thirteen meters below me receiving the *racimos*, the clusters of dates. The cachorona used her little claws to move around behind me and across my loin. My sweatshirt was tight and I could stop her progress by flexing my shoulders, but when I did that she whipped me with her tail. Her tail was the roughest, scaliest part of her. The animal was making me buck like a horse.

"What are you doing?" Cruz yelled. "You'll fall."

"Think of it, old lady, a cachorona went down my neck."

"What are you going to do? Don't fall."

"I'll fall, *Madre. Nothing* can make me fall."

"Come down, then."

"I'll come down, *Madre. Nothing* can make me come down until I get the dates."

I stayed up there until I sent all the dates down. It was September and still hot. As soon as my feet touched the ground Cruz lifted the back of my shirt and released the cachorona. With all that and the work, the ticklishness of the cachorona and the fear of height, I was sweating a lot.

After José López sold his cows I went to work for Jesús Guttierez. The López family had been good to me. They took me into their family and they had eight children of their own. Their children and I have always been like brothers.

With Jesús Guttierez I helped milk thirty-two head of cows every morning and was given a horse to ride when I day-herded them. I also cut grass for them with a machete. I loved the smell of the grass when it fell. For me, grass was never heavy and I was able to carry great bundles even larger than myself. I liked to watch the cows eat it because they appreciated it as much as I did.

I met Cruz at a dance at Colonia Los Timos on the fifteenth of August, Dia de las Marias, a Saturday in 1952. She was thirteen and I was sixteen. We danced together and from that moment we were never apart again. She lived at El Datil and came to the dance with her mother, brothers and sisters. I had known her since she was nine, but I never loved her until that night.

Cruz's mother was *indigena* and spoke the Mayo language. Her father was *medio indigeno y medio razón,* half Indian and the other half rational. He was a bricklayer and died when she was very small.

I paid court to Cruz at her home for one month. Then, on the sixteenth of September, a national holiday, a Saturday, I went to see her and we found that we were in accord. Tuesday, at 10 at night, riding *un caballo entapojado,* a bronc that had to be blindfolded before he could be mounted, I went and got her. The bronc tried to buck all the way back to my ramada, but he couldn't throw us. When she got down from that bronc she became my wife. After that ride away from her home we never hid from anyone again.

Three days later her mother came and castigated me, and then we talked. She was angry because we were so young. I said my circumstances required that I have a wife who would make me a home. In 1955, when Concha was born, we married.

I had been taking my meals at Jesús Guttierez's table. Before Cruz came to live with me I never in my life sat by my own fire. I was never close to anyone else's fire, not in the winter evenings, not even when I was irrigating on cold nights. The other irrigators always built fires so they could stay warm while the water filled the borders, but even when I had to work barefoot I stayed away. I would rather withstand the cold than put my hands and feet under the stress of the change from hot to cold. The few times I was allowed near a fire taught me that.

I learned it also from Jesús Guttierez. He advised me not to heat my hands and feet at a fire and then chill them in the irrigation water. If I was cold, to warm up by shoveling to reinforce the borders ahead of the water. That was better for him and better for me, for it kept me away from the fire and kept me working. I was able to do more work and stay warm in a normal fashion.

So the first thing I did was make Cruz a *pretil,* a bench for her fire. I put four *horconcitos* in the ground, forked posts with the forked ends waist-high. I laid four *viguitas,* small beams, in a square that rested in the forks. Then I laid smaller viguitas across them as I would for the ceiling of a ramada. I laid a thick cover of brush over that, then covered that with the same batter of mud and horse dung that I used to make adobe that would stay together in fire. I let the batter air out and dry a day or two.

I found myself five burnt bricks to make two *hornillas* on top the pretíl. I placed them to form two open-ended squares side by side, enclosed places for two separate cooking fires.

I used good mesquite wood for everything. That is the best wood when *palo fierro* or *ejea* is not available. I got a good *azador,* a quarter-inch iron rod for broiling meat, and I found an old plow disk for cooking tortillas. I bought a fired earthen *comal,* a frying pan, from a neighbor who made them, an *olla* for a bean pot and an olla for our drinking water.

Cruz was very clean. She kept the ground swept under our ramada and she swept a large portion of ground around the ramada outside. In the summer our clearing was so clean and bright with the sun that not even an ant could venture near our home.

She doctored us with natural remedies. She used *hoja de chicura,* chicory leaf to stop bleeding and bandage cuts. For a fever she administered the tea from *yerba el índio,* the root of a vine that grew in the *callejones,* the fenced alleys between the fields. This medicine could reduce almost any fever and was good for infections of the stomach and as a purgative.

For stomach worms she made a soup from the root of the *estafiate,* a hardwood wand that grows straight as a rod. Those wands are used as handles for homemade rockets that are sent up in the celebrations and for warding away flocks of blackbirds from the crops. The soup will stampede stomach worms out of any orifice they can reach. Worms will abandon a host within an hour after *estafiate* is taken.

She boiled the leaves of the *álamo* tree and laid them, still warm, on strained or sprained limbs to leach away pain. She used *závila*, a soft cousin of the maguey, to cure festering wounds, and cool and heal burns. She stripped off the bark and laid its cool, gelatinlike salve on the wounds.

She boiled *golondrina*, a wild parsley that is named after the swallow for the way it spreads its leaves upon the ground as a swallow spreads its wings when it lands. She pasted it on our children's head sores and other sores. She taught me that golondrina is good for everything inside a person and out. Before that, I only knew it was a favorite feed for cattle.

Her best remedies were preventatives. Every day she made us all drink a glass of the tea of *musso*, the short, ribbed cactus that looks like a cross between the saguaro and the pitahaya. She cut only the branches with five ribs so that when they were sliced crosswise they became five pointed stars. She made tea of one star for each of us daily to keep our blood clean and prevent arthritis and cancer. I know musso cures those diseases, even when no other medicine will work and people have been given up for dead.

Doña Teresa, a woman who lives in Jijica, a pueblito downriver from us, drank musso and praised it every day of her life. She is in her nineties. She makes the traditional woolen Mayo blankets and when she finishes one she walks the ten kilometers to Navojoa to peddle it. She walks another ten kilometers in the selling. Her blankets are heavy, for they are thick and measure two meters by one meter, large enough to cover any man.

Concha was born in Los Timos where the *partera*, the midwife, lived. Then came Maria Elena. Our third child was a boy, Jesús Maria, called Pati. Our fourth was Umberto, Beto. Our fifth was Rolando, the one my compadre called *nalgitas de baqueta*, little leather butt. The one who took Cruz from me was born dead.

I started work with my compadre in October 1959. Rolando was born very soon after that. I had been working for Jesús Guttierez fifteen years when I looked up one day and saw the tall gringo who was later to become my compadre coming toward me. He asked me to look for three steers that got away from a shipment he had sent north on the train. He offered me a hundred and fifty pesos, at that time twelve dollars, to retrieve them. I made a circle in the brush on

La Estrella, my bay mare, and found them bedded down on the baseball field at Ladrillera.

The American was staying at the Motel del Rio, so I rode over and told him his steers were in my corral. He gave me a check on the Banco Nacional del Yaqui y Mayo, the first check I was ever given in my life.

I did not know the man at all, so I went to my friend Ramón Encinas, who worked at the motel, for advice on what to do with a check. He said to wait until he went to town and he would give me a ride to the bank. I had never been inside a bank. The check was made out *Al Portador,* To the Bearer, so I asked Ramón to cash it himself and he did.

Cruz was waiting for me at the market to buy provision. We took it home and that evening she helped me drive the steers down a fenced lane to their pasture. I still remember them, a red steer, a black, and a red-and-white pinto, all steers with wide horns for American rodeo.

When we arrived at the American's corrals no one was there to receive the cattle. I corralled the steers. The American drove up, saw his cattle were safe in the corral, and asked me how much I earned with Jesús Guttierez.

"Fifteen pesos a day," I said. That was $1.20 in 1957.

He said, "I'll pay you twenty pesos if you'll come over here every day on your mare and look after my cattle."

I couldn't accept until I asked Jesús Guttierez to release me. He said I could take the job with his blessing because now that I had a family I should try to better myself if I could. We were living on a parcel of his land and he allowed us to stay there as caretakers.

The American brought his son Billy to live with him and we all moved up the river to the Cuatro Milpas ranch at Chihuahuita. Soon after that we became compadres when he baptized Rolando and confirmed my other children.

My responsibilities were to care for Pajaro, my compadre's personal saddle horse, and to look after the cattle and the farm. We drew water for the cattle from a well, or drove them down the bank to the Mayo River. We seldom kept big numbers of cattle in the pasture. Most of the cattle were sold and shipped north right away. We kept only cattle that were refused by the buyers for being too poor or unsightly.

My compadre built us an adobe brick house and we kept Pajaro in a corral beside it. One morning I prepared to gyp him, make him longe around me on a long rope to exercise him, and he balked. This surprised me, because he always enjoyed his exercise. Something inside a thicket near the corral agitated him and made him fearful and he paid no attention to me. I handed him to Pati and went to get another rope so I could toss the coils at him to make him move.

I was several meters away from the horse when a coyote staggered out of the thicket. He was sick, drunk, dizzy, the flies were sticking on him, and he was slobbering. He stank of wet hide and hair, as though he had been dunked in the river, but he was dry and shrunken. Pati was holding the horse by a lead rope and would not turn loose of him. Without a sound the coyote walked up to the boy, bit him on the heel, and turned toward the house.

Pati yelled and Pajaro tried to jerk away from him but he would not let go. Pajaro dragged the boy on the end of rope and attacked the coyote. He ran over the top of him and kicked and struck him with all four feet, then chased him back into the brush at the point of his hooves. Then he dragged Pati back to the house and stopped.

This happened about six in the morning. We were sure the coyote was rabid and were still lamenting over our bad luck when my compadre came and took Pati to the Red Cross. About four o'clock that afternoon the coyote came back. Tiano Murillo and I ran him away from my house and followed him. I was carrying a .22 rifle my compadre gave me to hunt with, but I couldn't get a shot. When the animal finally showed himself clearly I was too nervous and shaky to shoot. I handed the rifle to Tiano and he killed him with one bullet.

My compadre took Pati to the Red Cross for his shots every day for two weeks. The injections were given him near the navel with a long needle. The boy did not cry until the last day. Two days after the last shot the boy said, "Eh, Papá, when is the gringo coming to take me for another shot?"

"Why, son?"

"I like to go with him."

"Why is that?"

"He buys me a cocktail of a dozen raw oysters every time."

That spring when we were through shipping cattle we still had thirty-five of the cutback cattle left. We grew a good crop of sorghum grass, put an electric fence around it, and turned the cutbacks out to pasture on it.

My compadre was waiting to be paid for his last shipment and was short of money. We needed to irrigate the sorghum grass. We ordered the water from Recursos Hidraulicos and hired some irrigators. Each shift lasted twenty-four hours. The field was very dry and we always irrigated it with contour borders, allowing the normal gravity flow of the water to cover the field from border to border.

I went to receive the water in the morning when the *sanjero,* the ditch boss, allowed our ditch to fill from the canal, but my helpers did not show up. I took the water by myself for the first twelve hours, but that work was easily done by one man because the water ran over a large, level portion of the field. I did not know what I would do with the water when evening came.

At sunset my compadre came out to see how I was doing and he brought a *trago,* a swallow, of José Cuervo tequila and my supper. When he saw I was alone he picked up a shovel and helped me, after a fashion, that whole night. The only shovel available was a large, square, scoop shovel that I used to clean up Pajaro's manure, not well suited for moving the gummy, riverbottom soil.

My compadre and I knew easy times and hard times. This was a hard time. His shovel made him work twice as hard as a man should and he wasted a lot of motion. The April night was cold and I started a fire in a *guayparín* log so he could warm himself when he stopped. I went away to look after the water for a time and when I returned I found him asleep by the fire. The warmth of the blaze caused a hill of *mochomos* near my compadre to swarm. *Mochomos* are red ants that could not do more damage to a man if they carried machetes. They do as they please most of the time, but I awakened my compadre before they were able to get a taste of him.

The sorghum crop grew lush and plentiful. A big, old, heavy-horned, swaybacked black steer we called El Señor Pando served as lead steer when we drove the cattle out of the pasture to water on the river. Later, after the sorghum grass was gone and I day-herded the cattle on the canal and riverbanks, he was the first steer out the gate in the morning, and the first to lead his fellows home in the evening. My compadre ordinarily would never own a swayback, but when he bought a small herd of cattle from the man who raised El Señor Pando, the man said my compadre could not have the cattle unless he took the old swayback too.

The Americans failed to pay for the shipment of cattle so my compadre left me in charge of the horses and cutback cattle and went north to collect. I did not see him or hear from him for six months. He did not collect the money, so he found work in his own country to pay his debts.

I also found other ways to make a living while I kept my compadre's cattle and horses together. The cattle fattened on the sorghum and certain envious people told me to sell them and pay myself wages, but I could not. Men came and offered me money for the cattle, but I could not sell. Selling, or killing a beef to feed my family seemed an ugly thing to do. I made up my mind I would have my compadre's livestock fat and healthy for him when he returned.

My neighbors said I was a fool, that he was not coming back. They said only a dumb brute would be faithful to a gringo. I was also taking care of his house and other properties. The neighbors advised me to sell his radio, his saddle, anything to relieve my burden, but I could not touch any of his goods.

I took other jobs, though. I could never steal if I was able to work. I took Cruz and the children and picked cotton on neighboring fields. Our cattleman friends Rafael Russo, Manuel "Botas" Hurtado, and Ramón Peral also gave me work when they needed a vaquero.

When the sorghum grass was gone I day-herded the cattle on the canal and riverbanks and wherever I could find pasture on credit. I took them home and shut them in their own pasture at night.

In October my compadre came back and we started working happily again. As long as my family was healthy all I needed in order to stay happy was work. Work has always been the cure for my ills.

My compadre began handling large numbers of cattle again and Cruz Gastellum, a rancher from Pueblo Viejo, came to work with us. My compadre brought his little daughter Paula to live with him. She was four. He helped form the Charro Association in Navojoa, and Lucha Villa came to sing at the inauguration of the Lienzo, our arena. We put on weekly *charreadas*. We were healthy with plenty of work, music, and fiestas.

We worked happily for three years and then the coyote bit Pati. A month later Cruz died in childbirth. She had begun intense labor about 3 A.M. Only her mother and I were present for most of the birthing because our regular *partera*, midwife, was not found, and her substitute came late. Cruz gave birth to the child inside an hour, but he was dead and Cruz was feverish. I knew I needed to mount my mare and hurry for help, but I couldn't do it. I just couldn't. I don't know why. I was fearful. My feet felt heavy, as though they did not belong to me. I couldn't get on the mare. I felt I was a long way away from myself and couldn't use my body.

I asked my friend Tiano to go to the Motel del Río and call for the ambulance, but it never came. Finally I hitched my mare to a cart and took Cruz to Navojoa. She made the trip well. We took the little man with us, even though he was dead.

I left Cruz with the nuns at the *sanatorio* and went back to Cuatro Milpas to see about the children. I thought the nuns only needed to clean her up and make sure there was no infection. On the way back to the sanatorio I asked my brother Enrique and his wife to take charge of my children until Cruz came home. Then I went to tell my compadre's housekeeper that Cruz was in the sanatorio.

I bought some lotion, soap and a comb for Cruz and returned to the hospital. The nuns were cleaning blood out from under her empty bed. The lady in the next bed told me no one had attended Cruz during the entire time I was gone. The nuns who were cleaning up the blood were making their first appearance at the bed.

I told them I wanted my wife.

They said she was dead.

I said, "How could that be? I was only gone an hour and she has been in your hands all that time."

"She suffered complications."

"Yes, the complications were your hands, you daughters of the fornication."

"You must resign yourself to the will of God. Everyone has to die."

"You are the ones who should have to resign yourselves to death. You are the ones who should have died. You have no children. My woman leaves orphans. You deserve to die for neglecting her."

It seemed impossible that Cruz was gone. I couldn't believe it. To me the sanatorio was the safest place in the world. They directed me to the patio where she lay. Her face was covered by a sack and I replaced it with my handkerchief. I embraced her and tried to tell myself she was dead. I could not accept it. She was lying on a cement slab where all the dead were placed. I couldn't stop crying. I wept until I was scared I might not be able to stop.

The man who officiated at Cruz's funeral is called a *mestro*. The Mayos customarily have one present at such occasions when a priest is not available. The priest blessed Cruz at the church, but the mestro did the praying for people who did not know or understand the priest's prayers. Our mestro's name was Zenón and he was from Capoguisa near Loma de Refugio. To pray the novena and come up with the right words at funerals was his vocation, but he was not a holy man like a priest.

We buried Cruz and I thought I would soon also die. I couldn't get back to work. I took the children to live with their grandmother for a while, but she did not like the responsibility. My compadre then hired my *comadre* Delfina Valenzuela to come to Cuatro Milpas and look after my children. She did not stay long because her husband took a job in another pueblo.

I was forced to take care of the children by myself after that. I felt sad, helpless, and nearly dead. My children were small and cried for their mother every day. I didn't know what to do. It was hard for me to return home in the evenings and face the cries of my children. All our joy was gone.

I did no work at all for a year. I was unable to control myself. I was anxious for everything but my work. I was anxious enough to die. My compadre's paychecks never stopped, though. He visited the children often and I, more than often, was not there to greet him. I mostly sat under a tree and drank mescal. Thank God my compadre did not lose faith in me.

Conchita, my oldest, was ten. After a year of terrible hardship she took hold and began to cook, wash, and doctor the little ones. In another year Marilena was big enough to help and we all started pulling evenly together again.

I returned to my duties with my compadre and felt responsibility for my work again. Heavy winter rainfall brought a strong demand for cattle. My compadre shipped a steady flow of steers, stags, and oxen to the north and I did not have time to think. We worked seven days a week. In a year we shipped nearly nine thousand cattle and we were almost happy again.

We worked hard and long in this way for several years and our setbacks were mostly only financial ones. We rode good horses. I remained in charge of taking care of the horses, the farm where we grew feed, and the cattle. My compadre went into the Sierra Madre every fall and spring to buy cattle and send them out. I stayed at Cuatro Milpas to receive them and to doctor and strengthen them for shipping.

I had more time for my family than my compadre did. He was never home. His son Billy and his daughter Paula were often with me. They were beautiful children.

Billy was respectful, obedient, good, and serious; in a word, noble. Like his father, he was mischievous but never showed any signs that he had not been raised well. He was a happy boy.

The little girl Paula was beautiful and good, but she was not happy. The old lady who had taken care of these children when they were infants got too old to help anymore. She began taking long vacations at home in Nayarit. She was very old. Finally, during a long absence in which my compadre could not find her or even communicate with her, he hired a young woman.

This new woman, Alma, took over the household with great efficiency. She was a hard worker and honest. She loved Billy almost to adoration. But she did not love Paula. She saddled Paula with too much hard work and the light just went out of the little girl's eyes. She was not beaten, but she was humiliated. I can think of no better word. New clothes that arrived for her from her grandmother and aunts in the States appeared on other peoples' backs. Her only diversion seemed to be when she could visit Cruz and my children, swim with the horses in the canal, play dolls and fill her little stomach with Cruz's gordas. That was the way I saw it.

Then my compadre's new housekeeper began importing her family. First came an unmarried brother, then her mother, then a young sister, then another unmarried brother. They came to stay.

My compadre tried to put them to work, but they stopped when he went out of sight. He tried to find them work, but none of the opportunities they were offered worked out, because they did not really need to work. Alma gave them everything they needed at the new home my compadre built in Chihuahuita. Little Paula's work increased, though, and her clothes also showed up on the backs of Alma's relatives and even friends of the relatives.

If they had been workers, I would have lost my job. I was able to stay because when cattle work was to be done they disappeared like ghosts, like wraiths. My wages never stopped when there was even a little hard work to do, but when the cattle were gone and the housekeeper was left in charge of running the finances of the ranch, my wages often stopped.

My compadre gambled on cattle in large numbers. When the demand was good in the north, an abundance of good rain fell, and the Mexican government allowed the exportation of cattle; when the cattle were not dying in a drought and my compadre could keep them healthy for shipping, we prospered. Often we shipped great numbers of cattle and he came back with nothing, because the government closed the line for some reason before he could cross the cattle and get his money, or the cattle sickened and the profits were expended in feed and medicine, or the buyer's check was no good.

One year, when the cattle sales did not pay off, the only resource left to us was the farm, so we planted twenty-five hectares of *maizmilo* for a cash crop to sustain us. The crop was lush and both our families armed themselves to protect it from *dañosos,* the birds, and animals that would prey on it. With this work in sight, Alma's relatives decided to take a vacation at their home in Jalisco.

My compadre's family and mine left the house long before sunup and could not rest until after sundown for the sixty days that the *motas,* the heads of grain, were vulnerable. Blackbirds and *cuervillos,* the vicious bird that is larger than a blackbird and smaller than a crow, mourning and whitewing doves, rabbits, and quail attacked in hordes.

The boys were armed with *hondas,* slingshots for throwing rocks. The girls were given no weapons, though little Paula came out with a popgun. Any noise like that would make the birds rise off the field, but only deadly weapons could make them fly away. My compadre and I carried skyrockets and shotguns. The children were stationed around the field and my compadre and I patrolled on horseback.

The blackbirds invaded every morning before sunup. They were so many they darkened the sky. They thinned out during the heat of the day, then attacked again at sundown in double their morning numbers.

When a flock appeared over the crop we sent the rockets into the middle of it to scatter it. Most often they left us then for other, unprotected fields.

During the heat of the day the blackbirds changed their tactics and attacked by stealth. They fluttered in one by one, staying low inside the leafy crop. When we least suspected them, we would look up and see a whole flock blackening a spot on the crop.

Our children were paid a bounty for killed animals. All my compadre's remaining capital and my job were in that crop. We protected it through the latter half of June, all of July, and the first half of August, in the very heat of summer. The heavy afternoon rains gave us the only relief we knew from the sun and the blackbirds. When rain did not fall, the temperature reached 115 degrees and higher and we swam in the humidity. Our poor children could not stay awake. The field was oppressed by the sun, but surrounded by the shade of heavy brush. The children spent more than twelve hours a day as sentries and a stop in the shade often meant a lapse into slumber. We sometimes carried them sleeping to their posts in the morning and carried them back to the house at night.

We prayed for rain. I think the children must often have prayed for darkness to fall at noon, they were so tired.

My compadre and I patrolled on young horses we were breaking. We gentled them by lighting the fizzing rockets and shooting the shotguns and riding them many miles around the field. We knew no holidays, no Sundays. Dove and *pichiguila*, tree duck; *patagonia*, blue rock pigeon; rabbits and quail were our meat. My compadre was broke. Even my wages were suspended. The money that remained was for food, medicine, and tools.

A winter tourist who came down from the States to shoot birds gave my compadre an old 12-gauge shotgun and ten cases of reloaded shells, all the ammunition we needed. The rockets were only good if the birds knew they could be killed if they ventured onto our field. If we did not kill them from time to time the rockets only caused them to rise and resettle on new plants.

We were many. I was feeding seven and my compadre was responsible for all of his and all of mine. We were not in the field to kill game, but we killed to eat when game came in range.

Our favorite meat of all was the *pichiguila*, the tree duck native to the region. The pichiguila does not fly in flocks. When she goes she goes alone very fast in a straight line. We might only see ten go by in a week that were in the range of a shotgun. A lot more passed us too high and too fast.

One day I was irrigating the garden out of the canal and left the shotgun under a *jito* tree. Cruz was under the jito with Rolando talking to me, keeping me company, and she looked up and saw a pichiguila coming straight at her. A pichiguila does not keep herself aloft like other birds. She does not loft herself. She has no serenity when she flies. She agitates herself with great velocity. She only rests in the places where she lands.

I don't know what possesses her, but once she decides on a course, the pichiguila never seems to swerve from it. She always flies with all her might. When she launches herself from her nest, the wind from her wings scatters the leaves off the trees, as though she must make the flight in a headlong manner, as though she must end the flight as soon as possible, in the next heartbeat.

Cruz did not know one thing about a gun, but without a word she shouldered the shotgun and fired. The charge met the poor bird head on. The impact of the recoil on Cruz's shoulder pitched her backward into the full irrigation ditch. I was given a lot to look at, with the meat plummeting out of the sky toward the jito, and my woman going head over heels into the irrigation ditch. When she resurfaced she laughed so hard I thought she would drown.

The birds became our enemies, especially the blackbirds and the *cuervillos*. The cuervillo is black as the blackbird but the size and weight of a pigeon. He is not plump, though. He is wiry and nervous, and he is omnivorous and gluttonous. I have seen a pair of cuervillos swoop down together and catch a blue rock pigeon after the pigeon was shot dead in the air by my compadre. They caught him and flew away with him before he ever hit the ground. I've seen them prey in pairs, kill a rat and carry him away between them.

The cuervillo has a scissor bill like the blackbird and he can eat his weight in grain or meat, or I am sure, other cuervillos. We learned to hate blackbirds and cuervillos. We could eat the doves, quail, ducks and other game birds and they fell readily, but sometimes the blackbirds and cuervillos seemed impossible to kill even when we fired point-blank into the flocks.

Their voracity was an ugly thing, the way they crouched over the heads of grain and clutched at them and made them tremble as they fed on them. They themselves trembled and jerked with greed as they snatched at the grain.

We would be going along thinking the field was clean and then there would be a cuervillo tearing into a mota and sticking to it in spite of our shouts and rockets and stones from the slings. We couldn't shoot them off the motas without destroying a large patch of grain and we did not dare shoot a rifle near the field. A rifle bullet has too much carrying power, the brush hid everything beyond the field, and we could not always see where the children were.

The cuervillos seemed to be satisfying more than only their hunger. They seemed so full of hate they wanted to rape our field. That is what they were doing. We would look up and catch them in the act of rape. Before we even knew they were on the field they were already half finished with the violation. I often needed to remind myself that all animals have a right to eat. Everyone does, but the cuervillos and blackbirds have no grace about it.

One day I was hunting away from the field with the .22 and about noon I shot at a *liebre,* a hare, lying under a tree. She fell over dead. When I picked her up I could not find the wound that killed her. I picked her up by the ears and she revived and started bawling and she bawled all the way to my house.

I asked Cruz what to do with her and she said we must pardon her life. We kept her in the house and fed and watered her that night. The next day Cruz opened the door so the liebre could go out, but she only went as far as a shady, wet spot under the *tejabán,* the shed, and lay down. She seemed to enjoy being near the children. She stretched herself happily on her belly on the wet ground under the olla with her front feet crossed in front of her, her hind feet stretched out behind her. After seeing her in that pose, we would never have been able to eat her. Later, thank God, she got up and left us.

After several years of bad luck, my compadre took his children and went back to Arizona. Many years later, after my children were grown and married and I no longer was responsible for anyone but myself, he visited me while I was irrigating the Cuatro Milpas for another man. He told me he was coming back soon to take me home with him and retire me with Pajaro. The papers are difficult to regulate and the distances are great between his world and mine. He had offered to help me many times through the years, but was never able to do it. I could not see myself retired in Arizona. I kept on working where I always worked.

I knew not to expect anything. I swear I did not think I was counting on him coming back for me, but when two months passed and he did not come, I despaired.

My brother kept saying, "He's not coming."

My brother's boss would look at me and laugh and say, "How can you expect him to come back? He's not coming, especially not for someone like you."

"He's never lied to me," I said. "He's never told me one thing and meant another."

"He's too far away to think about you."

"Who knows how far away that has to be? Not me," I said.

Finally, one day I bought a bottle of Viva Villa mescal and got drunk. Villa began to drag me in the dirt. I drank enough to kill myself, but could not whip Villa. I did not give up, though. After two weeks of the fight, my kids ran me off. My brother would not have me either because I was too drunk to do his work for him. I slept in a rundown stable where my brother's boss used to keep his horse, when he could afford one.

I maintained my own vice. Nobody bought my Villa for me and I don't know how to steal. I worked every day I could and drank all I could every night. My brother's boss owed me six months wages. I had a blanket.

Then my brother and his wife beat and kicked one of their little daughters half to death, called her a whore and threw her out, and she came to share the stable with me. She was the only person in the world lower than I because she was sad and only had me to protect her.

I was not sad. My son's wife Prieta worked in the restaurant at the gas station. She came to see me from time to time and that was enough to bolster me. I always told her I was doing well. She never backed away from me even when she found me down on my face in dirt as fine as ashes.

I love La Prieta more than anyone else in the world. She is a happy girl unimpressed by evil. She is not afraid that an old drunk can bring the end of the world upon her.

Once I woke up without a cent in my pocket and all my mescal was gone. Prieta watched me closely for a long time. I tried to hide it, but I was in awful need of a drink. Finally she said, "How repugnant old drunks are. I think I'll just kill you."

With that she wound up like a baseball pitcher, kicked her foot at me and threw a bottle at my head. I ducked and it tore through the brush behind me. I looked for a place to hide from the next missile, but saw she was laughing at me. The bottle had crashed heavily through a tree, but it was intact. I retrieved it and it was a full liter of Villa in its plastic, unbreakable bottle. The sweet girl had saved it to cure me of my hangover.

Pati and Prieta have five children and they live in a one-room ramada. They use walls of tin in the winter and take them down in the summer. I often slept on a cot outside their door.

One winter's night I awakened about 2 A.M. in a terrible state of nerves as drunks do when they find themselves alone in the night-time of the world without a drink. I had cut myself off the mescal and every nerve in my body was lying out raw on the surface of me.

The night was black and my nerves made me afraid and there was no light anywhere to console me. I became aware of another presence nearby. I heard the whisper of a breath and a small clamor of moaning. Something rubbed against my cot.

I rose up like Lazarus and there above me a large white shape breathed a cold breath upon me. I jumped up to run away with no thought of direction, rushed straight through the door of Pati's ramada, and slammed face-first into the back wall. The sound of Prieta's laughter made me realize that she had pulled a joke on me. I did not speak to her for a whole day. When she served me my noon meal she asked me if I was angry, but I would not answer. She could not stop laughing, though, and by evening I was laughing too.

She does everything with a straight face. "Don Plácido," she said one morning. "Last night I prayed to San Antonio to please let you die of the *cruda,* the hangover. You keep me awake every night with the sighs, groans and moans of your suffering. I truly believe it is time that he take you away to your glory, whatever that may be."

I said, "Why would you want that? I won't leave you anything and you don't have enough money to buy a coffin."

"Don't worry, I have enough to buy a *petate,* a bamboo mat. I'll just roll you in it and drop you in the well."

The next day when I awakened, she said, *"Oiga* Don Plácido, I'm so relieved you did not die last night."

"Why?"

She handed me a sheet of paper with some writing on it. "Because I want you to sign this paper making me your sole heir. I know you must have a pot of gold hidden somewhere."

"What makes you think that?"

"You never have a nickel in your pocket, yet you always have money to buy all the Villa you can drink."

My brother Enrique might not have believed my compadre was coming for me, and he might have been too quick to let me do his work, but he is a good brother. I never drank in the cantinas. I took my bottle down to the orchard to do my thinking and drinking until

I slept. In the morning he knew where to find me and always came for me with something to eat. I would get up and hurry and feed and water the stock and do my work and as soon as I was through I'd take off to get my Villa.

"Ahi va el pajaro," Enrique would say. "The bird is taking wing again."

Then when I passed them by, certain people would jeer, "Here comes your compadre, Plácido. He's almost here, Plácido."

Enrique's wife, Tolola, could not stand to see me suffering the *cruda* and have no drink with which to cure it. She was capable of stealing to find me something to drink.

One day Elisa Russo came for me. Lucky for me she caught me working in the field, though I had not bathed or changed my clothes for weeks. I was irrigating barefoot with my pants rolled up to my knees.

She honked to call me in from the field, then stepped out of the car and shouted, "Plácido, come on."

"Where are we going, to jail?"

"To get your picture taken."

"Like I am?"

"Just the way you are."

I laid my shovel down and got in the car, muddy feet and all.

I lost my birth certificate in the flood of 1949, so we had to go ask my older brother to sign a statement as proof of my birth date. His wife would not open the front door when she saw me, so I went around to the back. My brother made me wait a long time. Elisa honked her horn and got his attention out front. I trotted around to the front in time to hear her say, "What, you come out for me and not for your brother? What kind of man are you? Just sign this and crawl back into your cave." My brother signed the statement without even reading it and Elisa took it to a notary and stood over him until he sealed it.

She took me home with her, bawled me out about being such a drunkard, gave me two beers and fed me. She then told me not to despair, because my compadre was coming for me the next day.

After that she took me to sit for the photographer. She did not approve of the first picture because it caught me with my eyes shut and she thought I looked like a drunkard, so he took another and caught them open.

Then she hurried me to the *comandancia* to obtain a letter of good conduct. They found nothing against me and prepared it readily. I've never been in jail, not even for drunkenness, not even on suspicion. Even if they had found something against me, they would not have presented it. Nobody would have opposed Elisa Russo's recommendation. She also supplied a letter of recommendation from the Cattleman's Association where she is Secretary. The letter stated that I had worked honorably as a vaquero in the valley of the Mayo all my life.

When we finished arranging all my credentials Elisa asked me if I wanted her to take me home. I had been paid the day before and I thanked her and said no, that I wanted to go to the butcher shop to buy some soup bones for La Prieta.

Elisa said, "Are you sure you do not intend to buy one big shank of mescal instead?"

"Yes," I said.

"Ah, *sí*, you've reformed."

"Yes."

"Yes, Little Jesus, I'm sure you have."

I did go and buy the bones and other ingredients for a soup, but also a bottle of Villa. When I got back to El Datil La Prieta said, *"Ay, ya trai su biberón, no?* You also brought your pacifier to suck on, no? At least change into the clean clothes I pressed for you. Bathe and get ready for your compadre. Sober up."

"No," I said. *"La cascara guarda el palo.* The bark protects the tree. And a man can't throw a rock without showing his hand. My compadre knows me. I'm not going to hide what I am. He can take me this way. Right now I shall have a drink."

There I was in the morning, with my empty bottle and my face in dust fine as ashes, when my brother came. "Wash up," he said. "Get hold of yourself. Your compadre is here."

That brought me out of the dust at last. "No," I said. "I don't need to get hold of myself. I don't care if he sees me as I am and neither does he."

He came early because he knows about people who drink too much. He wanted to get hold of me before I headed down the road to drunkenness again. He took me to his room at the Motel del Río and stuck me in the shower. Unfortunately, that morning there was no hot water, but this did not concern my compadre. He would not let me out of the stall. He made me bathe until my *huevos*, my balls, climbed up inside me to save themselves. He let me out to dry off and warm up awhile, but he stuck me in again and made my huevos run for cover again.

When I came out the second time a breakfast of bacon and eggs, frijoles and three cold beers was waiting for me. He had brought me new clothes from Tucson and a new hat and jacket. He set out in his pickup to do some errands and took me with him to air me out, to *oriar* me. He strengthened me with food and beer that day to bring me back to life and prepare me for the night I must endure without a drink of the hard stuff. My topsoil was dry by sundown.

That night he dosed me with red wine and talk and from time to time I was able to sleep. He said I sang in my sleep, proof that he stayed up and watched me all night. The next day he made me stay in bed and rest while he dosed me with food and red wine to keep away the demons. That night I slept better and the next morning we struck out for the north.

My compadre dosed me with beer and conversation all the way to Hermosillo. He thought I would have been dead in another week. He said the clothes he brought me hung on me like a shroud on a skeleton and that I looked more like a harp than a man, but we laughed a lot. I wanted to die. My stomach cramped, but I never once thought of turning back, or of asking him to stop the pickup.

In Hermosillo that evening we ate a good supper and my compadre took a separate room. After two nights of caping a drunken bull, he needed rest. I discovered the television and it kept me occupied enough so I could forget about my craving for drink several minutes at a time. I needed to be sober the next morning to pass the inspection of the Mexican Passport Bureau.

I stood in line ten hours for my passport. My not having a birth certificate caused me some trouble, but my compadre hired a good man named Carlos Hardy to go with me, a learned man with a gift for debate. Don Carlos convinced the authorities that my affidavit was proof enough of my date of birth.

When I came out of the office with my passport I felt better. A little beer with my meals was enough to keep me from having a nervous fit, but I still could not sleep. That night I sobered up completely in preparation for being run through the chutes at the American consul.

The Mexican guards at the consul barred my compadre and Don Carlos at the gate. I had to go in alone. A lot of people, people of

reason who owned more than I, were allowed to pass through un-
molested, but I was the one they searched with electric wands.

I was shaky and half sick, but unafraid of the institution or the
men and women who ran it. I was afraid for my compadre, for he
seemed to have more at stake and be more anxious over my acquir-
ing a visa than I was. One thing I did know, in that building and
everywhere else in Sonora I am equal to everyone else and have the
same rights. I could take any of the people who ran that institution
out on a moonless night in a wet field with a head of water coming
at us and nothing but shovels to defend ourselves with and twenty-
four hours to prove ourselves and they would have to start asking
me questions.

Since I am such a slow reader, I was sure I would have trouble.
When my turn came I faced an American who helped me fill out the
paper. He asked me what I intended to do in the U.S. and I said I
would visit my compadre. I presented a letter from his university
friends saying that I was their invited guest and a letter from my
compadre saying that I would be staying in his home. They asked
where my compadre was and I said the guards would not let him in.
They investigated all my other papers and showed me where I was
to sign my visa and that was it. That evening we headed for the
Border.

We celebrated by sipping a bottle of Villa, though not heavily, on
the way to the Border. One little bottle of Villa between the two of
us in six or seven hours is not very much and we had a lot of it left
when we reached the American Customs and Immigration station.

People must have thought we were wanted for murder by the way
we were searched. We must have smelled like the Viva Villa *vinata*,
distillery, itself. My compadre was mortified, because he had not
anticipated this. They made us sit down and wait six hours before
the supervisor himself came and made out my papers.

My compadre was angry, at first. Later, he said they probably
figured they could not arrest us for drunk driving, but they sure
could detain us long enough to sober us up. He explained that
drinking can be a serious offense under certain conditions in the
U.S. Our celebration did not mean a thing to the U.S. Immigration
Service, but our lives must have.

At my compadre's house I was given my own room and bathroom, my own kitchen, my own bed and blankets and a blanket
Billy gave me. Billy and Paula visited often with their children. I

thought I would have found it a strange place, but at first I felt much at home.

The weather was colder in Tucson, but once in a while in the evening my compadre and I took a little swallow of strong spirits before supper. We took care of nine saddle horses together. His wife Patricia and his mother-in-law treated me like a king, poor things. I rode horseback with my compadre's little grandchildren. I was *agusto*, retired. Once a month I dictated a letter for La Prieta and at first she answered promptly.

Every evening I went out in the pasture and brushed the horses. They fought for a share of my attention. Each was almost as big and good as Pajaro, almost. To me, no horse will ever even grow a hair as good as Pajaro's. These were good horses, though. My compadre and I were again riding horses that would be considered good in any country.

As a retirement gift my compadre gave me a saddle, as he did thirty-three years ago when I first joined him. After I rode it for the first time he asked me how I liked it. *"Está bueno,"* I said.

> *Está bueno para el santo que la monta,*
> *Y los milagros que hace.*

> It's good enough
> For the saint who rides it
> And the miracles he performs.

I stayed four months before I was stricken with a terrible *tristeza* that I have never known before. During my stay I counted heavily on hearing from my children, especially La Prieta. I received two letters one month apart in the beginning, then nothing. I sent letters home, but they were not answered. At Eastertime my compadre was visited by Billy and Paula and their spouses and their children and I began to long for my own family.

From one day to the next I grew physically and morally weak. My compadre was busy and I did not want to bother him with my problems. Then I stopped sleeping. My mind was in a turmoil for an entire week. One evening I cried at the supper table in front of my compadre and his family. That night my heart ached so badly I knew I would die if I did not go home immediately. The next morning I told my compadre of my illness. In order to impress on him how much I needed to go home, I said, "If you're a man, you'll help me."

That day he took me to Nogales, Sonora, and put me on the bus.

The Widow's Gift

A legend among horsemen in Spanish-speaking countries holds that the Moors once gave the Spanish queen Isabél a herd of fine palomino horses as a gift after the culmination of a treaty. The queen was ecstatic with the gift and the gesture, but the Moors were only laughing at her and making sure the Spaniards who rode the palominos would be afoot the next time they attacked.

The Moor was afraid to find himself afoot on the desert with his enemy in sight, but he considered being mounted on a palomino horse worse than being afoot. He knew the Spaniard loved to parade into battle and the Spaniard did not know the palominos would continue to parade during the battle.

The Shane family had worked hard all summer raising a crop of milo maíz on their ranch on the Mayo River in southern Sonora. The summer was hot and dry. Every day Miguel and his wife Vicenta and their three children were up at 3 A.M. to do their chores and go to their stations around the field and meet the assault of the blackbirds. The assault began at dawn and ended at dark every day.

Each day, by noon, thunderclouds tumbled over the Sierra Madre mountains in the east, but did not bring the rain the family needed. The combination of humidity and heat stifled the family in the field.

Miguel carried a bundle of hand rockets called *cohetes* for scaring the birds. To light a rocket he scratched the base of its cylinder with his thumbnail and fired the loosened powder with a pitch *tizón*, firebrand. He cast the rocket away toward the flock, it took off with a rushing swish, spiraled and trailed smoke as it chased the flock, then burst in an explosion of fire and noise.

Miguel gave his two boys a peso apiece for every blackbird they killed with slingshots. His girl was too small to do anything but yell and beat the brush to try to scare them, but the boys were deadly with their slings. They erected tall bamboo poles around the field and hung dead blackbirds on them, macabre warnings to other birds who might try to raid the Shane milo maize.

During the day the birds flew low into the field singly to keep from being seen. The Shanes never became aware of them until they had massed together in one spot. Then, all of a sudden, someone would see them swarming, crouching, clawing, and devouring the *motas* of grain and not making a sound. At sundown, the birds massed together and attacked in flocks from all sides again and the family fought them off until they retreated at dark.

When the hard work of harvesting the crop was finally done, the family was sunburnt and hard as ironwood, worked down and sleepless, but ready for rest and play. Miguel had promised them a trip if the crop was abundant, but the price of grain had gone down and it made no money. Even so, no one was unhappy about having worked hard for little pay. The children had not grown but they were much stronger. Miguel had ridden and trained a dozen colts in the hundreds of circles he made around the field, firing his shotgun from their backs, lighting and throwing rockets. He marketed a dozen gentle colts besides the milo maíz. He joked about the summer's growth in his crop of children. He said since there was no market for his children at that time, he would have to be content to grow them out several more years before they would be worth anything.

Don Gilberto Salido, a wealthy rancher and horseman, drove up to the front porch one day as the Shanes were finishing the noon meal they called *sopa*. Miguel invited him for coffee and they sat awhile and discussed thoroughbred horses. Don Gilberto had recently brought 30 brood mares to his ranch from Kentucky.

"Miguel, I have a favor to ask of you," Don Gilberto said.

"Tell me," Miguel said.

"I was a very good friend of Señor Thomas Greenbriar of Greenbriar Farms in South Mountain, California, near Los Angeles. He died last year and his widow has been selling his splendid mares and shipping everything off the farm. Before he died, he gave me a colt as a gift and sent me a bill of sale and the colt's registration papers.

"Yesterday I received a telegram from the widow asking me to come for the colt or send her the papers so she could sell him and send me the money. Evidently, the woman is about to liquidate the estate. Naturally I want the colt."

"Do you want me to go and get him for you, Don Gilberto?"

"Yes, you speak English and you are a good hand with a horse. I will pay your fee and all expenses. You will be doing me a big favor."

"Is the colt gentle? I only have my pickup and a rack. The rack is a box that lies in the bed of my pickup. I won't be able to haul him if he is bronco."

"I'm sure he's gentle," Don Gilberto said. "The gringos start loading and hauling their colts when they are only babies. This horse is four years old. Can you go?"

"I'll be glad to. If I find I can't haul him in my rack, I'll rent a trailer. I've been promising my family a trip and this is a good chance to show them famous Los Angeles."

"Fine. I'll leave four hundred American dollars with my office secretary for you."

"So much? I don't think I need that much, Don Gilberto."

"Listen, everything you do up there with the gringos will cost you dearly. Enjoy the trip and if you run short of money, call me collect. I pay for everything."

"Well, thank you. Is there anything else I can do for you in the United?"

"Only enjoy the trip. Mrs. Greenbriar will like you. She is eccentric, but very nice."

The Shanes washed and polished their pickup. They packed their best clothes. Miguel fixed a shelter in the back of the pickup for the boys and Vicenta laid a camp mattress on the deck for them. The whole family would have to ride in the cab on the return with the horse in back, but everybody would have more room on the way to Los Angeles if the boys rode in back. Miguel wanted to drive to Los Angeles without stopping so his family would have time to see the sights before he loaded the horse and returned. The Shanes had friends in Los Angeles, hunters he guided in the Sierra Madre every fall. The friends often invited Miguel to bring his family for a visit.

The Shanes left the ranch one morning at 3 A.M. They figured leaving early guaranteed a good trip. The first leg to the border was pleasant, fragrant, cool. The northern half of Sonora was green from the summer rains. Cattle and horses were fat. The mesquite trees were heavy with *pechita,* the long, juicy bean that was good cattle feed.

In the late afternoon they reached Tucson, Arizona, and serviced the pickup, then started across the Papago Indian country. Fifteen minutes later the red pickup began to fail. The red light that indicated an overheated motor went on. Miguel turned off the road and stopped. He felt lucky that a lot of traffic was going by. He was sure someone would stop to help him.

He lifted the hood. The radiator cap was gone. He only needed some water to get back to Tucson. No one stopped to help him after three hours.

He was about to start walking toward Tucson when an old pickup loaded with Papago Indians stopped. Miguel had turned his back to the traffic and his head was down, so he did not know anyone had stopped until he heard someone say, *"Pariente,* kinsman." He turned to see the pickup full of people and their packages and sacks of groceries. The driver was hefty, sweating and smiling. "What do you need?" he asked.

"A little water, *pariente."*

The Papago lifted a jug off the floor and handed it across his passengers to the window. "Take it all," he said.

Miguel emptied it into the radiator.

"That should help you get back to Tucson. I would follow you, but I have to take these people home tonight."

"Thank you, pariente."

"No need to thank me, pariente."

Miguel drove back to the gas station that had serviced his pickup in Tucson. The same man who waited on him earlier came out of the office.

"Fill it up?" he asked.

"Hell, no. I came back for my radiator cap."

"What radiator cap?"

Miguel smiled good-naturedly. "The one you forgot to put back when you looked in my radiator when I bought gas here a while ago."

"Mister, if I poured your gas when you were here, if you were here, I would not have forgotten to replace your gas cap."

"No, you remembered the gas cap, but forgot the radiator cap. Don't you remember servicing my truck about four hours ago?"

"Seenyor, this is a busy station. I can't remember every vehicle that comes in."

"You haven't seen a radiator cap lying around, either?"

"I just told you I haven't."

"Well, sell me another one, please."

"Yes, sir. What kind do you want, the three-dollar, the four-ninety-eight, or the five-ninety-eight?"

"The five-ninety-eight, please."

The man sprang away to his office in his white shoes and his white suit with its smart white cap. Miguel filled the Papago's jug while he was away. The man came back, opened a brand new box with a flourish and removed a shiny radiator cap. He filled the radiator with water and screwed the cap in place.

Miguel paid with a ten-dollar bill. The man opened a cash box with a key that was chained to his belt. "Let's see." He looked at a list taped to the inside of the lid of the cash box. "That'll be six dollars . . . and thirty cents tax."

With quick, efficient scoops of his fingers, he took the change out of the box and counted it into Miguel's hand. "And thank you very much, sir," he said.

Miguel got back into the pickup with his family and started the motor. *"¡Gringo mendigo!"* he said under his breath. "Gringo beggar."

The motor continued to overheat, the radiator would not hold water and Miguel barely made the 100 miles to Ajo. No garages were open and the motor was barely pulling them along when they stopped at a motel. The family rented a room and made their supper of food Vicenta had packed at the ranch. Miguel could not open the windows and the room stank of gas. The family slept with the door wide open.

In the morning Vicenta and the children went to a restaurant for breakfast. Miguel took the pickup to a garage and walked back to join them. "Little Red needs new gaskets or something and the mechanic needs to check and see if the who-knows-whats are melted. He won't be able to give it back to us before five o'clock."

The Shanes waited and rested in the motel all day. Miguel and his oldest son played chess. The youngest son practiced with his lariat. The little daughter worked with her paints, Vicenta with needle and thread.

That evening the man from the garage drove the pickup to the motel. "All it needed was a head gasket," he said.

"Did you find the cause of its heating up?"

"Yes. You needed a pressure cap on the radiator. Your cap was the cheapest one they make, worse than having no cap at all."

Miguel made the Los Angeles Freeway by late afternoon. The family liked the smell of the salt air off the Pacific Ocean. Miguel needed to find a place where he could stop and read his map. The map was in English, and Vicenta did not know how to read English or Spanish. Miguel saw a Highway Patrol sign and turned off the freeway. He drove another ten minutes before he found the office, but it was closed on that day, a Sunday. He lost another hour finding his way to the South Mountain Freeway, and a while later realized he was going the wrong way.

A patrolman on a motorcycle overtook him and started to pass. Miguel signaled him. The patrolman seemed not to believe he was being signaled and tried to ignore Miguel. Miguel overtook him and made signs of hopelessness.

The officer understood that. He signed for Miguel to follow him, leaned on the cycle with much professional verve, swung in front of the red pickup, and guided the family off the freeway to safety.

"Officer, we're in need of guidance," Miguel said.

"Aren't we all," the patrolman said, smiling.

"We're looking for Greenbriar Thoroughbred Farms."

"Do you know what town it's in?"

"In South Mountain."

The officer was not impolite, but he could not look at Miguel while he was talking. As he gave directions he watched the freeway like a herdsman watches his livestock when it is on the verge of stampede. "Where are you from?" he asked.

"Chihuahuita, Sonora. It's your home, if you ever come down that way."

"Be careful who you invite to your house. I might come some day and stay forever. And be careful on the freeway. I don't imagine you're used to this kind of traffic."

"Don't worry, I'm as careful as I would be if those people were pointing shotguns at me."

"Listen, they're pointing cars at you and in their hands cars are more dangerous than shotguns."

That evening Miguel chose a motel near South Mountain called

Knight's Sleep. A giant cartoon of a mounted knight jousted on the sign over the office and other funny-looking knights held forth on the walls in the rooms, on the furniture, on the linen. A large television set graced the room.

Miguel went to the office and called Greenbriar Farms. A girl answered and said Mrs. Greenbriar was not able to come to the phone but she would make sure the lady received the message that the man from Mexico was in town to pick up the colt. She said Miguel would be able to contact Mrs. Greenbriar by phoning in the morning at ten o'clock. Mrs. Greenbriar would surely be able to see him tomorrow, she thought. Just at the moment she was busy with visitors to the farm. Miguel could hear music and talking in the background.

Back in the room, the whole family was gripped by television, their faces soft and rapt with its enchantment. Miguel went out to get supper. The man who ran the office said a drive-in up the street sold big hamburgers and milkshakes, the Shane family's favorite supper.

Miguel drove up, but did not drive in. The acre parking lot of the drive-in and the parking spaces in the streets surrounding it were solid with cars. At first Miguel thought he had come upon some sort of church meeting or maybe the funeral of a great man. Surely only worship or tribute could take so many people away from their homes on Sunday. Certainly the appetite for hamburger had not caused such a hegira. Miguel did not venture to go in after hamburgers. He found a restaurant, ordered an expensive supper to go and drank a beer while it was prepared.

That night Miguel began to feel the trip would not be as enjoyable as he hoped. So far it had not been the diversion his family needed. As the long evening dragged on and he could do nothing but watch programs of pastime television, he wondered what kind of person this widow was. Why had she turned away from him with the excuse that she was entertaining visitors? Was he not also her visitor? To be of service to her and Don Gilberto, Miguel had moved his family more than a thousand miles. He was accustomed to being offered hospitality even when he traveled 100 kilometers away from home. This woman was not even able to bother with phone contact. In his country the welcoming of a stranger was a revered custom. In his country it was considered a privilege to welcome a stranger, to offer him food and drink and a place to rest, and to be happy when he accepted it.

Miguel felt he and Vicenta and the children were like a family of hungry, spotted longhorn cattle bunched together for protection in the corner of a modern feedlot full of thousands of sleek, fat, white-faced Herefords. He knew of no common side of the Shanes to show the gringos in order that his family be safe, now that he had not been welcomed to Greenbriar Farms. He had expected to find haven for his family there after he braved a trip of a thousand miles into a strange country. He had hoped to find an ally in Mrs. Green-briar so that his family would feel enough at home to enjoy the trip. He would have been so good to Mrs. Greenbriar if she visited his ranch in Chihuahuita that she would have returned to South Moun-tain feeling part Mexican.

Miguel was up at 4 A.M. He went out alone and walked around the block. No one was astir. He snorted a challenge like a Mexican bull but it went unnoticed. All the chutes were empty and all the other beasts in the feedlot were asleep.

At exactly 10 A.M. Miguel called the Greenbriar number again. Mrs. Greenbriar's voice was low, soft, and cordial. She was terribly sorry she had not asked Miguel for supper but her niece had not notified her that Miguel was in town. How long would he be in town? Would he care to come to her house right away? Of course he would want to see the beautiful colt as soon as possible. She gave him directions to the farm.

Miguel took Vicenta with him. She was dressed in her best blue suit, her short hair in pert, shiny curls. Her straight, tiny body did not weigh eighty pounds. She was brown and hard from doing her part in the sun for him.

Miguel had been on pavement ever since he stopped to talk to the motorcycle patrolman. The family was hours inside the paved towns and had seen very little earth. Now Miguel and Vicenta were sur-prised to see that South Mountain was bare of pavement. The dry stalks of that summer's corn crop stood in rows on its slopes.

All of South Mountain was owned by Greenbriar Thoroughbred Farms. The farm's stately, tile-roofed ranch house was on top the mountain. The house seemed a monument of disdain for the en-croachment of pavement, a holdout against high prices of real es-tate, a place for horses to run, build muscle, heart, and wind.

A sign off the freeway said: "This road leads to the headquarters of Greenbriar Farms, home of Tiger's Stripe, the Greatest Thoroughbred Racehorse in the World."

Miguel drove up the winding dirt road to the top. The paddocks and stud barns were being dismantled. Their white boards lay scattered on the ground.

The road ended behind the house. Miguel stopped under the shade of tall eucalyptus trees. No one was in sight. A noble old fighting rooster herded his hens together protectively when Miguel, leaving Vicenta to wait in the truck, stepped onto the walk that led to the front of the house. He rang the front door bell and waited. Tall fir trees stood at the edge of the front stoop. In front of the house the ground fell off steeply into the cornfield. The field had been plowed in horizonal rows against the steep slope like farms in the Sierra Madre. Miguel did not think anyone could have done that planting with a machine.

Miguel saw that he was standing above a layer of brown haze that hung over the pavement below the crest of South Mountain. He was on top of a mountain in the clear sky. Little cars skittered back and forth trying to get through the choked traffic on the freeway, but were quickly absorbed and forced to creep inside the advancing humpy mass of smoking steel. Miguel smiled as an old longhorn might smile when he saw the vaqueros had missed him and were driving his hapless companion bovines on to the slaughterhouse without him. He was free again for a little while.

He rang the doorbell again. The house was of brownstone with thin lines of mortar showing between the bulging stone blocks. The headquarters home was dignified, solid, and old. The front picture window was curtained against the sun. Miguel turned to another window on a corner by his shoulder. A face was there staring at him.

Miguel's eyes and the eyes in the pale face locked. The face's eyes were colorless, solid, and unexpressive as polished agates. Wispy hair around the face was like a wraith. The lips were still faintly streaked with a residue of last night's lipstick and deep cracks eroded the upper lip. The face quickly hid the lips by folding them in. The erosion of the upper lip had been formed by the expression the face assumed at that moment. It prissily clenched and ungenerously hid its lips. Then the face was gone behind a curtain.

Miguel's eyes relaxed and opened again. They had narrowed and slitted with involuntary viciousness at the sight of the face. They would have done the same if he had been surprised by a poisonous snake and had prepared himself to kill it.

After a while the front door opened and the woman welcomed him, grinning dazzlingly above a transparant negligee. "So you're the man from Mexico Gilbert sent for Tiger's Cub?" She extended her hand.

Miguel took it and shook it. "Yes."

"Well, please come in. Gilbert and his family have been nice to us on our visits to Mexico, so please feel at home." The eyes in the eroded face studied him with a flat stare.

The front room was cluttered with expensive waste. Glasses containing the leavings of high-powered drinks and smokes were strewn on the tables and floor. The room was dark and the paintings on the walls were dusty. Several bronze nudes from the Hollywood thirties rested on fine heavy wooden tables. They postured with seemingly innocent faces, but the legs were spread and the outthrust teats voluminous in case someone might be interested. The door to a bedroom was wide open and revealed a big, round, mussed bed, drinking glasses on the floor, discarded underwear.

"Please forgive the disarray. I had a little gathering here yesterday. Tell me about your trip. You do speak English, don't you?"

"Yes."

"Well, fine. What do you do? What is your occupation?"

"I have a ranch and I train horses."

"How interesting. Have you had breakfast?"

"Yes, I have, thank you."

"Well, surely you could have coffee."

"Yes, I can always drink coffee."

"I know. With lots of sugar. Mexicans use a lot of sugar in their coffee. Come in the kitchen while I warm it."

"Do you mind if I bring in my wife? She's outside in the truck."

"Oh? . . . Sure, by all means."

Miguel went to the pickup and opened the door for Vicenta.

"*¡Diosito!*" he said softly. "It's an ungirdled mess. We'll wait a minute so it can put on its clothes."

After a while Miguel and Vicenta went back to the house and knocked and waited for a long time. When the woman finally showed herself again she was in a housecoat and wearing Persian carpet slippers that showed off her naked, mottled feet. She did not smile when Miguel introduced the neat, dignified Vicenta.

Vicenta stepped trimly into the room with the open, good-natured pleasure that a good housekeeper shows when entering a strange home that is beautiful outside. Miguel watched her ignore the disorder and admire the fine, rich wood of the furniture. She stopped once to touch the top of a table as she followed the woman into the kitchen.

The woman had laid two cups with no saucers at each end of the kitchen table. She poured the cups brimful of coffee and remained standing. "There's plenty of sugar," she said. The sugar bowl was there, but only one spoon. "Have you seen the horse?"

"No, we haven't," Miguel said.

The woman stepped over to a speaker on the wall and pressed a button. "Clair?" she called. She released the button.

No answer.

"Clair, Clair, Clair?"

Vicenta smiled at her. Mrs. Greenbriar saw the smile, coldly turned her face toward the wall and the speaker.

"Yes, what is it?" a man's voice answered.

"Come up here, will you? The man is here for Tiger's Cub."

"O.K."

The woman leveled the polished stone eyes at Miguel. "My man is coming to show you the horse."

The coffee was so hot it could not be swallowed. Miguel wished he could be finished with it. His and Vicenta's seats at the kitchen table with coffee so hot it could not be drunk held them in place like laboratory slides for the eyes of the woman. He wanted to get out from under the gaze.

"What a fine couple you make. So brown," she said. "Are you out in the sun a lot, or is that your natural color?"

"We are never out of the sun," Miguel said.

"You mean you've been outside all your lives?" She giggled. "When will it end?"

"Never, God willing."

A screen door in the back opened and a big man stomped into the kitchen. He wore heavy, square-toed cowboy boots; soiled, farmer's blue-jean trousers with new leather gloves folded under the belt; a loud, checkered cowboy shirt; intricately combed hair; and what Miguel was sure the man believed passed for a large, shy, wise, just-an-old-cowboy smile.

Mrs. Greenbriar smiled sweetly and introduced Miguel. She did not introduce Vicenta.

"This is the man they sent for the horse," the woman said.

"Miguel Shane, your servant." Miguel stood up and offered the hand that had been broken less than a month before by a striking horse. The big man squeezed it unnecessarily hard. Miguel had long experience with the phonily hearty American handshake that tried to intimidate. Hotshots like this one substituted it for an open heart. That way they could get all expression of good intention over at the start. As he tried to ignore the pain, Miguel scolded himself and asked himself why in the name of saints he had let him do it. He did not like to admit a sonofabitch like this could sneak up and hurt him. Well, now at least he knew him well.

"I'm Clair. My servant, huh? I like that."

"In a manner of speaking."

"Where'd you learn to speak such good English?"

"My father is an American. I was in the U.S. Marines four years."

"Your name's Shane, huh? Well, a real *accomplished* man from Mexico, an *Irish* Mexican."

"Can we go see the horse?"

Before he went out the back door, Miguel looked back to see how Vicenta was doing. She was still dutifully sipping her coffee and holding her handkerchief under the cup. The cup had been so full and the coffee so hot, she could not manage without spilling some of it. Miguel knew she would sit there as a dutiful guest and accept all the hospitality offered her until the coffee was cool enough to swallow. She would stay because she felt she must at least show appreciation and keep the woman company, or at bay.

The colt was a palomino and standing in a paddock by himself. He was the only horse in sight. Every other paddock and stall was empty. When the men appeared he preened and pranced like a stud horse, then stopped and snorted and nodded at them. He stood in old manure a foot deep. A two-foot pile of manure that had been tromped up against the gate was proof to Miguel that the horse had not been out of the paddock in probably a year.

She's turned a sound young horse into a damned gooberlip, Miguel thought. He had become like his owner, all appetite. Her appetite did not keep Mrs. Greenbriar fat, however. Her appetite for chemicals kept her skinny. The horse was so fat the tallow had formed in pones on his sides and belly and there was no definition between his belly and hips. His legs and chest were flat and undeveloped. His neck was thick with fat. The hooves had grown out long and curled like the runners on a sled, causing him to stand abnormally on his heels.

His feet are gone, Miguel observed. His feet and the uneven spots of cold sweat, the residue of sweat salt on his shoulders, show me they fed him so much they foundered him. They've ruined him. As any horseman would say, even in California, he ain't worth a nickel. But how could he be? A horse can be no better than his owner. He's probably the last horse that will ever walk on this ground and he's the epitome of his owner, all belly from his front teeth to his asshole. He's never done anything except put away the groceries and be proud of his big, fat, untried balls. Old man Greenbriar would probably be alive today except he couldn't live without his balls. The woman took them away from him probably because she was sure she could put them to better use, then never did a thing with them.

"Has that thing ever been hauled?" Miguel asked.

"I've been here a year, ever since the old man died, and I've never seen him outside this paddock and I've never seen him touched by human hand."

"What in the hell are you graining him for? Why didn't you let him run in the pasture? That way he could at least keep himself in shape and his feet trim."

"He's too valuable, man. They say the old man turned down 40,000 dollars for him when he was only a weaner. You don't turn out that kind of animal."

"You don't? Well, all the good has been grained out of him. I bet you couldn't find anyone who would give you forty cents for him now. How much grain do you give him a day?"

"Only about ten pounds. He's a mean sonofabitch. If I fed him any more he'd charge right through his cage and eat me."

"Two pounds would be too much."

Clair picked up a bullwhip that was hanging outside the gate. "I use this to keep him from trampling me when I have to go in there," he said.

"I can't see myself heading down the freeway with that thing prancing over my family's heads. The first big truck that came along would spook him right onto the pavement. It's a cinch I can't haul him in my rig."

"I'll haul him as far as the border, if you can't do it," Clair said.

"How much would that cost?"

"I couldn't do it for less than six hundred dollars."

"Hell, sorry as he is, I'd ride the sonofabitch to Mexico for that. No, I'll see if I can rent a trailer."

"Suit yourself. The offer stands."

You're standing there ready, aren't you, thought Miguel. With a bullwhip.

Miguel went back and found Vicenta sitting in the pickup.

"Didn't you and the spook have anything to talk about?" he asked.

"She showed me the coffeepot and told me I could have all I wanted and left."

"Very nice of her. I hope she comes to see us sometime."

"She probably has a lot to do."

"Yes, I'm sure she does."

Mrs. Greenbriar and Clair approached Miguel from around the corner of the house. She had combed her hair, washed, changed to a modest slack suit, tied a ribbon in her hair, applied makeup sparingly and attractively.

She sure knows how to change her masks, Miguel thought. She's formidable. Lucky for me I caught her with the mask off. She can fool 'em with the masks off, too, though. Look at Clair.

"Well, how do you like our prize gift to Mexico?" The woman called, then she skipped down the walk toward Miguel just like the ex bright young thing she was.

"He's a good keeper, ain't he?" Miguel said.

"Well, we've always taken the very best care of our horses. That is why we have such a wonderful reputation in the racing world."

"That's what I've been telling the man, Lola. That's a fine, fine animal out there," Clair said.

"We would never let you take him without Gilbert's personal guarantee that you are capable with horses," the woman said.

"I'd like to catch him this evening, halter him, and tie him to a post overnight so I can handle him tomorrow," Miguel said. "I need for him to at least remember his halter training."

"Oh, we would never let you tie our horse to a post. We always get along with a minimum of handling. That is an expensive, spirited animal. It would break his spirit to tie him up all night."

"I can see that. Such as his spirit is. I have to see about renting a trailer, now. Could you have him inspected this afternoon?"

"Inspected? For what? Why? He is a perfect animal. Why inspected?" the woman said.

"Yeah, why inspected?" Clair echoed.

"You have to bring the state brand inspector out here so you and he can give me permission in writing, on a form, to haul the horse away from here, especially since I'm taking him out of state. We also need a vet to come and take blood for a Coggins test."

"We've never had to do that, even when we moved whole caravans of horses to the track in Tijuana."

"Mrs. Greenbriar, I'm sure someone must have taken care of that part of it without your knowledge."

"No, I'm sure they never had to do anything like that," Clair said. "She would remember, wouldn't you, Lola?"

"Of course. It's ridiculous. We never brand our horses, anyway."

"Is he tattooed?"

"Tattooed?"

"Don't registered horses have their numbers tattooed inside their upper lip?"

"We never did that."

"Ma'am, if he is the son of Tiger's Stripe I'm sure your husband had him tattooed. If not, it doesn't matter. His markings are all the inspector needs for a description on the form."

"Well, this must be something new. I'm sure it's not necessary for a Greenbriar Farms colt."

"Would you please see to it anyway? It might save me a lot of trouble down the road. I can't leave without the legal hauling papers."

"Oh, then, of course. *Anything to save you trouble.*"

"Thank you. I'm sure he's too spirited for my rig, so I have to rent a trailer. If I get squared away I'll be here to load him at three-thirty tomorrow morning."

Mrs. Greenbriar went back to the house. At the door she turned and motioned for Clair to come to her. They talked and Clair came back to the pickup.

"Lola wants to give you the game chickens. She wants to know if you can catch them today and take them away."

"No, thank you."

"She says she won't charge you for them or anything. She wants to get rid of them. They mess on the paths."

"Thank her for me. Tell her I appreciate her thinking of us, but those chickens would take all afternoon to catch and I have other plans."

"The offer stands. I'm going to see about the inspector and the vet, so I guess I won't see you until early tomorrow morning."

Miguel started the pickup back down the road to the freeway.

"She must have a thousand dollars' worth of chickens," Vicenta said.

"They're good chickens. Someone's been feeding and watering them and they've multiplied. No coyotes or bobcats here."

"Why don't we take them? We could bring the children and catch them in an hour."

"I don't trust offhanded gifts. Why didn't she tell us herself? A gift should hurt the giver and be given with a smile. Let her get someone else to clean up her chickenshit. How did you like her eyes? We would have spent an hour like germs under a microscope."

They found the children in despair. The wrong twist of a button had deprived them of television. Miguel found the picture for them and told them he would take them for a drive that afternoon, maybe to Disneyland, or to play miniature golf. They paid him no mind. Their television was back, all of it free, and only for them.

Miguel went to a pay phone and began calling trailer rental agencies. After an hour he gave up. No horse trailers were available for out-of-state hauling. He called Mrs. Greenbriar.

"Oh, it's the man from Mexico," she said.

"I wanted to let you know that I won't be able to leave early tomorrow as planned. I can't find a trailer to rent."

"Where are you?"

"At a pay phone near the place we're staying."

"Why don't you come on up here and tell me about it?"

"I have my children with me and we have plans for the rest of the afternoon, thank you. I also need to find a way to haul that horse."

"All business. Just an all-business Mexican, aren't you?"

"That is what I came here for, Mrs. Greenbriar."

"Why did you call me just now?"

"Only to tell you I can't leave with the horse in the morning."

"Why tell me your troubles?"

"I thought you would like to know."

"I really don't care. I gave a man a horse. Now his hired hand comes around bothering me with his troubles. How he gets his horse is no concern of mine. It is Gilbert's responsibility to take him off my hands in the safest and most humane way possible. So get with it and don't bother me with it anymore." With that she hung up the telephone.

Miguel went back to the room and lay down on the bed and shut his eyes. He felt like packing and going home, but he did not want to have to tell Don Gilberto a mean woman made him give up. He did not want a fight. The woman was making him hate her even though he thought he had defended himself well without trying to rile her. He won the first encounter when he caught the face in the window. He gained more when he refused to see her in her negligee as anything but an uncombed, crusty, vulgar old blister. Then she decided to put the Bunsen burner to the test tube in which she thought she held him and tried to unman him by attacking his competence. The tactic probably always worked well for her so she would keep it up. If he watched for it she might not succeed in making him feel so bad next time.

By evening Miguel had arranged for his friend Buster Vernon to haul the horse to Tucson. The Shanes went out and visited friends and the miniature golf course. When they returned the manager of the motel called him to the phone.

"Is that you, man from Mexico?" the woman asked.

"Yes, it is."

"Did you and the kiddies and the wifie have a nice evening?"

"Yes."

"Well, I've been very busy doing your work for you and I've arranged everything. Clair will haul the horse. He is leaving tonight. I want you to follow him to the border and arrange his crossing so he can take the animal all the way to Gilbert's ranch. That way I'll be sure he won't be mistreated. He'll be hauled safely and not in a crate as you planned. My only condition for arranging this is that you follow Clair all the way and help him."

"Mrs. Greenbriar, Clair wants six hundred dollars for hauling the horse."

"A thousand dollars. He will take him all the way to the Salido ranch. That is a reasonable price for Gilbert to pay for a forty-thousand-dollar horse."

"You're right, but it won't be necessary for Clair to haul him. A friend of mine, Buster Vernon from Tucson is bringing a semi load of horses to the auction at the Los Angeles Horse and Mule Barn tomorrow. In three or four days he is going back empty and will take Tiger's Cub as a favor to me. He'll also arrange for all the inspections and tests we need."

"Well, I have to think about that. I don't know this man."

"I've known him all my life. He's a fine horse trainer and he hauls livestock professionally."

"How many times do I have to tell you? Tiger's Cub is not ordinary livestock. You can't pinch pennies and cut corners in the care of a horse like this. How do you plan to get him from Tucson to Gilbert's ranch?"

"After I cross him into Mexico I'll hire a truck, or a railroad boxcar."

"Promise you won't haul him in that crate of yours. I don't want a Greenbriar Farms horse crated up and hauled through the countryside with women and brats. I'm still afraid you'll try to haul him in that crate."

"Mrs. Greenbriar, if you'll remember, it was my own idea not to haul the horse in my pickup."

"Have you the slightest idea how much trouble I've gone through to solve your problems? Now I've found a solution and it doesn't meet with your approval."

"Ma'am, you told me you didn't want to be bothered with this problem anymore. I'm sure the transportation I've arranged will be acceptable to Don Gilberto."

"Well, I'm going to call *Dawn Gilberto*. I'll let you know what we decide."

"All right, Mrs. Greenbriar," Miguel said, but the woman had already hung up the telephone.

Late in the night the office manager called Miguel to the phone again and this time Don Gilberto was on the line.

"*Que jodidos* is happening over there?" he said. "What have you done to the poor woman, Miguel?"

"Nothing, Don Gilberto."

"She telephoned me in *tears* a while ago."

"Don Gilberto, that woman doesn't own a tear."

"She is afraid of you. She told me that you are a vicious man and you nearly attacked her in the privacy of her boudoir."

"How can anyone 'nearly' attack anyone? Honest to God, I've been courteous to the woman."

"She doesn't want to see you again."

"Don Gilberto, for all but five minutes Vicenta was with me when I talked to that woman. I think her real trouble is that she was drunk last night, hungover this morning, drunk again this afternoon, and is finally seeing spooks."

"Well, after talking to her, I think you're probably right. See what you can do to calm her. Humor her. She says she wants to send the horse, but you've been fighting her."

"I've arranged to bring the horse home my own way, even though for the life of me I don't know why you want him. He's been so neglected he isn't worth a nickel, yet the woman thinks he's made of gold."

"Well, it's your responsibility, Miguel. You be the judge. I'm beginning to wonder if the horse is worth the trouble. For God's sake, don't fight with her."

"Very well, Don Gilberto. I'll do what I think is best for you."

In the morning at Greenbriar no one answered the doorbell. No face appeared at the windows. Miguel turned to leave and Clair walked up.

"I thought you left for Mexico," he said.

"No, I came to find out what the lady wants to do."

"I don't think anyone will be taking the horse anywhere. She told me the whole thing was off."

"She finally backed out, did she? Well, I've come a thousand miles to wait on her, so she'll have to tell me face-to-face."

"Let's go see her, then. She's in the house."

Clair walked in without knocking. Mrs. Greenbriar was waiting in the front room. Her last-stand mask consisted of a cotton print sundress, high heels and stockings, a ribbon in her hair, and only a touch of makeup. The agate eyes were rested and alert. The house was neat. She posed in the center of the room as though for a portrait. The hand with the wedding ring of Greenbriar rested gracefully on the shiny dark top of an old hardwood table.

She's like a spooky old cow defying me to try to flush her off her *querencia,* her mountain haunt, Miguel thought. I have no dog to set on her, so I'll just leave her here. Sooner or later somebody will gather her with money and drive her away happy.

"My business with this man was finished yesterday," she said to Clair.

"I told him that, Lola, but he insisted on seeing you."

"Mrs. Greenbriar, the last time you spoke to me you said you would let me know how you decided to deliver the horse to Don Gilberto," Miguel said.

"Oh, did I? Well, I've decided not to deliver a forty-thousand-dollar property into the hands of incompetents. I'm afraid he will be mistreated to spite me, so I've decided to exercise my woman's privilege and change my mind. My horse is not leaving this farm."

"Ma'am, he isn't yours to keep. He belongs to Don Gilberto Salido and I have the legal papers that empower me to take charge of him."

"And I have a feed bill against him amounting to forty thousand dollars that began when my husband gave him to Salido."

"Ma'am, Don Gilberto would not understand how he came to owe you money. He only wanted to receive the gift of his friend."

"The horse is too valuable to give away to Mexicans. He is the racehorse son of the finest racehorse stallion ever raised in the state of California."

"He might have been valuable before he was foundered and his feet ruined, his training omitted, and he ate himself out of his own hide. Racehorse? He couldn't run fast enough to scatter his own manure."

"I'm keeping him."

"That's fine. You deserve each other. As Don Gilberto's representative I've signed the papers over to you." Miguel offered the envelope that contained the bill of sale and the horse's registry to the woman.

Clair stepped over and took it from him, opened it and studied the contents. "It's true, Lola, see? He signed it for the other Mexican. You've got the papers back. This is mighty decent, don't you think?"

The stone eyes slid over Miguel. Miguel thought, I hope she's remembering the continuous feed bills and wondering how she's ever going to get the son of a gun out of his pen without being tromped and rolled in the shit.

"What is it you want?" the woman demanded quietly.

"Nothing from you. I'm giving your horse back and going home happy," Miguel said.

The Mulatos River Journal

For Kay Powell, one of only two, great, mighty sprinters, and for Lawrence Clark Powell, who always likes this kind of stuff.

Part I

When I boarded Dave Coughonour's Cessna 206 in the spring of 1968 to go into the Sierra Madre with him I realized no one would blame me for not going. My wife did not want me to go. Two months before that, I had been down to the Mulatos River prospecting for gold with diving gear and a venturi-powered sluice as a favor to Dave. I took three friends to help with the expenses. We found a good hole and enough sign of coarse gold to give us a fever. I was going back now with a very small grubstake from my friends and help from Dave Coughonour. This was not a venture for a cattleman with a wife and two children, horses to feed and his everyday bills to pay.

A lot of people did not want me to go, but I did not look back. I wanted to clean a certain piece of bedrock in the bottom of the Mulatos River. We took off early from Tucson and flew down the Sonora River past Cumpas, Moris, Sahuaripa; past Iglesias and Pilar; past the Tayopa rock pillars, Mulatos Canyon and the familiar red rock above our old camp. The first cordon of high mountains east of those red rocks is on the spine of the boundary between Chihuahua and Sonora.

Two cows were grazing on the airstrip at Trigo, Dave's ranch headquarters. We circled while a little boy dashed out and ran the cows off the strip with a stick. On our first trip there with Dave early that year we had killed a burro on landing. The burro was grazing just inside the fence that protected the end of the strip. Dave cussed when he saw him and turned on final approach. The burro kept grazing with his head down.

Dave held the airplane on an angle that would put his wheels down on the first few feet of the strip beyond the burro. Then, just as we crossed the fence, the burro looked up and saw our iron eagle swooping upon him and he turned and ran with all his might straight up the strip with the airplane. I was watching him closely. The left wheel struck him on the poll knot between his ears and killed him instantly. The 206 bounced about ten feet in the air and then settled on the strip safely. Now, I saw the burro's carcass settling into dust outside the fence as we landed.

We climbed into Dave's pickup and drove the three miles to his house. His young, dark, trim wife Licha was angry because the day before two of the mechanics at Dave's mine had drunk all the *soyate*, moonshine mescal, trying to clear their heads and get over a bad *cruda*, hangover, and she had none to give us.

She gave us a fine cup of black coffee and a plate of fried eggs. We rode around the ranch in the pickup with Dave *resongando*, complaining, about the work he always ordered done when he left the ranch, but was never done.

Dave always reminded me of a great turkey gobbler. The serranos even called him *Cocono*, Wild Turkey, because he was a flier and because that was as close as they could come to pronouncing his last name, Coughonour. They pronounced it "Coconór." He was a heavy man and tall with a florid nose and wattles on his chin, thin hair he did not worry about combing, thick fingers and thick, loose lips from which perpetually hung a wet nonfiltered cigarette.

We stopped where his crew was building a new mill for the mine. I watched Cucho, the head mechanic, plumb with a nail and string for a conveyor that began at the top of a sandstone and granite hill above the mill. A new well for the mill was already completed and shored with new, peeled, pine poles notched together in a funnel.

We took a long nap after lunch, for we had been up since two-thirty that morning. We got up again about four and walked around David's farm. We saw a wild turkey hen with her little ones in the timber at the edge of the farm. Dave went to talk to the man in charge of the farm and I went around the truck garden by myself with a flock of geese hissing at my heels. At supper Dave's wife fed me until I was about to bust, then noticed what she was doing to me, had pity on me and stopped.

I had been having trouble sleeping, but that night I slept the sleep of a saint. In the morning Dave added four dozen turkey eggs to my provision and we loaded up and took off for Mulatos. We went in to the strip below Mulatos that lies beside the river. The approach is from downriver. The field is on the edge of a bend in the river and runs up to the bottom of a mountain. Once a pilot commits, he has to land, for there is no room to go around. The mountain stands like a wall on the end of the strip and wraps itself around both sides.

David unloaded me on the end of the strip and left me standing alone with my gear. I laid everything in the shade of a big chapote tree, then lay down and slept a little while, waiting for Adán Martínez to come for me with his pack animals. I had notified him I was coming.

I awakened and saw him on his buckskin mare across the river, his little shaggy dog following him. I had sent word that I wanted him to help me, but did not give him time to answer, so I was not sure he even knew I was coming. I watched him ride on and dismount on the bluff by his father-in-law Guillermo's house. I waited to see what he would do and I said to myself, if he comes down toward me when he remounts, he'll be for going to work; if he doesn't, as we said in the Marine Corps, I'll be fucked, because I'll be in the big middle of the *Sierra oscura* with no help I can trust.

Adán came out of the house and rode off the bluff, disappeared behind a hill and stayed out of sight a long while, but he came in sight again at the foot of the airstrip. He rode toward me without saying anything until he reached me and I was sitting on my bedroll facing him all the way.

"*¿Qué hay, Adán?*" I said.

"You're alone this time," he said. "Why?"

"I don't like to start anything I can't finish. I came back to clean out the bottom of that hole and *desengañar* myself, remove all doubts that the hole contains or does not contain gold."

Adán said he would help me and explained why he was late. I asked him if he had a *culeca,* a brooding hen, and he said he did, so I gave him a dozen of David's turkey eggs to put in her nest. He took them and went home to get a mule to carry my gear. He returned quickly and we packed the mule. I rode his mare and he walked leading the mule off the field and down the river.

We stayed on the red trail above the river, down past the old houses and corrals of the Aguilar spinsters, passed through the gate and closed the *trancas,* gate poles, then down to the river again and across the rockiest place in the trail until we saw the red rocks that marked our prospect.

Adán rode the mare across, then sent her back to me and I got on her and led the mule across. We unpacked on the sandy beach on the edge of El Desengaño and while we were pitching the tent Adán asked, "Didn't you bring even one *trago?*"

I answered, "No, I was short of money." Then I offered him twenty pesos a day wages and ten percent of any gold we took out of the hole and he said that was fine and we shook hands on it. Then he left and Joe Brown was alone and looking over his shoulder all evening like a coyote a'shitting and shooting by the buzzards to scare them away from watering above the camp.

I lay tired in bed and listened to the voices, all men, singing and speaking softly and clearly in the river, but was unable to understand what they were saying. I imagined that a loquacious *espanto,* ghost, of a Spaniard in cockscomb helmet came along and squatted in front of the tent and asked for tobacco. Then two more, one very young, one surly and middle-aged, and both suspicious, came and stood behind him to show me he was with friends.

The Spaniards might have led me over the mountain through the spiny brush to the lost Tayopa, or some other lost mine that was maybe not as good as the Tayopa, but good enough for a man to have hell carrying all the gold he needed back to camp.

In the Sierra the people believe that when the Spanish crown recalled all the Jesuit priests from Sonora two hundred years ago, before they left, the priests cast bells in gold and painted them with bronze and hid them in caves. Men have looked for them until they used themselves up and went away failures and I decided I would never be that kind of a man. The Tayopa gold has never been found. With that thought I went off to a very sound sleep unafraid of anything because now I knew the Spanish ghosts.

I arose early but knew I would have to wait awhile for Adán because he was going to Mulatos for soyate before he came to work. I breakfasted on fried turkey eggs, picked and cleaned and put beans in a pot on the fire and sat in the morning shade under a *tepeguaje* tree to watch them. Tired of that and because the tepeguaje's shade was meager, I dove to the bottom of El Desengaño and worried the hole and tried to figure how best to work it. I watered the beans and walked downriver to look for other holes close to bedrock and decided El Desengaño was still the best. When I got back the beans were burnt beans.

Adán came with the machinery and we blew up the tubes and assembled everything. I dove with the compressor and air mask and the short Hollywood venturi sluice. The machines worked and we brought up *orito,* a little sign of gold, out of the sandy overburden on top of the bedrock. We quit tired from the underwater work and the day's hot sun.

People had been going by on the Camino Real across the river all day. That trail was used by those people's people long before Coronado. I think Coronado used it too.

My Granny Sorrells had given me a small cotton mattress for my camp bed. I shook out my bedroll and one of the cotton balls detached itself from the mattress and I felt obligated to save it. Probably it had been in my family couching my uncles and grandparents long before I was born. I slept like a dead man on that mattress that night.

In the morning I agreed with Adán that we shouldn't work on Sunday. I put on clean clothes and we went up on the mountain looking for meat. A yellow dog had taken up with Adán and he tried to follow us, but Adán chased him back to camp with rocks. We found a turkey feather, hid ourselves under a big *nopal* and called for turkey with a cedar horn caller, and nothing.

We climbed and Adán told me about the way the old man who drawled had defended his pistol. The *judicial* policeman demanded of him, "Do you have a pistol?" even though he could see the old rancher was carrying one.

"Yes."

"Well, you have to give it up because I am authorized to collect all pistols in this region."

"Very well," the old man drawled. "But these pistols cost two thousand five hundred pesos. I'll give up this one only if you pay me pesos for it."

"We are not buying pistols. We are confiscating pistols, old man."

"Then you will have to take my pistol the best way you can, so do your best."

"There are two of us, old man, so give it up peacefully."

"Maybe there are two of you but there will only be one of you after you knock me down."

"What caliber did you say your pistol was, old man?"

"I didn't say, but it is a caliber .44."

"We happen to have confiscated a box of .44 shells. Would you like to have it?"

"How much will you charge me?"

"Nothing. We will make you a present of the *parke.*"

We walked down an oak ridge and surprised a black mare grazing in a high, hidden swale with a yearling filly and a foal beside her. Before she became aware of us, Adán threw his hat under her. It sailed under her belly, then curved up by her side and she did not see it until it hit the ground under her nose. She jumped and kicked away as though afraid she had been marked for death by cata-mounts.

We walked up to a piney thicket over a canyon and called for turkey, and nothing. We climbed to El Palo Dulce and talked about wolves and Adán said years ago a white lobo prowled the mountains of El Pilar.

We saw no sign of deer or turkey. We went down another ridge back toward the river, past an old, degenerate *pardo,* light brown, bull whose bone was too light for his heavy Swiss body. We stopped at a small, clear, cold spring. Adán scooped leaves out of the hat-sized mouth of the spring and waited for the water to clear up. He said there were many *panales,* beehives, nearby. We took a good drink and watched the sooty wild bee traffic come in to land and drink in the spring.

We slid down a steep leafy side of the ridge on poor footing to a place called El Pinalito and called for turkey, and nothing. We talked about elk and the kinds of deer Adán had never seen and the pet antelope my family raised on my parental ranch the High Lone-some.

Adán told about the doe fawn some Indians raised. When she grew up she went away once but returned after three days, and they said, *"Vale más trosarle el buchi.* The best thing to do is cut her throat. What if she goes away again and decides not to come back?" So they cut her throat and ate her without remorse.

Then we climbed down to the cliff by the *toro prieto* tree the Indians say is medicinal and rare. If they all grow on the cliffs like that, I can see why they are rare. We could not even stand still there. Then, Adán got serious, because from high atop the cliff he saw his brother riding a mule on the river trail toward our camp. He shouted, "Hoooaaah!" and was too far away for the brother to hear, so he started hurrying down, hurrying, not saying why, but I knew he must be worried about this brother stopping in our camp. David said all his brothers were bad and to keep away from them.

We hurried past the adobe ruins of the house of the cow thieves by a great, dusty, horny *encino roble,* white oak. Adán said the daughter of the head cowthief had been so loose she took on any man who would stop off the Camino Real to service her. She wore big skirts and pulled the skirts over her head so as not to see what they did or who was doing it to her.

Adán really hurried us when we reached level ground. We trotted over the rocks by the river past the caliche gold hole to camp and Adán glanced quickly around to see if everything was all right, but tried to keep from letting on to me that he was worried. The camp was in peace. The yellow dog was there waiting for us, yawning.

Adán brought out the quart of soyate he'd brought that morning and we talked about ranches and cattle being no good anymore because of the money and the dudes. I shot old Meat in the Pot, my .45 Colt, at a squirrel for meat. He was sixty yards across the river and I took only half his tail with the first shot, then was very close for three more shots as he ran farther away. Adán was happy with my shooting and I was glad to be close to the target without killing anything. Adán went on home and promised he would bring meat from a young sow he would kill that evening.

In the night I got up to throw away water and took a drink naked under a full moon, surprised how dark my skin looked in that light. Went back to the robe and was almost asleep when I felt a tug across my knees. I shined the electric lantern all around and under myself looking for a *coralillo,* a coral snake, and nothing. Almost asleep again, I saw a gray mouse in the moonlight trying to get into the tortillas, so I gave him one to let me sleep. I wondered if a gray mouse this audacious ever stowed away in a space vehicle, then slept.

I slept late and old Tomás whistled to announce himself and get me up. I was sore from the working and the hard climb of the day before. He already had the fire built and was getting more wood when he woke me.

"*Vienes solo ahora*. You come alone this time," he said. "I thought old Tío Pablo would be with you. They said *un tal José y un tal Pedro* were down the river." Tío was one of my friends who had come down with me when we prospected the river earlier that year.

I told him I did not have any work for him right then, but maybe I would later and he said, "Fine, *hablando claro, después no hay lío*. Clear words spoken now will protect us from later disagreement."

I said I was short of money, but if he wanted to hunt I would give him a day's work and part of the meat. He said he did not own a hunting piece, so I offered him old Meat in the Pot. He said that was all right, he was not afraid of it. He once killed a deer with an old .44 he owned. The thing was so decrepit it required him to hold the wobbly cylinder in place before it would allow him to pull the trigger.

I ate turkey eggs and potatoes and old Tomás made a can of fruit disappear. He was a good hand at eating, but also good help around the camp. He washed the dishes before he strapped the pistol across his chest and glided away up the trail.

I washed my shirt and socks, then started up the breather and went in to clean debris out of the hole. Adán came and we sluiced overburden off the bedrock until almost out of air and cramped and personally out of gas. Went up to camp and ate Adán's fresh *chicharrones* with sweet coffee, then back in the water to clean against a shelf of bedrock. Came up with coarser gold every time I brought out the sluice pan, then one little wire and one good-sized nugget and the operation started losing its amateur status.

I came up out of the hole late in the afternoon weak and staggering. I drank soyate and Tang because I was too tired to eat. Later I stuffed down chicharrones, beans and tortilla only because I needed to eat if I was to work. I've always been a good doer and a good keeper. Went to bed while it was still light and slept hard. In the morning, was able to get out early and go again.

I recalled being in Nogales only a week ago getting my gear ready to come back to the river. I was in a hardware store buying a tire-patching kit and a *pata de chiva,* wrecking bar, when a dude who had been a longtime rancher of a place that was settled in 1860 by my great-grandparents came in. He owned that ranch so long hardly anyone remembered he was a dude. With him was a hotshot

contractor-developer who as a youth followed my uncle Buster Sorrells and my father Paul Summers around like a puppy dog. Now,
forty years later, he still blamed them for his marrying his first wife,
"a Meskin." He once whined to me he was too young to marry that
first time and he blamed them for not stopping him.

This same successful bigshot contractor-developer once confided
in me that he had always wanted to kill a man. He managed to avoid
service to his country as a soldier while it struggled through three
wars, though.

They came in the hardware both now very successful because no
one knew how helpless as men they both truly were and rich because they had a knack for making other men do their work and
take their risks. Their way was to wait until people depended on
their word as men and they gave it, then backed out of it to make
money.

Both were in fine business suits on their way to the Valley National Bank party and conscious of being dressed shiny. Then they
saw me there brown as an Indian and wearing a big hat, boots, clean
Wranglers and a dress shirt and just as ready to fall outside to do a
job of work as I was to run and play and it made them look at their
hole cards.

They probably remembered how much they used to wish they
could be like my uncles and father and my cousin Buckshot. They
fidgeted in line behind me waiting for service and did not speak to
me, though they had known me all my life. They were afraid and
too timid to lose their well-dressed self-assurance to say hello. Finally the dude said, "Let's go, I'll get them tomorrow." I was
almost through at the cash register, but they did not want to have to
say hello when I turned to face them. I didn't speak to them because, as successful customers of the Valley Bank, they were invited
to its party. I, as an unsuccessful one, was not and it pissed me off.
I'd wanted to be successful in business a time or two, myself.

I paid for my gear and followed them down the street. They
stopped talking to each other while they tried to keep me in the
corners of their eyes. I swear, it seemed to me they wobbled on their
puny legs while they tried to watch their backs to protect themselves
from me. I wouldn't have done a thing to them. Sonsabitches are
safe from me.

Mary from the bank was standing down the street all dressed up
talking to my wife. She was glad to see me, but said she didn't like

my mustache because she said it looked like I was trying to prove myself a man and didn't need to.

Then she asked, aren't you coming to the VNB party? I said, no because I didn't know you were having one. She said, of course you do, we sent you an invitation. I said, well, maybe we got it and threw it away before we read it like we do all the VNB mail.

Mary smiled and said good-bye and hurried on down the street so she could get fixed up and go to the banquet and smile at the dude and the developer and others who needed to hang around among themselves to feel rich. They get in there together all their lives where nobody can touch them, or wants to.

I wondered how Mary was going to like herself in my book *Jim Kane* when it got published, if it ever did. I wondered also if I was just going to keep getting it back forever from the publishers.

Adán rode up in the morning on his buckskin mare with Adancito, his oldest, the *guerito* behind his saddle hugging him. I was getting ready to dive and the brother of Bigotes came fooling along with the Arab Moreno boy, owner of the Palo Dulce ranch. The brother was short and brown with straight features. The one they called the Arab was flighty and sneaky-looking, tall and thin as a snake. He tried to pan with Adán's *cuchara,* a long, wide spoon shaped out of a cow's horn used for panning the finest gold left in the bottom of a pan, and got nothing. I went in the *charco* and moved big rocks away into the deep, main stream, then hitched up the dredge and vacuumed the bedrock and when I came back up everybody was gone except Adán.

Adancito stayed far away on the edge of camp and only peered out from behind a rock now and then because he was afraid of the motors. He had suffered recently from a fever and cold, or heat stroke, Adán was not sure which, and after a while he softly told his father he wanted to go home. Adán always spoke to him gently. Yes, he spoiled him in the way the gentle serrano must spoil his child in that hard place. He protected him in his way but even so the life was extraordinarily hard for a child. Children did not play much. Just going along quietly was the best a child could do, the only way he could get along. Their bodies are always in a press of rock and spine, their voices muted by the mountains, so the gentle fathers cater to them a little. After all they don't have energy for mischief.

Worked too much in the fine sand that day. At noon I surfaced, ate good beans out of the blue pot and rested. Then found myself sick tired in the heat. Adán scratched out a bench for visitors to sit on against the bedrock with his hands. It's easy for him to scratch something good out of the Sierra, scratching rock almost a symbol of his life there. Nothing ever becomes much more civilized there than a bench scratched out on rock and sand smoothed over by hand.

In the afternoon we found ourselves in the plush. The gold was coming coarser and coarser at the top of the *peña* every day.

When we were through, Tomás came in. He looked dry and caked carrying old Meat in the Pot and was apologetic. He saw three deer, shot under a doe and she jumped but didn't give him another shot. He shot Meat in the Pot seven times at other varied targets, wasting eight shells four hundred miles from a resupply of ammunition and left me disarmed for one night. I was sorry I loaned him the pistol. The Mexican saying that you should never loan your horse, your pistol or your woman always holds true.

Adán in the morning rode in on the bay horse that once bit me on the leg at the airfield. We talked awhile about mules and horses. The horse is almost one hundred percent noble, but the mule is a betrayer and is always hoping and waiting for the hour in which he will be able to excel in an act of treason.

I told about my mother's seven- or eight-year-old uncle who was kicked and dragged to death and then dragged out into the middle of a pond to drown by a pet burro. Adán told about the black horse he sold to the man who got drunk in Mulatos. On the man's return home, high on the *faldeo,* the dizzying brow of a ravine, his saddle slipped and he fell off. He passed out right there and way in the night awakened upside down under the horse on the very edge of the ravine. The horse had been standing still for hours and remained still as a rock until the man righted himself. The man wept with gratitude when he told Adán about it.

We went off to work and started bringing up coarser and coarser and cleaning and working and we filled the little jar, calculating an ounce. In camp we talked with soyate and Adán told about the time he met Pimienta Anaya at Tarachic. Pimienta had started for Sahuaripa ahead of 120 cattle he bought in Mulatos and his *mayate* was with him. A mayate is the one who plays the male role in an affair between two queers. Pimienta was the sissy son of a very rich, powerful Hermosillo cattleman and he only dared consort publicly with his mayate when he went to the Sierra to buy cattle. As far as

Adán knew, no one had ever told Don Guillermo, the father, about his son's habit of prancing around the Sierra with his mayate.

Adán was on his way home from Sahuaripa when he met Pimienta. The young man was in wasted shape from the lunatic time of dissolution he had been spending with his lover. He was afoot with only an old blanket to cover him. When he recognized Adán he tried to straighten up and soberly stated that he was on his way back to Mulatos to buy more cattle, but Adán could see he was naked under the blanket, had spent all his money on soyate and marijuana and had lost his hat.

Adán turned back to Tarachic so he could look after him, but at his first opportunity Pimienta got away and hid. Adán helped the vaqueros into town with the cattle, but no one was there to receive them until old Don Guillermo came in. He refused to pay for the cattle until Pimienta reported to him. Then the vaqueros told him Pimienta was hiding himself in Tarachic.

Don Guillermo's brother, the old uncle of the boy, hired a plane and went back and circled Tarachic and landed. Pimienta and the mayate ran out to the field to see if they could hire the airplane to get out of there and when they saw the old uncle they ran and jumped in a deep pool in the river. The uncle hired some help, laid hands on them and took them back to Sahuaripa.

They put the mayate in jail and later flew him to Hermosillo. Don Guillermo whipped Pimienta with a reata and kept him locked in a room until the necessary payments were met and the cattle trucked to Hermosillo. Then Don Guillermo faced the vaqueros who had been witnesses to his son's dissolution and remained faithful to their task, and paid them.

Adán told another tale about a poor little *cura* who was hot for a young girl in his parish for a long time and finally propositioned her. She said yes, she would do it if he would take her in front of the whole congregation on Sunday. So the very next Sunday he went to his pulpit and told the congregation to shut its eyes for one hour and to keep them closed or they would go blind. He mounted her in front of the altar and an old drunk in the rear pew, *lo que nunca falta,* the irreverent one who never fails to be present at such solemn occurrences, said to himself, I can't stand this. I'm going to open one eye and if it goes blind I'll still have the other one. So he opened one eye and saw the *curita* forking the girl and he shouted, open your eyes, he's going to fork us all.

Very tired, I had eaten a bunch of prunes for energy and they passed through like fine sand through a swamped sluice. Adán came in with his mare mule and we packed up and moved camp upstream to the wide beach on the Desengaño hole. The sweat poured off us in that sun by the river and the shade was good in the new place under a boulder big as a house by a big tepeguaje.

I saw Tomás go by on the trail carrying something very heavy over his shoulder and followed by his woman. He did not say hello and went on without looking at my camp. I thought it was because he did not want me to have a good look at his woman. I knew he was ashamed of her, because he told me she wouldn't even let him smell it anymore. She was followed by her worthless, thieving son. The son stole three one-gallon cans of food from us the first trip by letting them fall off a pack animal Ingeniero Carranza had dispatched to us. Adán saw him pick them up on his way home. That was a day before we hired Adán the first time.

The next day Adán told me that on his way home the night before he caught up to Tomás at the *trinchera,* the rock wall, by the old campsite we made on our first trip. He saw the heavy load Tomás carried was the harvest of an *enjambre,* a huge beehive bursting with honey. Tomás jumped the trinchera to hide, but the weight of the sack was so heavy he was unable to get it out of sight behind the wall before Adán saw what it was. Adán shouted to ask him if he would sell five pesos' worth of honey, and Tomás, without looking back, said no there was only enough for him a taste.

Adán accused him of being ordinary for not leaving some honey with José, his *patrón.* Was he not in José's employ during the two days he hunted when he found it? But Tomás and his poor woman and their coyote son went on without saying more. Tomás was always hungry and stricken by his poverty.

The next day while we were resting at noon we talked about Las Viejas Aguilera, the spinster ranchers of Mulatos. I told Adán about the time about five years ago when I was conned by Rosa, the meanest one, into giving her a free ride with all her *compras,* bought goods, in my airplane from Agua Prieta to Mulatos.

I had landed my airplane in Agua Prieta to cross cattle at the border and she was in the office at the airport when I went out to fly back to Nogales. She asked me if I was José Brown the cattle buyer and I said yes. She said she had been waiting there for several hours to find out if I would be interested in buying her cattle. I told her that I was always interested in buying cattle from the Sierra, but I would not go all that way to look unless her price suited me. She said this would be convenient for me, because at that very moment her cattle were being held on the edge of the upper airstrip at Mulatos. I asked her how much and she told me her price and it was just right, so I loaded her and about five hundred pounds of new goods and flew the two hours down to Mulatos.

When we got there and I had unloaded all the goods on the edge of the strip for her like a gentleman she pointed to the herd and told me I should go down and see if I liked her cattle enough to buy them. She could not go because it was too far for her to walk and she did not want to leave the new goods.

Cattle bearing her brand were down there all right, but she had already sold them to Pimienta Anaya. When I looked for the woman to confront her with her awful transgression, she was gone.

Adán told me once a vaquero who worked for Las Viejas Aguilera had found himself in need of a saddle and they owed him several months' back wages. He was in charge of their cattle *al partido,* on shares, so he called witnesses and the cattle inspector together and cut out three yearlings, part of his share of a calf crop. He then branded them with his brand in front of the witnesses and sold them for a saddle, a pair of chaps and a pistol.

The viejas came home to Mulatos the day the cattle left and immediately dispatched the judicial police to bring them back. They put the vaquero Jesús and the inspector in jail. Jesús became very ill in jail, lost his job and was forced to return the saddle, pistol and chaps. The viejas also took away the cattle he had earned on shares, he was put on probation for a year, and was never paid his back wages.

That same Rosa once asked Adán to retrieve a calf that had strayed downriver. She promised him twenty-five pesos. He brought the calf back and she sent word that he should put him in an upper pasture a day's ride away from Adán's home. When he got back to Mulatos he went up to get the money. The servant woman who came to the door told him Rosa was asleep, to come back later. When he came back and found Rosa awake, she said to please come back later because she was very busy. He went back later and she was still busy so he went home. He went back about a week later and she told him, "Oooo, I paid you a long time ago." Adán said many thanks but please don't ask me to help you anymore.

I went down in the hole, bright light shafts piercing clear blue water, and dredged the peña and moved a big rock to where it would go and came up and stayed out until the hole cleared again. Then I used the wrecking bar to clean and loosen tight, greasy caliche against the bedrock and made twelve quick trips out with that stuff in the sluice pan. I watched Adán pan out the first one and saw the coarse gold in the tin pan before he ever needed to refine it in the *batea,* the wooden one. I went right back in because the hard work was becoming very satisfying, but then the pump on the sluice began shooting out water and my supply of gasoline was used up and I was forced to quit.

The little short brown youth came by with the Arab, followed by a wild-looking black bitch dog and a hairy little bobtailed puppy. The brown shorty did not want to sell me the pup for company because he said they cost too much to get.

Adán panned out the first of the twelve sluice boxes and showed a little of the color so the short brown youth wouldn't think he was hiding anything. Later, after the visitors were gone, we panned the rest of it in the batea and the sight of the little golden individuals massed together brought a great shot of joy to my breast so even my skin felt the pleasure of it.

That evening Adán and I drank coffee and decided that he would have to go the next day to Mulatos for gasoline and soyate. Some trucks were expected to come in with provision for the *taniches,* the stores, and they might sell him gas. We couldn't work without gasoline and soyate. Adán left with the empty gas can and the money and was not going to try to come back the next day.

I cooked soup by the stream quietly and washed dishes and picked beans and put them aside to soak. I was not so tired that day and was able to enjoy smoking my pipe before bed. The pipe tasted awful good and I liked seeing the coal glow inside the bowl as night fell and I watched the satellite go by.

Part II

The people of Tayopa say sometimes on windy nights they hear bells and see lights on the top of a certain tall mountain. The sheer rock sides of the mountain cannot be climbed.

Adán's mother was from Tayopa and one evening her brother saw a young woman cross the meadow below a rock corral by their house. The woman wore a pink dress that almost touched the ground and was covered with gold coins. The brother called out to her thinking she was one of the Reys who lived nearby but she would not turn back. She climbed to a high *cordoncito,* a sharp ridge above the meadow, sat on a rock and disappeared.

Another time, Adán's mother Doña Ernestina said, Alberto Taylor—a Mormon from Casas Grandes—and another man passed through that meadow looking for a drink of water. The main drinking pool was muddy from cattle so they looked for another place to drink. A young woman passed nearby wearing a brand-new white hat, a large hat of a type not customarily used in that region. Taylor shouted to her several times to ask where he could find water to drink but she did not answer or look back. She climbed to the ridge and disappeared.

Doña Ernestina believed the woman was a spirit who tried to show the people a treasure. For many years after she married and went to live in Mulatos she wanted to go back to look for that treasure. Finally Adán and one of his brothers took her back and she pointed out her father's old corral, the meadow and the ruins of the house. Then she showed them the rock on the *cordoncito* where the woman sat before she disappeared.

Adán and his brother found the rock had been recently overturned and a fresh hole dug in the ground. Later, a vaquero told them that only eight days ago a monk from Tayopa had taken a treasure from that spot.

In the night I saw a bright orange flash of light like the flare of a match on the side of the mountain above the Camino Real. I kept watching and then a white pinpoint of light floated down over the rock to the opposite bank of the river where Tomás said the peña was very close under the surface of the ground. Several times the same kind of white light winked higher on the mountain so briefly I might have imagined it. They could have been fireflies, but the fireflies around my camp did not give off the same light.

Long in the night a strange sound awakened me and I identified it as something heavy being dragged, then again the same strange sound of something being dragged and I thought my panniers were being moved. The voices of the river were now coming deep and clear so I thought maybe the Spaniards were back.

I went out in my shorts with the pistol and the lantern and looked around the fire and at my panniers hanging in the tepeguaje, and nothing. I snuffed the lantern and sat on a big boulder of *tapustete* and watched a bright moon heavy as gold round the mountain above my camp.

Tapustete is a heavy, metallic purple rock the serranos call *guía del oro,* guide to the gold. Pebbles of tapustete appear with the kernels of gold each time a pan full of placer is washed out. The tapustete, iron, silver and gold make up the last residue in the pan. My Desengaño hole was surrounded by five big tapustete boulders big as houses. The rock pillars on the mountain above my camp were tapustete.

I went back to bed and before dawn heard several bell animals in a train on the Camino Real, heard the voices of the *arrieros* as they passed. Then later I heard horseshoes striking rock as a horseman approached my camp from downriver. He was singing softly and the words were indistinguishable. His voice was soothing and the song beautiful and suddenly I realized he was almost on top of my tent and about to ride me down. I started up out of my robe, but calmed myself. He was bound to be able to see me and was singing because travelers always sang as they approached a camp. Singing or whistling was done as a courtesy, so they would not surprise the camp.

The horseman rode right by me, between my tent and the river. The song was in Spanish, but I could not distinguish the words. There was no trail on my side of the river, only piles of jumbled boulders. I stepped out of the tent and looked for the horseman, the bell animal and the packtrain across the river, and nothing, they were all gone in the dark. I went back to bed and slept.

At dawn horsemen passed singing across the river, headed upriver, sounding as though they could be riding to catch up to the packtrain. They seemed to be right across the river on the Camino Real and I got up to build my fire, but missed seeing them, too.

I made coffee and put on the beans and waited to wake up. The whole canyon was still asleep. I heard a deer on the rock across the river, but moved too fast to find a better place to spy on him, and he saw me, or heard me, and was still. I looked for him a long time but never did see him.

Later, an old man rode by on a black mule, his straw hat and full mustache sharply white against his dark brown face. His face was so dark his features were obscure. His seat made him seem part of the mule. His body was armored by thick, billowing *chaparreras* and thick country-tanned brush jacket. He rode very slowly downriver and did not see me, or at least did not let on he did.

Adán came in on the buckskin mare with Adancito and I asked if he was able to buy gasoline and he said no not even enough to put in your eye. I usually only discover the day is Sunday and another week gone when he brings Adancito. The little boy always comes down from Mulatos to visit his father as soon as school is let out for the weekend.

I told Adán about hearing my panniers being dragged in the night, the singing horseman, the packtrain and the lights and he said they were probably espantos. This part of the river was famous for its rich placer. A prospector can hope he is near a rich placer if espantos manifest themselves to him. I showed him the sand between my tent and the edge of the river. The singing horseman left no tracks there and Adán said no packtrain passed his house or left any tracks on the trail.

He told about the *charro* who used to ride a white horse through Mulatos in the night. The people often saw him circle the church and then leave through the pass of Del Curis. One night an old man followed him on a bronc mule, but the charro disappeared in the pass. The mule put her foot through the crust of the earth in the pass. While she struggled to free herself the old man looked down and saw the corner of an ironbound chest underneath her hooves. A crowd of people was coming up the trail, so he waited until the next night to go back and uncover the chest. It was so heavy with gold coin he needed two pack animals and the bronc mule to carry it home.

A rich old man from Chihuahua who owned a large ranch and many cattle was having trouble with his children. They were all boys and grew up mean because their mother died when they were small and the father raised them by himself. The time came when they grew so mean they wanted to kill him and divide his wealth among them.

One day a child of one of the old man's vaqueros cried to her mother that she was in the grip of a *culebrón*, a big snake. The mother ran and found the child sitting by a big boulder with the snake coiled between her legs. When the snake saw the mother it slithered quickly into a hole under the rock, and the hole disappeared after it.

The people of Mexico call a hidden treasure an *interés*, an interest. A snake is the sign of a devil's interest. The mother called the owner of the ranch for help. He investigated, but scolded the mother when he found no snake and no hole.

Finally, after the boys made an attempt to kill the old man, he sold everything, portioned it all evenly among them and went away broke. He became a woodcutter, carpenter and lumberer complaining always to anyone who would listen that it was better by far for a man to be born poor and have nothing all his life than for him to be rich and lose his wealth. A rich man did not know how to pick up an ax, but the old man learned to pick up an ax and how to cut *tablitas,* shakes, for roofing and how to *gambusear,* pan for gold. He became expert at those jobs, but he complained that the labor stole years from his life.

The old man never forgot about the rock of the snake. After working among the prospectors, miners and laborers of his region, he appreciated that the child's encounter with the snake must have been sign of a devil's interest. He began to dig a shaft at the spot where the mother had seen the snake, but strange manifestations terrorized him while he worked. He became so afraid that his work intruded on the realm of Satan that he was forced to sip constantly at a jug of soyate for support and often became too drunk to work.

Several men tried to help him but were scared away by big rocks that flew by their heads and struck the sides of the shaft. The workers were never hurt, but when they looked down to see the big rocks after they heard them bounce on the floor, they saw no rocks.

The old man still works the mine of the snake and the rock. He tries to recruit men to help him *a medias,* for half interest, but seems doomed to work it alone.

At one time, Don Jesús Rey, the father of the brown shorty and Saul the *Bigotón,* was very poor and had only his woman to solace him. His sons were still little boys and dying of hunger. One day he went to Mulatos to the store of the father of Las Viejas Aguilera and asked to be trusted for *veinte centavos,* twenty cents' worth of coffee, veinte of flour, and a package of Argentino cigarettes worth fifty centavos to stave off the hunger. Aguilera said no he couldn't, so Don Jesús went home like a whipped dog to tell his wife he had been unsuccessful, the *hijo de la desgraciada,* son of a disgrace, Aguilera, had refused him.

"Ni modo," his woman told him. "Go down to the river with your batea and see if you can find some gold."

Don Jesús said, "What hijos de la desgraciada will I find?" but went down to the river anyway. He was washing dirt he scratched from cracks in the bedrock by the river when he saw the top of a thick bamboo tube standing out of the water. He pulled it over and it contained three balls of gold weighing over a kilo apiece. He went back to Aguilera and said, "Now, hijo de la desgraciada, are you going to trust me for the provision I asked for?"

"I can't," Aguilera said.

"Well then, hijo de la desgraciada, sell it to me then," and laid down a kilo lump of gold. "And pay me for this."

"But Don Jesús, where did you get this?" Aguilera asked after he burned the mercury out of the ball and weighed the gold.

"That is of no importance to you, hijo de la desgraciada. Hurry up with the provision because my old lady is flogging herself with hunger."

Don Jesús bought cattle and moved to Obregon. His sons bought ten or fifteen new hats and two or three new pistols and ten or fifteen boxes of cartridges. They used the hats for targets until all the cattle were gone and everyone was poor again. Now the brown shorty one complains about his worthless wife and his lumpy skin and wanders up and down the river like a hungry dog and Bigotes works irrigating and harvesting the fields of Obregon for other people, when he can.

Adán's sister became very ill and feverish a month before her child was to be born. By good chance a plane from Chihuahua came in with goods for the Mulatos mine. Adán hurried and caught the pilot before he left and asked him to take him and his sister and mother to the hospital in Hermosillo. The pilot said he would return early the next day and take them, but that day he needed to take a mine executive to Chihuahua.

Adán and his brothers carried the girl to the field early. The plane landed but the pilot said he couldn't take them to Hermosillo after all. Finally Adán lost his patience and called him a you son of a fornication and a *cabrón* who was flawed as a man.

He was able to catch a truck on its way from David Coughonour's Mulatos mine to Yecora. A trucker in Yecora charged the family fifty pesos apiece, at that time it was four dollars, to take them to Hermosillo. The ride over the dirt road from Yecora to the pavement at Esperanza was so bad Adán thought his sister would die. He did not eat or sleep for six days and took nothing but mescal to keep going. When he saw his sister laid out in the bed in the hospital in Hermosillo he collapsed.

He found work in an orange grove, a beautiful place, though he did not make much money. He and his mother stayed with his sister's husband's family. Doña Ernestina, Adán's mother, went to the hospital every day, but the authorities there would not let her see her daughter. Adán tried to see her on Sundays, but the authorities refused him entrance to her ward.

One day a brother of the husband came to the orange grove for Adán carrying an *amphorita,* a slender half-pint bottle, of tequila. He told Adán his mother wanted him at the house, but before he went, to have a swallow of the tequila. At the house Adán was told his sister had died giving birth to her child.

Adán wept with anger for not being allowed to visit his sister during her illness. The authorities demanded permission to perform an autopsy and said it was the law, but Adán said here the law dies or I do. You'll have to kill me before I'll let you touch my sister again. They wouldn't let the family have the infant for a long time, then only a few days after he was released, he died too.

I wrote this under the tepeguaje with the wild bees loading up so heavily with cargo from its flowers they fell at my feet when they tried to fly. I heard voices murmuring in the canyon across the river and three burros came over the cordoncito above the canyon in full flight and scattered down the trail. A young rider came after them and I waved and he waved. Later another boy returned on one of the burros bareback with his rope around the burro's neck. He answered my wave by raising the coils of his rope.

At the same Puerto del Curis where the charro on the white horse showed the chest of gold to the old man on the bronc mule, it was said, another treasure had been marked by a pipe sticking out of the ground. Many people looked for it, but no one could find it.

One afternoon an Indian carried his young son down off the mountain looking for a doctor and when he reached the pass he stumbled over the pipe. He pulled it out of the ground and went straight to the Mulatos home of Adán's mother. The Indian had been raised with Doña Ernestina's children and he called her "Tina."

Adán and his brother went back with the Indian to the pass and he told them where to dig. They dug a deep hole and worked hard until the Indian suddenly sprang over to Adán's side and shouted,

"¡El culebrón!" because he had seen a big snake stick his head out of the ground. Adán and his brother laughed at the Indian and stopped digging because they had seen no snake.

All the hot day Sunday I washed clothes and tidied my camp. Tall Miguel Moreno came by with a young boy and an Indian and asked to borrow my fishhooks. In the evening he came back to ask if I would sell him some coffee and I said no but I would trade him some for a *trago* of the soyate from his family's *vinata,* distillery. He promised repeatedly that he would bring me a liter, then took the coffee and went home.

While I was sitting smoking my pipe in the evening the black bitch to whom I gave tortillas the night before came by headed downriver. In bed, very dark before the first sleep I heard a horse sneeze softly behind the tent and go down to water by the sluice and breather motors. I heard him blow on the water and then grunt when he laid himself down in the sand and rolled.

After a while I got up and drank water from Tío's canteen and the horse was gone. Across the river a brilliant white light flashed rapidly at me, so rapidly it could not have been only one light. Then it crossed the river toward me and stopped close offshore. Lightbugs, maybe, but awfully brilliant. I was very sleepy, smoked a cigarette and sat up a half hour and watched for the light to return. I did not see another glimmer, so the flashes were not lightbugs. I saw plenty of real lightbugs.

Back to bed and instantly asleep I dreamed of meat to eat and arriving too late to begin the term at Notre Dame. I dreamed my wife laughed and swatted herself in the face with the meat and then two Jack Swaugers came to see me. Jack wanted me to see the crazy state in which he encountered himself, being two exact Jack Swaugers, and the two exact looks of consternation on his faces were so funny I woke up laughing.

After the second sleep I lay wide awake and far away heard a *cencerro,* a bell on a horse or cow, and waited for the animal to come nearer, but it moved away. I listened until the bell gave out its very last ring before the animal took the step that carried it out of earshot.

I was still wide awake but comfortable again when a rock struck the back of the tent near my head. I got up with the light of the lantern and found no rock. Then I thought maybe the black bitch stopped by on her return and hit the tent with her tail but she was not there.

I slept hard until first light and then heard arrieros speaking to their animals and the cencerros going by on the Camino Real, then clearly heard turkeys singing down by the old camp. Listened to two or three songs and then called back to the turkeys with the cedar horn. I slipped down to my old camp and called again and they answered, but they were leaving high and north as though they did not intend to stop in Mexico, so I went back to camp and built a fire for coffee.

I heard young voices playing across downriver, then heard one voice turn into that of a coyote singing, farther downriver. The next sound was a dog crying above the fire where my panniers had been dragged and I went up to see him but there was no dog.

I came back to camp and heard the *güero,* blond, Moreno coming and was able to look up and watch the spot where he came in sight. He was carrying a reata and the black bitch with the tawny and knowing eyes was at his heels. He said he was going below to get some cattle he sold and invited me to go with him to kill some of the wild goats that were running there. I said I was waiting for Adán so we could go to work and he went on.

Adán came to camp riding the buckskin mare and followed by his little shaggy dog. He brought me tortillas, but no gasoline. I told him about the *guijolos,* the wild turkeys, I'd heard and he said he would see if he could borrow a .22 rifle and stay all night so we could kill one. He said *El Güero Chupado,* the blond-headed Moreno boy, had killed one downriver the day before. Ever since that Moreno boy stole some coffee from two Americans, one fat and one lean, Adán has called him the Blond Who Sucks.

I told him about the lights and the rock and the cencerro and suddenly remembered the horse. I took him down to the river to show him where the horse sneezed, drank and rolled the night before, but that horse had left no tracks, either.

Adán told me about a certain *sahurina.* A sahurina, he said, is one who cries in her mother's womb before birth. If the mother tells no one about the cry the child will be born with supernatural powers.

This sahurina told three men about a treasure she saw in a dream. She told them the top layer that covered the treasure would be earth, the second layer, ashes, the third, carbon, and the fourth, a flat rock. Under the flat rock they would find gold.

The sahurina told them the exact spot to dig, but warned that one of them would die when the treasure was uncovered. The three men took this last under consideration and each to himself said, *"Ah, jodido!"* Which means, more or less, "Ah, the screwed-up aspect of the operation makes its appearance."

They went to the spot and began to dig. Under the earth they found ashes and under the ashes they found charcoal. Under the charcoal they found the flat rock. Then all three picked up their tools and went home.

Adán drank coffee and left so he could be on hand if another truck came into Mulatos. At midday, I fixed the extra face mask so I could dive *al puro resuello,* with nothing but the air I could hold in my lungs, and cleaned five sacks of rock out of the hole of the size that often stops up the nozzle of the sluice. When I finally quit I was cold.

I went to sit on a boulder to warm myself and an Indian came up the trail driving two young cows who were necked together. They were not getting up the trail too well and someone from my side of the river shouted for him to let them *resollar,* blow awhile. I knew how they felt, only they were hot and out of breath and I was cold and out of breath.

The Güero Chupado came along and asked for a light for his cigarette, then visited a short while and went on. I panned the tailing off a previous panning I had made, because I was looking for a wire of gold I thought I saw go into the sluice, but found nothing.

At dark I lit up my sweet old pipe. I bought that pipe in Duchesne, Utah, when I was packing for Jack Swauger building trail in the Uintas wilderness. The pipe cost a dollar and a coupon out of a pouch of Sir Walter Raleigh tobacco. Right then on the Mulatos River I considered it the best dollar I ever spent. In two years since I ran the packstring in the Uintas it had often been my companion.

In the morning Adán came and pulled a bottle of soyate, a pack of cigarettes and a sheet of jerky out of his *morral,* then from under his arm he brought forth a calico rooster. The poor old feller was trembling and *asoleado,* hot and panting from too much sun, but I did not concern myself with this. I got busy rinsing the dust out of my Dutch oven and building a big fire.

Adán tried to sharpen his old knife on the tapustete rock, but did not do a very good job. Then he said, *"Ni modo,* there's no other

way, Señor Gallo, please pardon me. But why did God make you?"
and wrung his neck. The old feller squawked once, so Adán wrung
his neck again, but that was still not enough, so he cut off his head
with the old knife and it was over. He took him down below El
Desengāno to pick and clean him.

I happily peeled the spuds and made the Dutch oven ready with
grease before Adán got back. I fried the liver and gizzard and we ate
that with soyate while I braised the bird. By the time he was brown
all over my shirttail was much longer because my belly was now
shrinking fast in anticipation. I poured in water and potatoes and
one diced onion, made a bed of coals for the Dutch oven, then
covered the lid with coals and was in business.

After a while I put in a little more water and basted him when it
got hot, then put on salt, pepper and garlic salt when the potatoes
turned brown. The coals just kept the old feller simmering. All this
time Adán and I sipped Tang and sotol and it fit inside us perfectly.

The little short brown one came by with an Indian and the black
bitch Pantera in pursuit of *La Bronca Vaca Josca*, the Wild Brown
Cow. Each time they spoke the miscreant's name their eyes wid-
ened. Adán made the observation that it would be *pelón*, baldly
impossible, for them to catch her as long as they tried it afoot and
carried such short reatas. She knew all the broken places where she
could beat them and get away and was in the habit of refusing to
join other cattle that might gentle her down and lead her into a
corral. They had decided to give up on her for a while after she
made a suicidal run off the high red rock bluff above Palo Dulce.

Adán asked them why the Moreno brothers were not helping
them and the brown shorty said the Güero Chupado Moreno
claimed his *fundillo*, anus, hurt him and the other Moreno, Miguel,
said he couldn't run *de cuesta baja*, downhill. Shorty brown said if
Miguel couldn't run downhill he sure wouldn't run uphill and the
Vaca Josca loved to run uphill as much as downhill. They did not
stay long, but the wild black bitch sensed the meat in the pot and
stayed.

Guillermo, Adán's father-in-law, knows all the stories and tradi-
tions about lost gold in the Sierra. His house on top of the bluff
over the river enables him to see and hear everything that comes
along the Camino Real. Adán asked him if he sensed or heard anyone go by the night I heard the singing horseman and the packtrain
and he said no he did not and maybe it was espantos.

He said long ago a very rich packtrain left the Mulatos mine going downriver and a band of Apaches followed it. The Apaches took to the *cordón* above the trail at a spot where the trail left the river, as it does across the river from El Desengaño, and went ahead to wait in ambush for the train.

The arrieros saw them, unpacked, dropped the cargo in the river, ran the mules up the trail as a diversion and fled back toward Mulatos. When the Apaches saw the empty mules they knew what the arrieros were trying to do and they caught them and slaughtered them. That cargo is still somewhere in the river.

I asked how anyone found out what happened if all the arrieros were killed. Adán said the mules were still saddled when they were found, but carrying no cargo. However, no one could tell by the tracks exactly where the cargo had been unloaded.

After a while we took our bird off the fire, let him rest and cool a little, then began devouring him. The gravy was as thick from the potatoes as it would have been with flour. The meat slid off the bones when we picked them up. The salt and pepper was just right and we were happy with the way the poor old feller turned out. We ate two helpings apiece and divided the bones evenly between the Pantera bitch and Adán's dogs.

While we were talking and smoking, I saw Adán's mare mule coming up the trail. He had loaned her to the Morenos. She was carrying only one ten-gallon barrel of a two-barrel load and had lost her arrieros. She crossed the river where she used to cross at the lower camp. Adán said the poor thing was looking for help and went down to catch her and bring her to our camp. Sotol leaked from holes in the barrel. We unpacked her and Adán gave her corn from his morral. She was glad to see him and relieved to be free of the responsibility of her burden. She sighed and chewed the corn and her big, bottomlessly dark mule eyes lolled with contentment. Every now and then she looked up at Adán with pure gratitude.

A tiny Indian came along looking for her and said she had fallen as she tried to lift the two full barrels of sotol over a steep climb in the trail. The weight of her cargo came to rest on the downhill side and pinned her down. He and his partner worked hard to unload her so she could regain her feet, but when she got up she ran away.

The other Indian came along with a black mule loaded with two ten-gallon drums of sotol. Adán told them to unload in our camp because the comisario was waiting for them at their destination with orders to confiscate the sotol for the government.

They unloaded the black mule in front of my tent and the second Indian went away. Adán and the tiny Indian were cussing the Morenos when they came along looking for their sotol. They complained about the punctured drum and gave me a liter of the stuff. Maybe its adventure was the reason, but it was such good spirit it barely dampened the lip.

The Morenos stayed and we passed the cup. Adán told about the time he was working cattle roping and branding on a hot day, took some of the Morenos' mescal to ward off the heat and got drunk. He felt so good he shot his new pistol in the air, then stuck it between his chaps and his pants. He went on to another roundup and when he was finished for the day he missed the pistol.

After dark he headed back toward the first corral to look for the pistol but fell off his horse drunk and slept the night on the edge of a cliff. In the morning he awoke afoot and *norteado,* not knowing which way was north, and without his hat. He worried that he would wander for hours, but luckily he found his horse and hat right away. As soon as he got back to the trail he spotted the brand-new pistol a hundred meters away.

Now complete again, he felt so good he detoured to the ranch of good friends who lived several hours off the main trail. He had not seen them in years. They gave him breakfast and a swallow of strong soyate and he enjoyed a fine visit with them. He now remembered the whole matter with great joy and attributed it all to the Morenos' good soyate.

The Morenos told about two *Inditos,* their word for simple, childlike Indians, who lived with their families in a cave on the side of a cliff on a high mountain. One day an American came along and gave them money for a house because the cave was on a steep, precarious place and he was afraid it might slide off into the canyon and crush them.

The Inditos kept the money, but stayed in the cave. One of them went to Obregon to work for the American, but returned periodically to visit his family. When he stopped coming back his family went out and made inquiries and found that he had been caught stealing food in Yecora and hanged like a little dog. Now only one of these gentle Inditos was left for them to enjoy.

Our visitors went home and Adán and I were hungry again so we uncovered the remains of the gallo. His bones were so tender they broke when we bit off the meat. After Adán left, the luscious carcass slipped out of my hands to the sand and I picked it up and crunched it with its new sand in my teeth, and that was good too.

In those days I liked to have partners to share my experiences, but none of them ever went all the way down to ride the river with me. Somehow the partners never wanted to see the bottoms of the holes as badly as I did. I had been resenting that, but now realized I didn't mind anymore. I decided I would not mind sharing what I brought out of the river, but would rather do all the work alone and make it a condition that they all stay away. I decided that if we kept the work as it was Adán and I could be assured of having a good camp far away from the big talk of financial deals and partners who expected to share without doing any work or going away into a fifth dimension of wilderness world alone.

All I needed was someone to talk to now and then. I dreamed about what I would do when I carried out the gold I found in the bottom of El Desengaño. I'd deposit my share in Don Roberto's Banco Nacional in Nogales, Sonora. When I needed money I'd go down and stay in the Fray Marcos and listen to the music and early in the morning go down the street and take out the cash I wanted. Afterward I'd go in the Frontera Bar and have a cold gin fizz. That way I wouldn't fool with checks at the VNB or ever pay one goddam cent to no government. I could stay home with my family and write stories and stay out of trouble. Once in a while I'd come back down here alone and work a hole with Adán.

After Adancito watched us a few days, he described the work to his mother: "They have two motors. One is my father's and one is the gingo's [sic]. The gingo's has two long tubes like snakes. The gingo starts his motor and the snakes, one white and one red, come alive and hiss. The gingo puts on a mask that is attached to the red one and buries himself in the charco. Al ratito, a little later, he comes up and waves to Papá and Papá starts his motor. Then the gingo waves at Papá again and Papá stops his motor and the gingo comes up with a little pan of gold."

The tall Moreno's boy's real name was Abdul. He said his father was an Arab from Beirut. He stopped by and told this story: A young man from Mulatos, a vaquero, was hunting on the Cerro San Fernando and found some old Spanish taunas, ore mills. He prospected there on that bad and broken cerro until he found the mine.

He would go alone to the San Fernando and bring back rich ore on a pack mule and process it in the mill at Mulatos. One day he took only his saddle horse and did not return. Searchers found the horse still alive and tied to a tree at the foot of the San Fernando escarpment three days later. The body of the vaquero was nearby. The vaquero had shot himself accidentally in the groin with his .30-30. The Spanish mine of San Fernando is still undiscovered.

Part III

A man named Miguel Roldán rode up to my camp on a nice-looking bay horse. He was well outfitted with a good saddle, a well-made, eight-strand reata, wide Sonora batwing chaps and heavy spurs on his *teguas,* his homemade shoes. Once, seven years ago, he served me as an arriero driving cattle from Yecora to Esperanza. We talked about that three-hundred-mile drive that took place just before Christmas, the good men who were on it, and the bad. We also talked about other mutual friends, the charro named Chuy Díaz from Via Juarez near Obregon, Ingeniero Carranza and David Coughonour.

I went back to work cleaning my hole *al resuello* and he decided to go in and help me. He immediately saw gold shining on the bedrock where I had been cleaning and was stricken with the fever. He brought some of that out in its sand and washed it in the *cuchara,* but he mishandled it and lost it on the way to the surface. He could not handle anything well without wearing a weight belt. He was too buoyant to hold anything when he swam to the surface. In order to keep it he needed a weight belt to hold him down as he carried it out.

He gave up diving for it and went to the dry bedrock against the mountain and found a little color. He dug deeper in the cracks with the wrecking bar and washed what he found in the cuchara. All this time I was hoping he wouldn't look in my pint jar and see the real *macho* grains of gold I had gathered. He washed up a nice little grain in the cuchara and was very happy with it and left it in the bottom of the batea where it would not be lost and it looked very nice to him there.

We went up to the camp to rest and he told me the only man in the region who would raise a finger in favor of the Viejas Aguilera was David Coughonour. He even knew of one of their neighbors who said he would kill the women if they ever appeared at their upper ranch. The viejas once had decided they did not want him as a neighbor there, so they denounced him to the Federals on a false complaint. When he refused to surrender himself to the soldiers, they beat him so badly they almost crippled him.

At one time Miguel worked for the viejas growing corn near the airfield *al partido,* on shares. One day a calf showed up on the field wearing the earmark of the viejas but his brand had been changed. He had been poorly vented with the Aguilera brand to make it look as though they had sold him, but Miguel knew none of the Aguileras' cattle were for sale at that time in the growing season.

The vaquero brother of old Tomás of the beehive was their neighbor at the upper ranch and he came along while the calf was still near the cornfield. Miguel discussed the wrongness of the new status of the calf with him. The vaquero advised him to take the calf to the comisario and report his suspicions. Miguel's report made the comisario suspicious of the vaquero. The viejas had been trying to make the comisario arrest the vaquero because they suspected he was bringing their calves down from the upper ranch and turning them over to the Morenos. The Moreno brothers were suspected of selling the calves in Sahuaripa.

The vaquero was accused of theft and put in jail. Miguel said he always felt bad about it because if the vaquero had only told him he was responsible for changing the status of the calf Miguel would not even have remembered seeing the animal. Anyway, it was all done now and everyone understood that the vaquero had cast suspicion on himself and no one blamed Miguel. The Morenos were never charged with any crime and the charges against the vaquero were never proven and he was released. He and his family vowed they would kill the Aguilera spinsters if they ever showed themselves at the upper ranch, though.

When Miguel went to settle with the vieja Rosa on income from the cornfield, she owed him 725 pesos. She gave him 25 pesos and said that would leave a *numero completo cerrado,* a round figure, for her to pay when he came back the next day. He came back the next day for his *numero completo cerrado* of 700 and she handed him 500. He said no you are mistaken it is 700 and she said no you are mistaken it is 500.

Miguel said to me, what could I do, she held the money and I needed it so badly right then I didn't have time to argue with her. So he let her cheat him out of two hundred pesos.

Miguel said he began to learn early that he must defend his own. Soon after he married he worked a farm in the mountains south of Mulatos and the Ingeniero Carranza and David held the mineral rights to the same property.

An American was there working the mine for them. He never gave work to Miguel, so Miguel went on about his own business. One day he cut some *lajitas,* shakes, for the roof of his wife's kitchen and carried them past the mine in a sack. The American called him over and accused him of stealing lumber needed for the mill. He showed the American how few shakes he had cut, but the American told him not to do it anymore, everything on that ranch pertained to the mine and was for its disposal only. Miguel held his tongue and went home.

Then one day Miguel returned from the farm to find the American drilling to blast right near his home. The American called Miguel over and ordered him to get his wife and children out of the house. He did not want to be blamed if they got hurt. After arguing for a while, Miguel *se encabronó,* turned into a sonofabitch, and refused to move his family. The American said you get out or I'll get you out. Miguel said we'll see who gets out. He went in and got his .30-.30, planted himself in his doorway and told the American to get his fat ass off his farm. The American and the workers discussed what they should do for a while, decided they did not need to blast and went away.

The next day David and the Ingeniero flew in and the Ingeniero started talking to Miguel from afar as they walked toward his house, saying, *"Como, como, como, como está esta cosa. Aver, aver, aver, aver.* How can we explain this thing together. Let's see about it and resolve it, please."

Miguel told him how the thing was and both the Ingeniero and David concurred that he had done right. Since then David has given him work from time to time.

Adán came another day with no gasoline, but with a gallon of *tesguino,* a kind of mountain man's corn beer that once even caused an Apache war in Arizona. Miguel Moreno came by moving slowly and talking very softly and sat down and went on talking with his head down. Adán and he gave me the recipe for tesguino and here it is:

Soak corn in water in an open container.

Lay a *tanda,* layer, of pine needles over it.

Lay another tanda of soaked corn on that.

Lay down another tanda of pine needles.

Irrigate every day until the corn takes root and the first shoots appear.

Grind and boil the corn in its own water.

Set it in the sun to absorb heat.

Place it in *ollas* lined with leavening.

When it cooks and foams up with its own heat, it is ready to be swallowed.

I warmed a pot of beans with chili I'd made and they liked it, eating two bowls apiece. Adán armed a *trueno,* a bomb, with a half stick of dynamite, lit the fuse, threw it into the mainstream, and it went off deep. Many fish came up and we swam and gathered them.

I started the motor on the breather and went down and found six bigger fishes on the bottom. When I came up a vaquero was squatting on a rock across the river and La Pantera was with him. He carried a short reata coiled on his belt and a longer one in his hand. He crossed upstream and turned out to be one of those sullen smart-aleck critics that crop up in any camp from time to time, but at least he was a quiet one.

Adán and the Moreno boy cleaned the fish, about thirty of them, and the sullen young one built a fire and cooked himself four fishes, smacked his lips on them and left with the tall Moreno boy. I put on a fish fry and afterward Adán slept under the big tapustete rock for a while.

When he woke up we decided if David came on the twenty-fourth of April we would still have time to work before the rains came, but if not Adán would go to Tarachic with his animals and two barrels of ten liters to buy gas. This would be a two-day trip and we would not work then until the twenty-seventh but at least we could be sure to have the gas and be able to work a full week before we needed more.

Then Adán built a fire for coffee water and told me the sullen one was his youngest brother, *El Coyote.* I asked how many were his brothers, and he said four and one sister. He said one was in jail in Sahuaripa. He sat down and told about the fights in Mulatos.

A group of people were drinking mescal one Sunday down by the river airstrip. A little Indian who made good soyate had packed two twenty-gallon *barricas,* barrels, down from his still to ship to Hermosillo on the route plane. Many poor people stopped by on their way home that day for a drink. Many stayed by the barricas longer than they should have.

Adán came along riding a sorrel horse he had just bought and a bunch of loudmouths stopped him and during the drinking Adán's horse got away downriver. An old man went with him to catch the horse and when they were on their way back they heard women wailing inside a ranch house.

Adán jumped on his horse bareback and hurried to them and on the trail near the house he saw pools of blood. The women, in full voice, told him someone had stabbed their *pariente* Benito Rey at the party up the river. The man cut him in six places and then ran to Mulatos.

Adán went back to the party and after a while he hired a *guitarrero,* girls came with their parents, and everybody danced until morning. Adán was asleep when the comisario came with five armed men and arrested the fifty men at the party. He confiscated the mescal that remained and loaded it on a mule. He lined up the men two by two behind the mule with three guards on the barrica, one in front of the men and one behind, and marched everyone dying of the *cruda* to Mulatos.

In Mulatos the comisario lined them up in the hot street outside the door of the *comisaria* and the first one they called to give testimony was Adán. They said now you are to give the truth about what happened at the party yesterday when Benito Rey was cut. Adán said of course, what else could I give?

The comisario said all right, give it.

The whole truth is that I don't know what happened. I wasn't there at the time of the cutting. I was chasing my horse.

Then others spoke up and said this is the truth.

The comisario then asked why Adán put on the dance.

He answered, *"Porque me dió mi pinchi gana.* Because I damned well felt like it."

The comisario swelled and straightened up with his chest puffed out and said well, I'm going to fine you twenty pesos.

Fine all you want, but I won't pay it. Fine the real criminal who did the cutting and is now in his home pleasurably eating his breakfast and curing his cruda. Don't fine us for dancing.

Then Adán's uncle the judge stepped forward and told the comisario to fine Adán ten pesos and forget it.

Adán produced the ten pesos and said here you are for your four *tecatonas,* your quarts of beer.

The comisario lost his temper and told Adán to leave but not to talk to anyone on the street. Adán bought some canned food for those on the street and sat and talked with them and the mean wife of the comisario gave Adán a liter of mescal from the confiscated barrica. Later the comisario complained about it and she threw him out of the house.

That night some *borrachitos,* drunks, came upon the comisario drunk and yowling at his door for his wife to let him in. He begged the borrachitos for a drink and they told him to go very much to the fornication, but he began joking with them and sucking up to them until they, laughing at him, gave him a drink.

The mean wife of the comisario sold the remaining mescal dram by dram. The comisario made five hundred pesos in fines from the borrachitos, everyone shook Adán's hand for telling off the comisario, and the man who did the cutting was never even questioned.

One morning Adán chased a heifer past the airstrip and a boy named Fidel Roldán, brother to Miguel, was there with his wife waiting for the plane that came regularly on a route from Hermosillo. They were newlyweds.

Fidel shouted to Adán, "Will you catch her?"

Adán said, *"Seguro que si."*

The plane did not come that day and the boy and his wife went in to stay the night in Mulatos. Later, Adán was out on the street when he ran into a man who was an enemy of Miguel Roldán's. This man once beat Miguel so badly he left him for dead. Now, after two years, he had returned from Hermosillo. He owned a new pistol and told Adán he intended to kill Miguel. He looked all over Mulatos and when he did not find him, got drunk.

In this situation, Fidel, Miguel's young brother, *en sangre fria,* unworriedly, with no rancor, encountered the man.

The man said is it you, son of the fornication? and shot him. Fidel lived an hour and a half.

The man went from there to the house of Miguel, pounded on the door, fired several shots, then mounted his horse and ran to the ranch of a tanner and woodcutter. There he asked for food and told the tanner, dying of laughter, that he had killed Fidel and still hoped to kill Miguel. Then he hid in the *tasolera*, a bin for cornstalks, at the ranch of his brothers nearby.

Adán got up very early the next morning without knowing about the killing and went in search of his *toro buey*, his work bull. The toro buey had been running near the ranch of the tanner. At the ranch, the tanner told Adán nothing about the killing, and to keep him away from the tasolera, said the toro buey was now running somewhere else. Adán was sure the toro buey was running above the tasolera, so he rode that way anyway.

Adán was armed with his carbine and would have been potshotted by the killer if he had gone near the tasolera. The coward would have killed any armed man who rode near him. Just before Adán reached the tasolera he saw the toro buey running high on a mountain with other cattle. He wondered at that because the toro buey was normally gentle.

Adán turned away from the tasolera and when the cattle saw him they ran along a ridge to get away from him. He hurried to get ahead of them and stopped at a ranch long enough to leave the carbine so he wouldn't lose it in the chase. He went on and caught the toro buey on the mountain and led him back to get his carbine. At the ranch the women asked him, surprised, if the toro buey was all he had come for and he said yes.

They said they thought he had been after Lorenzo Rey, killer of Fidel Roldán. Didn't he know about it?

He said no.

When the women told him about the killing it was the first he knew about it and he thanked the toro buey for leading him away from the tasolera.

In the night, the river—rushing sounds inside my tent—seemed at times at flood tide and at times would subside and be quiet. I heard the sound of someone running away from the tent and went out, and nothing.

In the morning, Miguel Moreno came by with a full stick of dynamite and told about being at the dance of the *Indias* the night before. One of them was good-looking, but her father took her away early because he did not want any mixture of Arab swelling inside his daughter. He followed her home *atarantadito*, a little dizzy with the need of his body, and slept with her brother and had to fight him off all night.

Miguel said that while he was in school in Sahuaripa he boarded with an Indian woman who slept with her brother. She said she wanted to keep it in her family and never gave him any.

Miguel's brother sired two children with an Indian woman in the Chihuahua Mountains this side of Madera. One day the brothers decided to go and get the children because they didn't want them to be reared by the Indian. The village heard the Moreno brothers were coming and stood together to keep them away from the woman and her children.

The brothers seized the woman's father, who was head of the village, tied him up and broke into his house. The woman was waiting for them with a rifle and they took it away. She got a butcher knife and they took it away. Miguel tried to hold her from taking up arms again and she bit and kicked him, so they tied her up and took the children.

I found some string and we hung the stick of dynamite on a stick of wood for a *bombillo*. I harnessed myself with the face mask and weight belt and Miguel threw the bombillo into a deep pool just north of El Desengaño. It went off just right and up came one big fish and one small one. I went down, and nothing. I went down again and found three small fishes on the bottom. Miguel cleaned them and black-peppered them and put them on my tepeguaje tree to dry, then walked downstream to look for a better hole.

I went into the mainstream and looked for more fish, and nothing. I washed my pants and socks, the pants with Bill Rush's name in them I got from Del Brooks. Then I swam to cool off and Miguel's Indian came by with a big string of fish. Then one of the little Indians came by with a string of little fish and both Indians were hurrying. Miguel came on very slow and gave me two little catfish. He ate one of my dried fishes and I gave him ten pesos to buy me some cigarettes and he went on.

The black bitch Pantera stayed with me and I gave her the pea soup. The sun was still so hot in the evening I went up to the shade of the oak above camp to smoke.

A boy came by burroback driving a pack burro, then a man carrying a rifle, then two more men, then later another, and they all looked at my camp to see the gringo. When they didn't see me because I was sitting apart from it under the oak they shouted, *"Et,"* and I shouted, *"Adios."* They all looked around for me and I was in plain sight, but they never saw me.

After sundown I went down to sew my pants. Pantera was still there and I gave her a Hershey bar the mice got to. While I was sitting in my shorts sewing, Miguel Roldán came by with Adán's sullen brother. He blew around the reason for his visit awhile and finally begged some .22 cartridges, promised me meat, and they left.

I fried the dried catfish for my supper and fed Pantera spoonsful of beans and all the tails and bones of the crisp, salty fish. She lay low in the sand as though afraid I was going to send her away, but she wouldn't come to me. I sat on the big rock and smoked my Duchesne pipe.

In bed and in the night after the first sleep Pantera was standing at the tent flap hoping I would awaken and when I did she came in. I told her to lie down and she went out and I knew she was gone and had only come in to make her *despedida,* her farewell.

In the morning I ate raisins and coffee and shaved with the back of the lantern for a mirror. Then I washed all the dishes, stripped and bathed and went up to the big tepeguaje tree to write this. That whole day I was so hot and tired and lonesome I didn't want to remember any more or write about it.

In the morning I awoke with hope again, after dreaming all night that I had rejoined the Marines as an enlisted man named José Bravo. I boiled potatoes and was frying them with jerky when I heard an airplane land at Mulatos. I was pretty sure it was David and after a while he lifted up and came over, no lettering on the underside of the wing, and I was sure it was David.

I expected Adán to return from Tarachic with the gasoline that day and he came right on time to go to work. He said the plane that landed was David's and he stopped on his way to Nogales to see how I was. He had not received my message about the gas until yesterday, but didn't bring any anyway. Adán said for him to say for sure what day he was coming and he said for sure the fourth and Adán told him we were having a small success but we needed gas to last nine days.

I got up and the ass had finally gone out of my Levi's. We ate breakfast and went down to the charco and got ready to work. Everything worked fine with the gasoline and I brought out two of the *ralavitos,* little sluice pans, and looked over and the air was coming out of the hose on the extra breather. We took that hose off and left the face mask on the bank.

Then the pump stopped working and we carelessly changed the

oil and left an oil slick on the pool. Then the canvas hose on the sucker was burnt by the exhaust and split open. We fixed it and the Briggs motor wouldn't start because the shaft in the pump was stuck. We took it apart and cleaned it and the Briggs still wouldn't start.

Frustrated, I went in and worked underwater for an hour and a half with my fingernails to bring up material for Adán's batea. One of the times I looked in my groin where something was bothering me and discovered a three-inch leech stuck to me there and I tore him off and put him on a rock in the sun to die.

Adán was bringing up very good color in his batea. Of the eight or ten pans I brought up not one failed to show one or two pieces the size of a grain of wheat and many smaller grains and a lot of fine dots of gold. Finally, after another half hour I was cramping so I came up for good and that pan was also good. Adán washed it all and we put it in the U.S. coffee jar and almost filled it.

Then, very hot, baked and tired, we quit and went hunting for the carton the Johnson breather came in. We found it where it blew into the river and was no more. Adán went home and me and Pantera ate the rest of the cupful of jerky and potatoes, a *gorda* with chili Adán left me and a tortilla with peanut butter; I washed the dishes and wrote this.

Pantera slept all night outside the tent by my head and every now and then she would groan and stretch and push my head through the tent. In the morning I was hopeful when I went to the fire even though I was out of coffee. I cooked my spuds and fried my jerky and Pantera lay down under my legs and kept looking at me. After a while she said ouch with a little moan because a flea broke an egg deep inside her. She watched for the culprit but he was wise enough and knew his country well enough to be able to retreat and save his life.

Early, David came from Nogales and landed and Adán said he asked, "What happened to my gringo? Has he been swallowed by a charco somewhere?" Adán told him, "No, he still swims well."

I went in El Desengaño and cleaned but couldn't do much without a dredge. I saw a shadow of a presence above me and surfaced and Adán was on the bank. He asked me if I had tried the pump. I said yes, but *está jodido,* it's been cuckolded, so we went to the camp to make coffee Adán brought. He also brought sugar, a can of sardines, a can of milk, cigarettes, four leavened breads and a liter of soyate. We drank a trago with coffee and ate bread.

Adán panned what I had taken out while he was in Tarachic and it was good, but not as good as the gold I brought out yesterday with my fingernails. I went down and brought up some *ensayes*, samples, and they were not as good as yesterday either. I went down again and wrung myself out all afternoon using the gardener's claw and my fingernails to dig a hole against the peña six inches square. My gasoline gave out while I was down and when I came up it was almost sundown.

Adán panned that and it was fair and I was disappointed, but then when Adán put everything together in the batea and washed it he turned it up and it was like a thick smear of butter in the bottom of the batea. He filled a whole Tang jar with the coarse gold and was afraid to wash more because he might lose the fine gold in the dark.

We began talking about stingy people we knew. I told him about Don Felipe in Navojoa who always complained in a drouth about the high cost of alfalfa hay. He bought it high, but it always cost him twice as much because then he would hoard it and not give it to his cattle. He did not have any complaints about the costs of ware-housing it.

Adán told me about the tight old man from Mulatos who ordered 250 kilos, *una tonelada* of cottonseed meal for his cattle. The trucker who was taking the order said *como una tonelada?* How a ton? And he answered, *sì*, 250 kilos, one ton.

His family wouldn't eat anything but beans and tortillas and no salt. The seven-year-old son needed ten pesos for school and went and sold a goat for fifty pesos and gave forty to his mother and she didn't ask where it came from, she knew. Then the buyer of the *chiva* sent some of the meat to the mother and the old man saw it. He took the boy and shook the story out of him, then hung him in a tree and whipped him with a reata like a dog.

I had my supper with some soyate and felt better, optimistic again. I decided to go out and try to get the pump fixed so I could make a fresh try at it as soon as possible. I wanted to get some real work done before the rains came. I decided to move camp the next day.

I gave Pantera three fishes and she was very happy with me and we played. She whiffed at the soyate to see what I saw in it.

Part IV

The next morning, the twenty-ninth of April 1968, I heard turkeys peeping high above my tent on the steep mountain. I climbed after them with my pistol and felt weak. At the first *encinal,* oak grove, I heard them peep again in a canyon below me. I skulked down through the brush and rocks looking into the canyon for the turkeys and underfoot for snakes. The turkeys subsided in the brush so I called with the little cedar box and a young gobbler walked up the bank across the canyon and looked at me.

I ducked behind a rock, but remembered I wanted to eat fresh meat again, said what the hell, raised up, pointed the pistol, and there he was in my barrel thirty-five yards away. The 265 grains *smashed* him. The ball ruffled and collapsed him so his feathers stuck out all around. I could see I did not have to hurry to keep him from getting away. When I lifted him he rolled inside his skin like canned meat inside a small, fragile sack. As I lifted his carcass, he was so killed his feathers sagged and stayed a moment to scratch the ground in parting, as though even they were more alive than he.

Adán came and we roasted the turkey in the Dutch oven like we did El Gallo. He was fatter than the rooster and browned with, I swear, a chef's glaze on him. We ate him and he settled heavily but gently and more comfortably on our stomachs than El Gallo.

I told Adán we were working now for nothing. We had prospected the hole well and knew the stuff was there. We agreed that I should go out and get the pump fixed.

In the morning Adán brought his mare mule and brown horse and we loaded them with a cargo apiece and he left for his ranch. He had been gone about fifteen minutes when Ted Farnsworth flew over with Ingeniero Carranza. They were expected. I decided to hurry and see if I could go out with Ted. I hefted the *mochila,* my canvas bag, and it weighed at least sixty pounds with the full jars of gold added to my clothes and old Meat in the Pot.

The trail was hot and I hurried upriver with Pantera at my heels and did not slow until I climbed the white cliff. From there I watched Ted lift off, head straight for me a moment, then skim overhead. I waved and said Ted, but he went on, of course.

I went very tired and sweaty to the shade with Pantera and rested. After a while I went back to camp and sat in the shade of the tepeguaje and smoked a cigarette, heard something and looked downriver and there very slow and low came Ted again hanging with his flaps down. He passed right over me and I waved and he went on and landed.

So I loaded up the mochila again, sure he must have seen me and got to thinking when he lifted off and had come back for me. I hurried upriver in the sun so Ted wouldn't have to wait, the air and light on the trail hot, still and heavy.

When I finally reached the camp of the Viejas Aguilera, about fifteen people were there, about ten head of saddled horses and mules and a waterlot full of cattle. One of the viejas was tending a fire. I asked for Felipe, the viejas' vaquero, and recognized two Hermosillo cattle buyers. They just looked at me as though they thought I was another serrano, or some crazy bigger than the ordinary Sonoran, or some gringo whose broken Spanish they did not wish to hear.

The old viejo *lambeon,* kissass, who hung around my camp the first day I came with Tío and the firemen, was there and I asked him for Felipe, the vaquero of the Aguileras. He said there's no Felipe here. I asked him if someone could loan me a *bestia,* a saddle horse. He answered the airfield is very close. I said thank you, I know where the airfield is and that wasn't what I asked for and went on.

As I stepped out of the mesquite thicket over the camp I met the buyers who had come in on the second plane. I had walked five times farther in the sun than they had and they were kicking up dust in the still heat, dragging their feet with fatigue. They asked me in desperation where the cattle were. I said about two hundred yards farther and asked if that was Ted Farnsworth's plane. They said yes and I hurried on.

I walked by the old camp we made when we first came to the river, Tío, Jim O'Farrell, Art Breitzke and I. We had come for fun and were lighthearted then, only a few months ago. Then, that first night we sat outside the tent in clear, bright blue moonlight and a horseman passed by singing and Tío and the firemen must have thought the place was idyllic.

The next afternoon we heard Daniel's black dog Caporal baying and watched him come by herding cattle toward the barbwire wing that channeled them into the Aguilera corrals. Daniel stopped and talked to us, confident the dog would pen the cattle even though no one could see what was going on. The corrals were on the other side of the *mesquital,* mesquite grove, from our camp.

That night we heard Caporal's voice again. His howls came from Daniel's house up the canyon this time and he was chewing on them because he was full of pain, his throat slit by a *solitario*. A *solitario* is a coatimundi who grows too old, bull-necked and mean to be tolerated by his tribe until he shuns and is shunned by it and goes away by himself until he dies. He may not die for years. Caporal had tackled one. His howls became weaker that night until he died. That was on the second night of my friends' vacation and it brought them to the real Sierra Madre, was their first experience with the wondrous cruelty of those mountains.

I could see the plane from the cliff at the bend of the river and no one was around it. I hurried on to the end of the field and knelt down on the river and drank and wet my head, then climbed to the field and walked down the strip. If he tried to take off before I reached him he would have to run over me.

I made it and no one was there. The plane was a Cessna 180 and the same color as Ted's, but the last numbers were 81U, not Ted's. The papers inside said it belonged to Rubén Morales of Douglas, my friend El Toro. I had blamed the two Hermosillo buyers for not knowing me, but I had not recognized El Toro, so I wasn't so keen an observer myself. The pilot had made two trips with his buyers to lighten his load for landing in that heat. El Toro was probably already carrying three passengers per trip and hot as it was, even though he probably carried no luggage, he might not be able to take off with me and my mochila. I went to the shade.

After a while, bathed in sweat, I saw Adán riding across the river on the cliff above Guillermo's house on his way back to camp for the rest of our gear. I shouted to him and he came over and looked in my face and saw I was *asoleado,* with too much sun, and said he would go alone to load the camp. I rode double with him down to the river and he gave me the jar of soyate from his morral for a sip with water to ward off heat exhaustion.

He went on and I walked all the way back in the sun and lay down under the mesquite on the field with my mochila again. The soyate made me feel much better and I took clean clothes out of the mochila and went down to the river to bathe.

Across the river below Guillermo's house a young woman was kneeling at the edge and washing clothes singing. She wore a straw vaquero hat and a towel around her waist. She must have just bathed, for her back and breasts were bare. I went on without staring at her.

Upriver I stripped and bathed in the deep cool water of a wide bend. I kicked across on my back and the sky was clear and hot as the glass peephole on a furnace. Refreshed, I walked back. The girl was gone and I regretted it, felt I'd let another wonder pass me by.

I was back under the mesquite at the airfield when the cow buyers came back and hollered something at me, but I saw for sure this time that El Toro wasn't with them so I didn't answer. They loaded and left.

The wind turned hot and searing under the mesquite and I napped with Pantera. After a while Adán hollered from up on the cliff and I shouldered the mochila and walked down to the trail that paralleled his route across the river. The vaqueros from the viejas' corrals were at Felipe the vaquero's house across the river, their mules tied under the trees in the yard. They stared at me and Adán rode smiling across their front.

I walked on and the vieja Rosa rode up behind me and hollered and came on to catch up. This was the first time I had been within talking distance of her since I unloaded her on the upper airstrip, the time she foxed me into giving her a free ride home from Agua Prieta. I bowed my head and kept going and she slowed so she could follow along behind me and ask questions.

Finally I stopped, out of breath from talking and walking in the heat. She asked how I was called and I looked at her and said, "What are you asking me?"

She cocked her head as if she expected me to recognize her.

I Indianed it and went on.

She said she wanted a ride on the airplane that was coming for me.

I said David Coughonour was not dependable and anyway would be loaded with cargo.

She said thanks anyway and I said *de nada* and went on.

Adán saw all this from the other side of the river. I left the trail then and walked down off the cliff and crossed the river and Adán loaded the mochila on his mare.

The old bastard that told me the airstrip was not far instead of trying to help me was bathing naked in the river when I crossed. He stared at me and crouched in the water to hide his parts.

Adán's house was surrounded with much greenery and the trees were leafed out and giving a lot of shade. His wife Lucrecia was handsome and plump with strong legs and a smile of fine white even teeth. She had a deep voice with the accent of the serrana, and the heavy, warm, plump vowels. Her eyes were tawny.

Adán right away brought fresh water and strong soyate to drink. I sat in the shade and rested and the soyate revived me. We ate sardines and coffee with milk and the sullen brother arrived and ate too, then sat around and stared at his feet, then finally left. Adán seasoned a bottle of good mescal with raisins, cinnamon, orange peels and *panocha*, brown sugar. He stoppered it and put it in a cool, dark adobe corner of his house to keep.

Then, at supper in lamplight, a vaquero came in from Tarachic and said he wanted to buy the viejas' cutbacks. He ate with us and seemed to be a fine boy. Adán told me that when he had gone to Tarachic for the gas he arrived late one night at this boy's house and was still too far from Tarachic to go on. The boy's father made him unsaddle right there and eat supper. He opened his house to Adán and gave him a cot to sleep on.

When supper was done, it was night, but the boy wanted to go on to Mulatos with his partner. The *compañero* led up a saddled mule that required a *tapojo*, blindfold, to be mounted. The boy said, *"Nombre sea de Dios,* in the name of God," stepped on him and lifted the tapojo.

The mule bogged his head and bucked away and disappeared up Adán's rocky arroyo in the night. After a while he came bucking and bawling back. The boy stopped him at the house, turned him around and made him go back up the arroyo out of sight to drill and school him a little.

The next day the boy came by to say goodbye. He had gone to the home of the Veijas Aguilera in Mulatos to tell them he was there to receive the *resaga,* the culls of the sale to Morales, and the viejas said, *"No, ya no.* No, not anymore." They did not want to sell them now, had already turned them loose.

After the boy from Tarachic was gone Adán and I made plans awhile and then he gave me a cot in the front room and I slept well. In the morning when I washed I saw myself in a mirror for the first time in three weeks and I combed my hair with brilliantine before breakfast.

I was there at Adán's for ten days before David came for me in answer to my telegram. He came one morning without warning and

Adán and I had to catch and pack the horses. I shouldered the mochila and hurried to the field ahead of Adán. David and his wife and Clay his brother and Clay's wife Rita were there stretching their legs outside the plane. I had never met Rita. David kidded me about the red bandana I wore on my brow and tied in back under my hat and Rita said, "You laugh like your dad."

I asked how she knew my dad and she said, "Oh, yes, I knew him very well. My sister was once married to your uncle Buster Sorrells." That made me feel good.

Adán came and we loaded the Briggs in the plane and all went aboard. Adán was forced to hold Pantera because she set up a howl when she saw I was leaving. I sat on the floor behind Rita. We roared off over El Desengaño by the red rock peaks above Palo Dulce, and on to Nogales.

In Nogales David's brother Marsden came out to the airport for me and David and his family went on to Tucson. We ate lunch at the Nogales Tavern, Marsden went home and a Mexican cowboy friend of my family gave me a ride to the Fray Marcos in Nogales, Sonora. I got a room and went up and slept until evening, then ordered up two filet mignons and four beers and ate and drank them all up and slept until nine the next day.

I walked over to the Cavern and talked awhile with old Nick Kiriakin and a poor, palefaced, unfortunate gringo wandered in looking for a friend after being rolled. I didn't feel a bit sorry for him. Misfortune was everywhere.

Nick remembered the fine times we'd had in the Cavern. Three generations of us have used it for a place to eat and drink, court our sweethearts, celebrate our mothers and fathers and listen to the mariachis. I'd been in there with my father when I was a button, and he'd been there with my grandfather. My dad gave me my first shot glass full of beer in there.

I went across the line to visit with Paul Bond in his store and then over to Dr. Gonzales for a tetanus shot. At noon I stopped in the Wonder Bar and ran into John Jones who was now the owner of my great-great-grandfather's ranch in Parker Canyon. We got to talking and then Hal Boyle and his boss who can't give him a job but works hell out of him anyway came in and he asked me if I was related to Joe Paul Brown. I said I am one and the same. He said Marlin Brady told him about the time I traipsed down the ramp in front of the fancy matrons in the De Anza Hotel lobby in Calexico. They were waiting for a fashion show to start and the models were late so I modeled for them my hat, Levi's and manury boots.

I loafed back across the line and finally phoned my thenwife. She said her friend Doug was going to bring her down that evening in his plane. I went up and slept again until they called me from the lobby.

We had some drinks and then went to our favorite place for *menudo* and beer, the place steamy warm from the great boiling pots of beef paunch stew, the cow's knuckles steaming and cleanly smooth in the stew with bleached corn, onion and chile *tepin*. The good paunch settled away all the alcohol and made us sober and thoughtful. Beef paunch menudo stew is best for bringing a body down from too much drinking, settles its wildness and sends it to bed content as an old cow who has chewed her cud. Some good mariachis came in and played for us, too. Then we went to the hotel.

Doug said he would not see us in the morning because he was flying to some business early, but would come back for us. My thenwife whom I loved a lot then went to bed with me and was softer and rounder in the right places including her heart than I ever remembered. We awakened early to investigate that matter more, then we bathed and went down to show her off at coffee. I took her to the shops and kind of hazed her around all day and we went to see my Granny Sorrells. Then we had lunch with the mariachis and *cabuama,* sea turtle stew, in the Cavern.

In the morning the little authority at the desk would not take my check, so I hired a taxi across the line and Joe Crevelone cashed it at the Coronado Hotel. I went back and paid and we made it to the airport in time to keep Doug from waiting.

He was very hung over in his twin Comanche and said he was bringing me bad news. His friend who was trying to help me get published in New York told Doug that David would end up screwing me out of everything I accomplished in the Sierra. That made me feel bad enough to bawl. I had known Dave Coughonour and his family all my life. I believed Doug was mad that anyone could be that wrong about David, mad as hell that anyone would believe he screwed anybody.

The way I saw it, Doug's friend had invested in Dave's mine and when it failed to meet expectations, he wanted his marbles back. Then he decided to get more than even and wanted David's marbles, too. When he gambled and lost and couldn't have all the marbles, he told everybody he got screwed.

Doug mistook my anger for sadness, at first, then I told him David didn't have to screw me to get anything he wanted from me. I'd give it to him.

Doug let us off in Showlow and we went home to Pinetop. My thenwife's mom needed to say something about my mustache, but other than that the homecoming was about O.K. I was able to be home in the arms of my family a few days while the pump was being fixed and I recouped my outfit.

Tuesday, 11 June '68. Drove down from Tucson and arrived at David's trailer in Tucson at 2 A.M. He woke me up at three and I followed him in my Impala called Carlotta to have coffee. Paddy Ryan, the old saddle bronc champ, was there coffeeing. He said he was working for the movies now. I could see he still had hopes and plenty of heart. He was working extra in the movies wearing checkered woolen trousers, his boots from movie wardrobe run over at the heels. He got in his clean Chevy car and drove away. I bet his old, bowed legs still fit a horse better than anybody else's.

At the freeway airport, David said he had waited till 9 P.M. the day before for me to come with my cargo and when I didn't come he loaded a sheet of steel and a roll of screen. There was no room for my gas, oil, packing or grease and I climbed in on top of the steel all doubled over. David said I know it's damned uncomfortable, but we'll be there in an hour and a half.

The light of the sun was rosy, the mountains purple as the man piloted the 206 up the Mulatos River, around Cerro San Nicolas, over El Desengaño, and landed. Miguel and Oscar came to the plane and David took the key to my car and left, promising to come back day after tomorrow.

I shouldered the rifle I brought Adán and walked to his house. Lucrecia smiled when I gave her the material I'd brought and told Adancito to go for his father. I followed the boy to the corral and Adán was milking his red cow while her spotted calf nursed on the other side. I said hello and went back to the house with him and he gave me a nice swallow of the *compostura,* raisin-cured mescal.

Adán's *culeca* hen came out with a tumbling, ravenous crowd of chicks hatched from the eggs David's wife gave us. The chicks were striped and feral little turkeys who ran with the hen's own yellow chicks and thought they were chickens.

I gave Adán the hat and rifle I'd brought him. Pantera came and sat at my feet and I didn't notice her until she carefully tasted the tip of my finger. I began to feel better after the hour and a half of riding on top the sheet of metal with my nose against the overhead of David's plane.

Lucrecia fed me and we went to the field and packed the beasts with my gear and went down the hot trail to El Desengaño. At the *nogal*, the walnut tree, we drank the last tragos of the jar of compostura. I told Adán about the time my Uncle Buster roped the bravo bull when we were having a picnic at his ranch, the Letherman place. He'd been wanting to catch a certain bull that came in to water while the family was at the picnic. After Uncle Buster caught him he rolled Uncle Buster's horse and then when Aunt Hazel ran to save Uncle Buster, he rolled her too and embedded her into the hardpan of the road in front of the house. Aunt Hazel had been Uncle Buster's first-grade teacher and was way too tough to kill, but the bull got away trailing the rope.

We went on, very hot. I shot at a big whitetail hare with M in the P, my .45., for meat. The rabbit was about a hundred yards away and much later the bullets arrived to where he had been sitting. We went on to El Desengaño and made camp there for the fifth time. I felt I had the flu and in the night sweated the cold drop, but in the morning I was better.

I was setting up the motors when Don Tomás came and kind of begged around for anything he might be able to get all day like an old dog. He did not go away until evening. He was working for the viejas again, but did not mind waiting to see what he could get from me.

I blasted away an overhang that had been threatening to drop on me when I dredged underneath it and began dredging again in the afternoon. I brought up good color right away. That evening it rained heavily upriver.

The next day I dove early and spent two hours cleaning and searching underwater, brought up a pan of very, very good, coarse gold, then really got after it. I made fifty-six trips and felt we were on the way to becoming rich, or at least able to pay our bills.

The next morning I stepped out of my tent and the water had turned to the red brown of a very rich chocolate milkshake from the rain on the Mesas Coloradas upriver. I tried to work anyway, but the water was so solidly impenetrable that I was only able to feel around the hole. I worked until I was so tired I had trouble finding my way to the surface.

I started again in the afternoon and tried to clean until the air buoy ran out of gas. I tried to surface, did not know where I was, came up under the big rock and started to drown. Adán ran and turned me around with the hose, then ran along the rock above me and pulled me out by the hair of the head. Because of the weight belt, I never did know up from down in the chocolate brown.

My chest hurt like hell so I quit for the day very discouraged. Adán left and I ate supper and wrote this. Pantera stayed with me with those eyes and she knew almost everything there was to know in the world at that stage because she was about to have puppies.

On the fifth day after the rain I decided to leave El Desengaño and find a clear stream. Adán came and put the mercury to our two days' work and it amounted to about three grams. If we could stay at El Desengaño and work thirty good days, I'm afraid the crowd who hates, envies or is contemptuous for the way I live would have to swallow their bile and no longer be able to make Joe Brown swallow his.

I dove once more to bring out the *pata de chiva,* the goat's-foot wrecking bar, and the dredge. Adán threw a bombillo and I retrieved a hundred catfish on the surface. I bathed and shaved and changed clothes and rolled up camp. Adán left with a load and I finished packing in the heat and sat down in the shade of the tepeguaje to wait for him.

Saul the *bigoton,* of the large mustache, stopped by to talk. He was also a *gambusino,* a placer miner, and agreed El Desengaño was a good place for placer to be because we were finding coarser gold on the bedrock as we went down. He was a pleasant man to talk to, especially when he told me what I wanted to hear.

Adán came back and we loaded the rest of the camp. I rode the mare with Pantera at her heels, and knew I'd failed again. A man who has to ride a mare ought to feel a failure, I guess. Everything was comfortable for me in Adán's home again. I ate a nice supper and went to bed without having uttered one peep of despair that whole day because I didn't feel any. It still wasn't in me to feel that way.

I woke up in the morning when Lucrecia brought in two buckets of water from her well. Adán and Adancito and I walked up the arroyo of Mulatos and the first two big pools were clear in a natural sluice on the bedrock. I felt good about them because they were so clear and still and the *peña* was right there and would be easy to follow. Everyone believed the Mulatos mother lode was somewhere in this arroyo. Its only drawback was that it was right on the Camino Real and a lot of traffic would be going by our workplace.

We went on very hot to Mulatos and stopped at the first house where an old woman sold mescal and it was awful. After a taste of it we drank coffee with her instead. Adán's sister-in-law came in and told the old woman one of her inlaws had been beaten up in town the night before.

The old woman said, *"Que va,"* and started to cry. She had a beautiful face, soft with beautiful lips, clear white skin and dark, dark eyes. She made her living selling drinks and food. While we were there her little granddaughter came in with a fine, clear smile, black curly hair, long-lashed black eyes and a dimple in her chin.

Adán's old father, dressed neatly, but crippled with arthritis, met us at his door with a drink of mescal. His mother was very pert and blue-eyed smoking a cigarette.

We went to Adán's father's billiard parlor. He had a fine table, but no one ball and the two ball was a six ball. I played and lost a beer and bought a twelve-can *cartón*. We kept playing and after a while I looked up and Pantera was having her puppies in the corner of the poolroom. The first one was born dead, but the second lived a dog and she didn't have more.

We ate noon *sopa* at Adán's house. All his four brothers were there. Adán and one brother were handsome men. The sullen brother was all puffed up all the time so it didn't matter what he looked like. It was my rotten luck that Adán's pretty young sister was sullen too. When the rains come, the river runs high and trashy, and washes away all the treasure, *all* the treasure. That was the way my luck was destined to run in gold and women, I guess.

Adán's brothers told us the old woman's inlaw who had been beaten the night before was the *guitarrero* Bernabé. He was the only peaceful brother of a bunch of feuding brothers. Someone, nobody would say who, had beaten his head with a rock and his family took him to the doctor in Sahuaripa.

We went back to the poolhall and the poolhall drunk hit me for twenty pesos as soon as Adán's back was turned. What the hell, I gave him twenty and the money for another carton of beer and sat by Adán's old father and played pool.

Then Adán and I made a *vuelta,* a turn, around the town and stopped at a store. A *comisario,* constable, came in drunk and saw a chance to lean on somebody when he saw me. He asked for my papers and since I was in there without any I said I was a Mexican. That shut him up enough so we got out of there and went back to the old woman's and her place was now full of drunks.

One drunk started spouting bullshit and telling me how honorable and what a good worker he was. I played dumb and listened awhile and went out on the street and there was the damned comisario again. He tried to lean again, but he almost fell on top of me when he did, he was so drunk, and I got away from him.

The whole town was now full of drunks. There was only one dirt road for trucks into town and that one was from Sahuaripa. All other avenues to Mulatos were for horses and mules and *teguas.* Not even boots and shoes traveled them well. Some people came fifty miles afoot or horseback to catch a ride out of the Sierra, or to buy flour, beans and canned goods, but the first thing the men did was quench their thirst with beer and visit other friends with soyate. Because of the drinking the women and children stayed off the streets in the afternoons and evenings.

Adán and I went back to the poolhall and got the little Pantera dog, put her puppy in a morral and headed down the high Camino Real for his house. About halfway down I slipped, my kneecap flew out of place and I went down. Adán pulled on my foot until the kneecap crawled back to its slot and I passed out right there from the pain. That was very pleasant, passing out. I came out of it right away and felt good until I tried to walk. I hobbled down the rest of the way off the mountain cussing the luck.

In the morning we loaded up and headed toward the arroyo of Mulatos to work and came upon Umberto, old black Don Toríbio and Manuel Valdéz drinking a real fine soyate by an old rock. We stopped to visit with them and old Don Toríbio told us he had been a gambusino forty years. After a while more men stopped to visit and everyone moved to the shade. By this time fifteen men were gathered by the trail with Don Toríbio, all of them having stopped to avail themselves of his jug and listen to the conversation, that being the most used form of entertainment in the Sierra.

A blond, heavyset man came by and asked Don Toríbio to introduce him to the American and when we started talking I learned he was a Federal Judicial Policeman called El Coyote. Three of his brothers lived in the U.S.

El Coyote said the reason the comisario asked for my papers was because the law was looking for Kennedy's assassin. I told him Kennedy's killer had been finished off five years ago. Maybe they were looking for M. L. King's killer. That disappointed everybody. They had been thinking John F. Kennedy's killer was still at large and they hoped for a chance to catch him, tie him to a tree and wear out their reatas on him. They had never heard of Martin Luther King. I told them King's assassin was caught at least a week ago in London, but they just looked blank at that.

Adán and I went on to the *tinaja,* the rock tank, above a place called Babicora and ate lunch, then fired up and went in the charco below it. Adán dove for the first time to cool off while we prospected against the bedrock to find the best place to start.

The boy Chito Coronado came by from Mulatos and I let him dive, then scrambled to pull him out when the compressor ran out of gas and he panicked. For a moment he was so still and cold I was afraid he'd drowned, but we gave him artificial respiration and a swallow of spirit and he got all right.

He swallowed no water, but he must have gone into shock before I pulled him out of the water. He was "cast" like a horse. I've known horses to cast and go into shock when they plunged underwater. I swear, he came up dead on his side like a horse in shock and that scared me so bad I was ready to quit and walk all the way out of the Sierra to get home. I wondered what the hell else could go wrong.

Umberto caught up to us at La Tinaja with some hot beers and I got dressed. We loaded up and I rode double behind Umberto back to Don Toríbio's. The mescal turned the world very cloudy for me there, even though I had hoped it would change it for the better at least a little while.

Next, I found myself riding behind Adán on an old brown mare who was falling off the mountain kind of wild and at the bottom Adán didn't pick her head up and she turned a *catatumba,* a tomb filler, head over heels, and rolled on both of us, burying my head in the sand. I came up laughing with sand all over my face and my hat crammed down over my eyes and ears. I stopped when Adán started spitting blood, but only his lip was mashed. That sobered us enough, thank God, so we could go into Lucrecia's house and sleep like gentlemen.

In the midnight morning after the first sleep, horsemen passed by going upriver. I heard Adán greet them when they paused briefly at the house, but they did not answer. Later, the sullen brother rode in on Adán's dun mare and she was lathered white from being ridden hard all night. Adán simply said he ran with the *guerrilleros* last night.

The guerrilleros were an element of youngsters who did not own anything or have enough to do, so they thought they might start a revolution so they could have something. They were the same element that kidnapped ranchers and visitors to the Sierra in the '70s. Then the soldiers caught a bunch of them in Chinipas, gave them *ley de fuga,* law of flight, turned them loose on the airstrip by the river where they could find no cover, machine-gunned them dead and put an end to the element.

The next morning we awakened to the sounds of guitars being smashed and the smell of burning clothes from across the river. The word came over that someone had eloped with that family's fretting, blooming daughter named Margarita.

This cheered me and Adán and we went up to the *tinaja* to work. I cleaned awhile until the dredge clogged and I was one hour in the sun unplugging her. I got going again and the pump came uncoupled. We went home in the dark finally beaten.

The next morning was the day the route plane sometimes came and I went up early to the airstrip, but nothing. I went back to the house and read *Leaves of Grass* all the long hot day. Adán had gone back to La Tinaja for the equipment. He came in late after dark dragging from fatigue. I shined the lantern on the packhorse and no air buoy.

Adán told me, "I went to the charco and set everything ready to load. I tied the horse under the tepeguaje and went to Mulatos to see about my *cartilla,* a proof of service in the militia, that I expected in the mail. In Mulatos they told me an old friend of mine had died. The mayor asked me to help bury him, so I bought some candles and sent them to the house while I took care of my business. Then I went and picked up my friend and carried him to the chapel, then to the graveyard.

"After we buried him I went to the old woman's house to have a drink because I was very hot. The comisario was there drunk and began to make demands because he wanted to arrest me. I wouldn't go with him so he left and after a while came back with a loaded pistol. I took it away from him, hit him over the head with it twice and then smashed it on the rocks. He went away and came back with deputies and me and my friends fought them a street fight and ran them off.

"I walked down in the night to load the horse and come home. Well, my horse had been moved and tied in the sun and someone had scattered all the motors and equipment.

"My horse was stumbling from having been tied so long in the sun. After I loaded him I turned him around to see if he was all right and he fell over backwards into the pool. The weight of the full load was drowning him, so I jumped into the pool and unloaded him while I held his head above water. When he finally tired to get out under his own power he lunged and kicked me in the chest with both hind feet and I went down in the pool. I finally got him loaded again and he bucked the motor off into the rocks."

Well, this finally finished the gold business. I pondered all night and finally decided that if Pepín the route plane pilot came in I could pay for a ride to David's. David could stop here on the way home and pick up both motors and Tío's gear. I was not giving up, though. I was coming back in September.

The next morning I went to the field and sat with Umberto in his clean camp and talked while I waited for a plane but none came. I started crossing the river to go back to Adán's house riding double behind Umberto on his gray horse. The horse, probably sensing that for the first time in his life he was carrying someone more unfortunate than he, almost bucked me and Umberto off in the river.

Adán had returned to the house with the air buoy and it looked like hell. The air intake tube was twisted off inside the engine and like Adán said, the whole thing was made into little pieces.

Through the long, hot afternoon with *Leaves of Grass* I was sure no human being could move in that heat unless he was underwater. About 3 P.M. I went to the stream and washed clothes and bathed. I came back clean with my Levi's damp and cool and found Adán detail-washing the gold from El Desengaño. Later he put the mercury to it and made it into about forty ounces of golden balls, at thirty dollars an ounce, twelve hundred dollars.

We burned the mercury out of the gold I took out of La Tinaja separately and produced a ball of about two grams, the product of about one hour's work, one hour that we were able to work in the forty-five days I've worked here. Every hour I was able to work in El Desengaño had been twice that good.

I knew I had discovered a bonanza if we would ever be able to work our hole right and move a ton of overburden off the bedrock a day. We had worked only three holes the size of a hat on the top of the bedrock near the surface in El Desengaño. The bottom, where the bedrock leveled off, had to be paved with gold after catching new gold every year for centuries.

Adán and I were proud we'd kept our mine quiet. After supper we talked and smoked in the dark and then listened to Lucrecia at work. She was never still. Here she was still working at nine at night and she'd been up at five carrying water, sweeping, loving kids, scolding, feeding, cooking, watering her garden, washing dishes and clothes, chopping wood with her hat on, breathing hard with her buckets of water and giving her breast to the little naked, cheerful Robe with her skin glowing.

She left the house in the dark with the flashlight and called to Adán from the corral that a whole herd of rabbits were on the hill. I got old Meat in the Pot and Adán the rifle and we made a circle with the lantern, and nothing. We came back and sat down and she went to the other side of the house and called again. We went and I shot at a rabbit and was high with the lantern light. When old Meat in the Pot went off, the smoke clouded the whole area inside the lantern light for five minutes. I made another circle and fired three shots at another and missed.

In the morning I sat and enjoyed listening to little Black Memo's musical talk. He was Adán's second son and was as dark as Adancito was light. I liked the way he pronounced his brothers' names with many inflections. "Ro o obe," he would sing in high melody instead of only saying "Robe" in an ordinary fashion.

Adancito and Memo watched the chickens and their little ones with more enjoyment than I ever saw kids get from TV. I remembered the way these kids enjoyed their lives when I wrote *The Forests of the Night*, without ever looking at this journal. In fact, I never opened the journal, or even thought of it, when I wrote *Forests*.

I was reading later and heard someone announce himself outside. I recognized Maurice's voice. He was the American who ran the

Victor mine. He was young, wiry and clean-cut, and always wore a green working man's uniform.

He came in for coffee and told about the many years he spent in South America. He was one of the few Americans I knew who was able to be happy working in the Sierra Madre. He helped me try to fix the pump and said he could fix it if we took it to the Victor, but without the compressor it was no good anyway. He observed that it was a good thing David had not been able to bring my twenty-gallon drum of gas when he was overloaded in Tucson. We would not have been able to use it all, anyway, and I said yes, a good thing.

We ate a good lunch and talked until the sun started going down. I told him the reasons I thought El Desengaño was rich and he agreed that it should be. He said the white grease I was finding in the cracks always held a lot of gold. I gave him my radio and batteries and magazines and walked him to the airport, then went and bathed and washed clothes. Now all my clothes were clean.

When I came back Lucrecia was gone to Mulatos in the new dress of the material I brought her. Adán said she made three dresses and shirts for each of the boys with the material. Adán and I had two good drinks, ate supper and stayed up until Lucrecia came back.

A big, general storm covered the Sierra the next afternoon. Heavy black clouds climbed over the high mountains with lightning in them. The lightning strikes braised the tops of the mountains and streaked off through the monster thickness of the clouds, then glimmered back through them, died, lived again, died, then struck again.

The storm gave a full hour's warning as it built. When the water came the drops were big, sparse and splattering for a half hour as the clouds built higher and doubled on themselves. Then gradually the high mountains across the river disappeared in a heavy rain that started over the Victor mine and came across a high *cordón,* ridge.

Across the arroyo Adancito hit for home carrying little Robe, stumbled, slid headfirst down a smooth, hard path on the arroyo bank and disappeared as the wall of rain reached him. Robe came over the sandbar running naked, his tiny legs serving him well, the tiny feet in *teguas* stepping surely. Adán ran from the house, scooped him up under one arm and ran back for the house laughing. Adancito came over the arroyo bank crying, but running like a cottontail rabbit. All three were soaked when they reached the *portál,* but Robe's wetness came shivering off into his mother's towel.

The storm was really fresh with lightning and a wonderful thunder that pounded back and forth across the river against the high mountains. The leaves on the oak trees seemed to flatten and reflect new light when the heavy thunder hit them. Watching the storm with its solid wall of water continuing, I was happy I was not at El Desengaño. The sand would not have held my tent stakes in that beating and the flood would be ten feet high, enough to wash away my camp.

Adán's five goats were caught by the storm on the face of a cliff across the arroyo. They huddled in the shelter of a boulder outcropping on a vertical slick of rock while the rain poured to wash them off.

A particularly horrible scream issued itself from Adancito on the portál. I hurried there and a big centipede that must have weighed a pound, its brown and yellow heavy old scales hiding its heavy meat, was writhing on the floor of the portál. It had come out of the rain and charged the Guerito before Adán swatted it.

We buttoned up the house and gates and went to bed as soon as the storm subsided. The storm's dying was good with *Leaves of Grass* and it was a long time into the night dying.

After I put away the book and blew out the lamp, I watched the storm's last glimmering over the mountain and took stock. After having done my best, though having failed again and still broke, I was still my own man. I did not have to apologize to myself, or sell myself to my backers with excuses, or tell lies to excuse my failure. I did not have money, but I had lived a fine natural time in the Sierra Madre Occidental for everybody. I did not have to make anything up to excuse that. During this whole winter and spring I had not been on the French Riviera, by God.

I could see my thenwife's mother's face, though. That smirk was the same one that appeared on other faces when they heard I was trying to be a writer. The ones that said, "So, now I hear you're trying to be a writer," the friends and "loved ones" who protested they were only criticizing me for my own good. I couldn't love anyone who required that I lie to them in order to have love. My thenwife would look lovingly sad when she handed me the truth of the back bills I had promised to pay with placer gold. Bills that could not be paid made everybody sad, no matter how great the adventure that prevented the payment.

June '68. I liked Whitman's poem *Me Imperturbe*, from *Leaves of Grass:*

Me Imperturbe, standing at ease in nature
Master of all, or mistress of all, aplomb in the midst of
irrational things,
     Imbued as they, passive, receptive, silent as they,
     Finding my occupation, poverty, notoriety, foibles, crimes, less
important than I thought,
     Me toward the Mexican sea, or in the Mannahatta or the
Tennessee, or far north, or inland,
     A river man, or a man of the woods, or of any farm life of
these states or of the coast, or the lakes, or Kanada,
     Me wherever my life is saved. O to be self-balanced for
contingencies,
     To confront night, storms, hunger, ridicule, accidents, rebuffs,
as the trees and animals do.

The next afternoon Adán and I set out to look for his brown mare mule. We walked up the gradual slope of the mountain on the south side of the river to a high, leafy, shady point in the oaks. Way down on a sandbar on the river we saw some cattle and one brown mule. We climbed steadily for a while, a good, steady, sweaty, hot pull, and then slid straight down the trail toward the river. We met the brown mule on the trail, but he was a horse mule, not a mare, and did not belong to Adán.

We followed the river around the bend of a mountain looking for tracks, but saw nothing but the river. It was growing wilder every minute. The black cliffs above us were covered with full beehives but they were inaccessible except for someone who could rappel from the top. The sheer cliffs were alive with grass, *amól* the small cousin of maguey, brush and swallows' caves and seemed to be coming more alive every minute now that the rains were heavy. In the south, more heavy black storm clouds were coming on.

We climbed out of the river and went up through a forest of spiny *vinorama* brush, around a jutting cliff, up to a high saddle sweating, and stopped there. Standing on the very edge of a high ridge, in the shade of some tall *tuna,* prickly pear, we watched the new storm come across black mountains to the south. The wind was strong on our faces and fresh and cool from the rain.

Adán showed me the high Puerto de la Cueva del Agua, Water Cave Pass, overhead and the Victor mine to the south. The corner of a canyon below it was green with many oak trees. We stepped back off the edge of the saddle and there was absolutely no wind and we crossed an old *mauguechi* clearing and crossed a fence and went down toward Adán's home. Pantera and the shaggy dog jumped a rabbit and disappeared downhill, and a moment later crossed a clearing far below a hundred yards behind the rabbit. We went down across a hard rock clearing from which every ounce of soil had eroded, past an old spring, down to the arroyo of Mulatos and across to the house.

Adán showed me a horsehair bosal made by young Toríbio the older son of Toríbio, a work of art in black and white horsehair with embroidered tassels. He then gave it to me with two reatas to take home with me. Later in the evening the storm came on high but was only arming itself with lightning while it passed on to the north.

Adán's guitar was hanging on the wall by the window in the room where I slept and every once in a while something would scratch a tone on it. We all heard it from time to time but paid no attention to it. That evening Adán took it down and looked into it and there was another writhing brown and yellow centipede big and heavy and mad as hell. How he got into the guitar is unknown but he sure couldn't get out so we shot him a dose of Black Flag and he rolled out and hit the floor like a pound and a half of raw meat.

David finally came for me and I came out. I went and cowboyed that summer, fall and part of the winter for Linkletter Enterprises at Lida, Nevada, and used the bosal and reatas there, an experience that became my novel *The Outfit*.

Part V (El Desengaño 1969)

In March of 1969 Art Breitzke from Chicago, old Tío and I formed the trip to El Desengaño again. Tío came to my home in Pinetop on the morning of the fifteenth and we loaded up his pickup. My thenwife came out to the pickup to see what she could do to help when there was nothing more for us to do except back out and drive off. We drove to Tucson and met Art at the airport, had some beer in the Last Chance and then drove out so I could introduce them to Rambo.

Rambo had been represented to me by David Coughonour as a

master mechanic. As soon as I got home from Mulatos the summer of '68 he came up and stayed a weekend to demonstrate the machinery he had put together for dredging the gold out of El Desengaño. The machinery consisted of a five-horsepower water pump mounted on a thirty-foot sluice, thirty feet of four-inch canvas and steel hose. A four-inch venturi nozzle with which to vacuum the bedrock was attached to the end of the canvas hose and to a water hose from the pump. The pressure of the water that was pumped through the nozzle caused the vacuum that sucked sand, gravel and gold up the canvas hose to the sluice. The sluice floated on tractor tires on the surface of the water.

Rambo demonstrated the thing in Pinetop and it cleaned the bedrock of every speck that would come loose. We were finally equipped to dredge for gold. All the machinery was first-class and smooth-operating. Rambo was an abrasive kind of man, but he seemed generous about contributing his work and machinery and I was happy to have him. I did not apply to him my one prime rule for taking gringos to the Sierra Madre: Don't ever take a salamander to the mother mountains. Their skins are too thin.

When we reached Rambo's compound he scurried around too busy to greet us and then after I introduced my pards he began telling us how to run the Desengaño and where the gold ought to be. I got us out of there as soon as I could and we went back to the hotel.

The next morning was Sunday. We checked out of the Santa Rita and went out to Rambo's again. He started up with "Where were you? I thought you were going to help me."

I said, joking, "I figured if we waited long enough you'd have it all done when we got here." He did not like that answer, though. His wife didn't even say hello and he didn't ask us in for coffee. The Rambos had been smiling and friendly when they availed themselves of my hospitality and were fed and bedded in my home in Pinetop.

Art, Tío and I drove to Nogales and got a room at the Coronado and charged out to run and play. Tío and Art were on vacation. We had the mariachis with our supper at the Cavern, got clip-jointed at the Alhambra, snubbed at the El Dorado, but stayed out stubbornly until we had a good time.

I saw my friend Felix Johnson on the street with his son Roy. Roy was just too damned angelic in those days to suit me, but Felix was always very proud of him and doing his best for him. Felix was always good with kids. When I was six and he was sixteen we had the job of driving cattle for my dad from the border to the Baca Float. Felix was always a patient pardner for a kid and always a gentleman, as dignified at sixteen as he was later when he became a parent. He died awfully too damned young.

Next morning we went to the Nogales tavern run by my friend Ramona to cure the cruda while we waited for David. I called his brother Clay and talked a long time on the phone to Rita. After cutting him open twice, the doctors had given up trying to cure him of cancer of the prostate and he was taking chaparral tea. Rita had high hopes that he was over the cancer. Now, 1990, his cancer is long gone. Clay came down and we drove out to pick up David. They both looked healthy as hell to my bloodshot eyes.

David said he had not believed I would be back and I told him I'd gone off to cowboy a season for Linkletter in Nevada. I paid him the fifty dollars I'd owed him since he brought me out the year before, plus two hundred dollars for our two new trips to Mulatos. The Coughonours left us at the Coronado after promising to take us to Mulatos on Wednesday. That afternoon I bought Art a good hat at Paul Bond's to replace his dudy cardboard hat.

Tuesday morning the bartender in the Cavern told me old Nick died. I went across the street for a haircut and visited with the old grayheaded cowman Durazo while we waited. I stopped to see Mantequilla Vasquez and he was busy and sober so he ignored me. I stopped to see Mary at the bank and stood away from her so she wouldn't smell the whiskey.

Then I went down to the store of a man I used to call a friend to buy Adancito's boots. The clerk was subdued and very polite and careful and the owner's wife was sitting behind the desk with her back to me and looked back at me out of the corner of her eye like an old bushed-up cow, as though afraid to look right at me, afraid I'd pounce on her. I stood there grinning at her as she slowly turned her head enough to get a good look at me out of the corner of her eye.

I gathered my pards together again and we went around town buying the provision and equipment we needed on the river. I was carrying a new washtub across the street and met Sergio Elias and Héctor Bustamante. They gave me *abrazos* in the middle of the street and kidded me about the laundry I was going to start in the

Sierra Madre. They were still handling a lot of cattle, their word was good and their money was good and they always stuck together.

When I was with David at Ramona's tavern Marsden, David's brother, came down to see me and they told me Del Mercer and his partner, a man from Nogales we all knew, had been accused of stealing cattle from Del's neighbor in Sonora. Del was framed by his own cowboys. Del was in the pen in Hermosillo, though, and his partner who never risked anything but his money turned state's evidence which means he ratted out so he could get off scot-free and keep his money.

I went back to Ramona's by myself and was glad to see Gene Sykes and Little Arthur Grimm, Jr., there. Gene looked as clean-faced as a little innocent boy and was holding his rum well. He told me about the wreck in which Panchito Elias was killed. Panchito put his head on Gene's shoulder after the crash, sighed and said, "Ay, Genito," and died. Gene's wife Pauline came by and I invited her for lunch but no she didn't want any part of a deal that included Gene, Arthur and I in a drinking bout and left. The next wise one to leave was Little Arthur.

I roared off to town again and that night met three actors at Felix Johnson's table at the Coronado. I was having a nice talk and drinks with Jim O'Connell and his wife and son. The big actor said the O'Connells looked like beautiful people. He loved everybody that night but the O'Connells were awful good people and always looked as good as they were. They were the best example I ever knew of branded-in-the-hide cattle people who never looked crusty a day in their lives, not even when they were coming in after working cattle all day. The real big actor of the three came to the table and introduced me to a shiny blond lady who was ready to absent herself from his company. They were making a movie with Cameron Mitchell.

In the morning my Mulatos pards and I came together again and went to the airfield. We loaded and with a no-time tailwind made it to Mulatos. On a bumpy approach David gunned the airplane with power and still greased the landing on that little half-mile strip.

It was March 19, St. Joseph's Day, 1969, my saint's day, so we cracked a bottle of Old Crow with Guillermo while waiting on the strip for Adán, finished that one and cracked another. The day was clear and warm and we sat in the middle of the strip and threw the bottle caps away. Adán appeared after a while on the buckskin mare followed by his dogs. The little Pantera we carried down from the poolhall was nine months old now. With her white clean teeth in the black head romping along behind the mare she was the spitting image of her mother.

I turned over the gifts my thenwife sent and the boots, then moved across the river toward Adán's house. Guillermo was so drunk we had to leave him folded lengthwise over his own heels on the airstrip. Art and I, arm in arm, fell off the cliff above the river and rested by the big rock we missed when we landed on our heads. We thanked it several times for not killing us, then went on. We had drunk both quarts of Old Crow at the airfield and were reduced to drinking soyate on the way to Adán's.

We stayed at Adán's two days and killed a beef and carved it up in sheets to dry. We weren't poorboying it anymore. Friday morning David came in with our equipment. Maurice Teewinkle of the Victor mine came in with Ted Farnsworth while David was still parked on the strip. When he saw the state of my companions, Maurice kept to his business and headed straight for the Victor. David said he would bring Rambo Sunday.

Saturday we moved camp to El Desengaño and it was unchanged, only a little washed away from the rains. Old Tío went to sleep, fell off his horse and dunked himself headfirst in the river on the way to camp. Nothing about him floated. I looked back and he'd gone to the rocky bottom in a foot and a half of running water and left no sign of himself. I ran back and pulled him out by the belt. His hat was mashed down over his face.

That night a cold storm blew in. In the morning I built a fire in the misty rain and heated water for coffee. When I opened the tent flap to give the pards their coffee the fumes of the sweated St. Joseph's Day mescal in the tent, and that which they had drunk thereafter, almost knocked me over.

Sunday it stormed all day and David landed and waited in Sahuaripa with Rambo. On Monday they came in and I met them at the airfield. Rambo acted pleasant and I was relieved because I worried he might not fit in the Sierra.

Adán packed the gear on his mule and Rambo and I set out for camp. I tried to gently warn him against jumping from rock to rock across the river. We were a long way from doctors and splints and it was easy to break an ankle jumping across rocks. He didn't pay a bit of attention.

The next evening he wanted to go see where old Tomás had been panning. Tomás had told Tío while we were working, "The gold from the big *pelota* rock north of El Desengaño is mine, from the big pelota south is yours."

So I said to Rambo, "Where do you want to cross?"

He said, "Where I jumped across this morning."

I said, "Remember where you are. You're not five minutes from a hospital like you are in Tucson. If you break a leg here we'll have to carry you out."

He said, "Don't worry, you won't break a leg." As if to say, "You chickenshit."

So at the crossing he leaped over the slippery rocks with the agility of a cockroach. I built up a place to cross and slipped in and wet my feet. We went downstream and he saw a lot better places to dive than El Desengaño and kept ignoring me and telling me where the gold was more likely to be. On the way back I sank the stepping stone again and he scampered over the big rocks like a cockroach again and after that he was superior as hell.

After we gave him a drink and some supper, he was pleasant while he bullshitted at the fire, except we noticed everything was, "Alaska I, Alaska me, I in Alaska." In the morning it was the same thing and he already knew more about El Desengaño than I did and gradually began to let me know he knew everything better than I did, that was that, there was nothing down in the Desengaño at all and I was a liar.

The next day it was the same thing and gradually the son of a bitch became overbearing. I was trying harder and harder to be cooperative because he made it so plain I was dumb and naturally the cause of him being so overbearing, until he hollered from the big rock on the edge of the hole, "Joe Brown, you son of a bitch, I think you are full of bullshit." He'd been at El Desengaño two days, we were still only cleaning the year's accumulation of overburden off the bedrock, but I was a son of a bitch for not already making him rich.

So now I started laying for him and figuring on how to get rid of him and still keep his gear. Once, I said you may think I'm wrong, but that doesn't change the fact that the gold is there where I say it is, but he sneered at that so I decided not to say any more. He was the only creature I had ever seen use a sneer in the Sierra.

Later, when we had the equipment running, two of us worked on the bottom and one rode the sluice to keep it clear of big rocks. Rambo wouldn't take his turn on the surface, because he knew the look of gold better than everyone else and wanted to work with it on his own firsthand basis, so I took three straight shifts on the sluice.

In the middle of the afternoon I noticed one of the tractor tubes on which the whole contraption floated was losing air and going down and told him about it. He just looked at me and said, "Aw, don't worry about it." So for fifteen more minutes I just watched the thing go flat and rode it down. The motor sputtered and sent up a bubble or two, but that was it. The canyon was quiet again.

Rambo's face came up out of the water white and he looked at me as though I'd sunk his contraption on purpose. Adán jumped in the water at my side to help me try to right the barge or boat or raft, but it wanted very much to collapse with its feet in the air and was bigger than us. Rambo went under with the breather and took the motor off the sluice and he and Art salvaged everything but one of my socks I was drying on the sluice.

It was a catastrophe and I felt like hell about it, a culmination of the goddam tension old Snicklefritz (David's name for him) had been building in us all. I got out of the rubber suit because I was thinking I might have to fight this son of a bitch, he's giving me those looks. When he came out of the water I walked over to him in case he did and he strutted around me all blown up like a rooster. I didn't budge except to look at him when he got behind me because I knew he wanted to Sunday me if he could blindside me. I caught myself looking at him out of the corner of my eye exactly the way the wife of my ex-friend looked at me in her store.

Adán and I pulled the sluice and the raft up on the bank and old Snicklefritz wouldn't speak to anyone. When he and Art finally came out and carried his precious little toy to the rock I followed after him like a puppy, waiting on him to appease him.

Adán said, *"Está cagado.* He's shitted himself. *Está enchivado.* He acts cuckolded. Let him sit in it."

I said, *"Está rajado.* He's given up being a man."

After a while he called me over to show me how the cam of the drive shafting spark plugs worked and fit together just to show how much he knew and I nodded and walked away, through with him finally. This made him awful mad. He ate Tío's supper without saying a word and swelled some more, then went back to taking the engine apart and wiping it dry.

About this time Andresito and his little brother came in for something to eat. They'd been coming in every day and at first old Tío wanted to adopt them and take them home, but now he wouldn't speak to them anymore because they stole his brown sugar.

He turned to me and said, "Are you going to give these little turds anything to eat?"

This pulled my stopper and I said, "You give them something. You asked them here. They're here because of you."

"Not me. I didn't ask them here."

"Just a few days ago you were all noble and wanted to adopt them. You wanted to educate them and clothe them and now because they stole your precious sugar you don't want them around."

"I can't stand a thief."

"Oh, you can't stand a thief. These little farts were thieving to eat before you ever met them. They were hungry before you came to the Sierra and they'll be hungry long after you are gone with all your noble ideas about thieving and adoption. You think they just started being hungry the day you swooped down on them in the iron bird like a bearded angel from the U.S.A.?"

"No."

"Well, the fact is even though they stole your brown sugar they are hungry and just little turds but hungry little turds. And of course you've never done anything worse than steal brown sugar."

"Well, I know they're hungry."

"You'll admit they're hungry, then?"

"Yes, yes, yes."

"Well, if you'll admit that, give them something to eat."

I walked away down to where Snicklefritz was brooding. I said, "Can I help you now?"

He said, "You can work, can't you? I'm working. I want to get this back together and get back to work 'cause if you don't want to work you can just forget about the whole thing."

"I think that's right. I think we'd better forget about the whole thing."

"What?" He started that swollen-up strutting toward me again.

"I said we'd better forget the whole thing and get you loaded up and out of here."

"What do you mean?"

"I mean what I said. If you're going to swell up with all that superior shit every time something goes wrong, I don't want any part of you in this operation."

"All I wanted was a little help."

"Hell, I don't know anything about your goddam motors. Everyone on this outfit is bending over backwards holding up his end and you want them to hold up your end too. You called me a liar, then blamed me because your goddam play purty capsized before you even bothered to look and see that the tubes were flat underneath it. That's it for me."

"I don't blame you for that anymore."

"Thanks a lot. Shit! Life is too short to have to work with somebody who's all swelled up all the time, so if you're going to be mad about working my hole you might as well pack your toys and we'll pack you out."

"Well, I want to work."

"Let's get something straight, then. We're going to work this hole and no other hole. We're going to see the bottom of it."

"Hell, I'll work any hole you say."

"Let's get after it, then."

I started helping him again to try to get along but I'd had it with him. When he started a bunch of familiar buddy joking again I didn't even try to get with him. I really wanted him out of there and figured to lay in ambush for him from then on.

Andresito and his little brother stayed close to me and helped me for the rest of the afternoon, though they could not have understood my conversation with Tío. I went to bed early and slept well at first but after a while woke up.

Art and Rambo were still up and talking with the soyate. Art was telling him the truth that he was a braggart, he worked too hard, his stories about Alaska bored him, he had been causing trouble way out where a man needed friends instead of trouble and he almost fucked up the whole trip. Rambo said he'd been on a lot of crews where they were always fighting and did his most successful work so his being mad didn't mean anything.

In my bed listening I thought, like shit it don't.

Art said, "You made one mistake and that was a bad one when you mistook Joe Brown's good nature for weakness. Because Joe Brown is a man and my idol. He's a man here and all over the Sierra people look up to him."

Rambo didn't have anything to say about that, but he did say a whole lot about himself and Alaska. Old Art just kept drunkenly pounding away about Joe Brown until Rambo decided to go to bed.

The next morning he was up early and I got up and joined him at the fire and he sure was happy. I started talking to him again knowing David was coming and I'd better start for the field. David had promised to land on his way back to Nogales to see if there was anything we needed, but knowing him I was not too confident he would do it. I fooled around and fooled around listening to Snicklefritz until David did come. I took off for the field and the morning was hot and gave me a good sweating walk as an occupation. When I reached the red hill I hollered and then went on and hollered again and walked down to the field. David's wife was with him. They kidded me about wearing the bandana on my head under my hat and asked, is your head tied up because your leg hurts?

I right away told them about Snicklefritz. When David said he couldn't be back until next week I sent Adán back to camp with a note to get Rambo. I knew he could not stay a week. Then me and Guillermo tried to keep the Coughonours entertained until Adán brought Rambo. After about two hours David's wife began to complain, *"Ya no vienen. No vienen ya.* They won't come, now. They're never coming."

David said, "That's what I get for landing here." There was nothing I could say to that except, "Please wait so you can take the son of a bitch out of here."

Finally Guillermo said, *"Ahi vienen ya.* Here they come, now."

I went to meet them and took Snicklefritz's duffel bag from Adán and helped them onto the field. Snicklefritz started taking pictures and he was really sweating in his tee shirt, had his cigarettes rolled in his tee sleeve, his upper arm scratched by the brush. I could see now he felt he was a helluva veteran and I was so happy he was leaving I could have sung and danced for a week. When David took off Snicklefritz waved like he was doing me a favor to look down on me from his vantage point. I waved back because of the great favor he did me by getting the hell away from my Desengaño hole.

I gave Adán the rest of the day off and walked back. The vieja Rosa Aguilera had come to the field with her vaquero while David was there and she acted so humble to David it almost made me puke. She rode her paint pony on ahead and I caught up to her at the corral. A bunch of her vaqueros were nooning there and I said buenos días and they answered but she didn't.

I stopped above camp when I heard the air buoy. Art was down in the hole and Tío was asleep under a rock. Art came out and we were both happy as hell we would now be able to work in peace.

We worked hard and with great happiness in the partnership for seven days. Each day the color doubled and got coarser and we brought up one little nugget that wasn't tumbled or shiny but dull and rough. Art took that gold with him. Wednesday morning early David came and took Art and Tío home. I sat down to write this ten minutes after David swooped over my head on takeoff and realized everyone was gone and I was alone at El Desengaño again.

Thursday Adán and Guillermo built me a ramada. Friday Adán threw a *trueno* and I brought out fifty good-sized fish. I wrote this alone at El Desengaño on Easter Sunday and was lonesome. I could safely say that was the lonesomest day of my life. Nothing was nice on the river that day. I'd drunk all my soyate by noon and even the goddam flies doubled up to give me misery in the evening. My hearing was bad from being cold underwater and I was *muy cagado* ready to quit and go home and stay until my ears got better, but there was no way I could go anywhere as long as the equipment worked. I decided I was just extra depressed from having made a hog of myself with the soyate.

I lay all night awake with the extra big drop of the dancing cruda and was up early the next day. I decided as long as I kept making a hog of myself with the soyate I'd never see the bottom of the Desengaño. This venture could go sour for a lot of reasons, but I sure didn't want it to fail because I couldn't stay sober. I'd suffered through a lot more last May and June when I was short of money and equipment. Now I had everything I needed and poor little me had to pass one Easter Sunday alone in the Sierra Madre and almost bawled. I accused myself just like my brother Gene Adams used to do. He'd look at me and say, "You drunken asshole."

If I didn't have any breakdowns I'd make a real dent in the Desengaño that week and I made up my mind I would work so hard I wouldn't mind being alone for a good day's rest next Sunday. I was making myself ready to work when the Panterita dog started barking above the peña behind camp. I told her to shut up but she kept it up. Suddenly I looked up and a big silver bird was swooping down from the *encinal* above and he was not a buzzard, did not flap his wings once. He looked more like an eagle than anything else and was as big and heavy. To tell the truth, he looked like a hatchet with those same sharp angles gliding heavily, but gracefully. He sort of sliced horizontally, then chopped vertically as he plummeted across the deep canyon and landed on a bald spot on the cordón. When he braked just above the ground and settled, the silver on his back glinted in the sun.

Then he strolled and strutted like an Indian chief, majestically, powerfully, up the hill and turned into a big, old, wild turkey gobbler. He was way out of range and I didn't want to kill him that way, by accident, so I loaded the rifle and walked downstream so I could get a shot if another crossed, but none did.

I sat and drank coffee until Adán and Guillermo came. Guillermo told me the gobblers were running alone at that time of the year. When the sun had warmed the bottom of the canyon I put on the wet suit to go to work. I was soon sweating half sick in the head and chest it was so hot. I put on the weight belt and the air mask.

Everything was ready, but what I'd been expecting to happen, happened. On the second pull the starter cord on the compressor broke and wouldn't rewind. I fooled around with it a few minutes Mexican style and decided Adán would have to take it to Coughonour's. He could catch the route plane tomorrow. I refused to worry about it anymore. I still had months before the rainy season began. This was only more proof to me that there was gold in El Desengaño worth working and waiting for. Adán loaded the apparatus on his brown mare mule and he and Guillermo left immediately. He had to go all the way up the mountain to Mulatos to get a blanket and a change of clothes, then come back down to the strip to catch the route plane the next morning.

Part VI

The next morning Juan Roldán came by. We visited awhile and I picked up the rifle and went with him to hunt for camp meat. At the crossing by the old camp, Juan took off his teguas and rolled rocks into the river for a bridge for me. He said I shouldn't go barefoot in the river with my lungs hurting. He said water is good, but *de más*, but to use it too much as I had been doing, was bad.

Panterita followed me across the river, but I scolded her. She skinned back across like a little goat and went on to camp without looking back.

The walking was easy on the Camino Real. Juan said, "I fixed that part of the trail last year during the rains. Even as old as it is, it will disappear if we don't keep it fixed." I said, "That's true and it's been here longer than Mexicans, longer than Spaniards." He said, *"Sí,"* silently with an intake of a breath, as though he knew everything about that trail, because he had been there since it was only the beginnings of a footpath.

We went down to his jacal at the farm called Las Vigitas. A skinny black and tan puppy came out wiggling to greet us. The roof was of long leaves of bear grass or palm, thatched in the same plump shape as the roofs in Japan. The walls were of rock without mortar. The new door of hand-split slats, a gate roughly nailed together with one side longer than the other, were unsymmetrical but useful. Only the roof had kept a normal shape.

Juan's *veranito,* garden, consisted of a watermelon patch in the river sand, a few small peach trees recently planted and one great, bare peach tree with branches so heavy they bowed to the ground. We climbed through a split rail fence and walked across two hectares where Juan said he would plant corn and beans, then down a leafy trail by the river.

As I walked along behind Juan I noticed his hair was pitch-black under the mashed hat, but silver with his sixty years on his neck. His teguas turned up sharply at the toes and his step was springy as a youth's, springier than mine at thirty-nine.

I started to sweat like I hoped I would, but it was a cold, feverish sweat and chilled my back. I stopped and drank from the river before going up the Arroyo de la Escondida, a steep, narrow arroyo full of stairstep *tinajas* in solid rock. Near the top we climbed across the sunny side of a grassy mountain, then walked through a thick, spiny *vinoramal.*

We stopped under some oaks and Juan picked up a heavy rock and said, it's *antimonio,* I never saw antimonio here. He pointed out a large red phallic rock on a high mountain southeast as El Chile, and another great escarped peak, La Ventana. The ravines that cut the side of the mountain were still in night shade, but the morning light was just glinting off the broad silver tint on the leaves of the thick oaks outside the ravines. The side of that mountain was many different shades of green and brown with no bare open country on it at all.

Juan said, "Over that *cordón* below the peak lies the *maguechi* called Las Mesas, a man-made clearing so steep that the bean and corn crops have to be planted with pick and bar because a plow cannot be pulled there by a mule or ox." That maguechi was also called La Marcada and was the largest clearing in those mountains, though only twenty hectares, about fifty acres, but if a man stumbled at his work he would roll a whole league before the bottom of the mountain stopped him.

As we stood there high on the mountain, Pepín, *el de la ruta,* the pilot of the route plane, lifted off the airfield with Adán. They were below us and climbed down the canyon past us.

Juan asked, "What does it mean when you hear bells?"

I told him about the belief that the Jesuits had cast bells in the gold they mined, then plated them with bronze when they shipped them to Spain, to keep from losing the gold to the Crown. Some people offered the theory that the Jesuits had been forced to hide and leave a lot of the gold behind when the Crown expelled them from Mexico.

Juan said, "One day two of my friends and I were clearing a maguechi there." He pointed to a spot at the mouth of a ravine. "And all three of us heard three loud and distinct peals of a great bell. We went to the spot where we fully expected to find it and found nothing but the bare rocks and sand of the ravine."

I told him about the theory that the Jevies buried their bells or hid them in sealed caves when they were forced to return to Spain. This could have been a bell in a cave an animal ran against, or something like that.

He said, "Could it have been the gold in the bells trying to discover itself to us?"

"Yes, maybe. Who knows?"

"The gold wants to leave where it is and go to the *parranda,* a happy binge, and be spent for pleasure. I believe this. One day one of my nephews and I were *gambuseando,* panning for gold, and we heard the sound of running hooves coming toward us, the *murmuro* of riders, the ring of their spurs and the roll of the crickets in the bits in the horses' mouths. The sounds came right over the top of us and we never saw a thing. Another time I was digging for placer on this river and I stuck my iron bar in the bank and turned my back and it fell ringing to the ground. I stuck it into a softer place to make sure it would stay and after a while it rang to the ground again, but this time at the same place it had fallen before, at least three paces away from the soft ground."

I told him about my singing horseman, the horse that rolled and drank at my hole, the pack train, the men dragging the panniers. During the telling Juan kept saying, "It's the gold telling you it's there. There's gold there." When I finished he said, "You know, when the gold wants to get out, it finds a way to tell you. You know another thing? It is trying you to see if you deserve it. When it decides to give itself up and that you are a man and won't *rajar*, give up, it will surrender itself to you. You know another thing? It won't surrender itself in its pure form to one who doesn't drink. Only to one who does. It wants to be spent freely and generously."

We walked out of the oaks and zigzagged sweating up the sunny side of the mountain on the edge of a deep ravine. Above the ravine we topped out on the rim of a grassy bowl shaded by oak where we found a lot of deer and turkey sign. We rimmed the edge of the bowl and found another bowl, and another, and they were fine, hidden shelters for game and livestock. We rimmed around to the north side of the mountain and came to a small, grassy plateau where the javelina had been rooting, then followed that same rim to the edge of another deep ravine.

While we stood high in the wind a flock of *patagonia,* blue rock pigeon, came whistling straight at us. They came headlong, as though completely obsessed by their speed and as if no moderate inclination governed them for their safety at all. Even their eyes seemed wild with a craving for hurtling themselves into the wind with all their strength and I recognized very well the state. It was a preoccupation with their power and talent for flight and the more they put into it the more they loved it.

The birds saw us so late they could only veer slightly to keep from hitting us. An abrupt change of direction would have scattered them or dashed them against the cliffs. They had to risk hitting us in order to stay together and the veering was almost suicidal. They seemed to scream by us, though I remember no sound, and went on searching low over the mountain for their nests. Their way of flying is such that they are not able to slow before they reach their nests and then settle down together. They make several swift passes closing the circle around the area of their nests and as each one recognizes something of the terrain he peels off to land. None slows down during the passes until he has recognized his own home and goes down alone.

We walked past a bunch of cattle lying under San Nicolás Mountain on an *hechadero,* bedground, where they could see for a long way in all directions. We descended into a deep ravine and at the bottom stopped at a spring and drank clear cold water. We followed the canyon down always back toward the river, then rimmed out to oak ridges again, then straight down to the river and back to camp footsore.

That night my lungs hurt and they still hurt the next morning. I took nips of mescal all day to help them and stayed close to camp scared of pneumonia.

The next day the wind started up early and Adán's brother Guillermo, El Indio, came by looking for a heifer. Then a pair of mescal *contrabandistas,* one riding a good-looking blue mare mule, the other bearded and rough-looking, came by and sold me a quart and a half. Jorge Moreno and his little brother stopped by with the Rey brothers and they stayed the whole livelong day.

The next day David brought Adán back with the repaired air buoy. Adán said the Coughonours treated him very well. He also told about a shootout in Yecora between a vaquero from Canela and the *comandante* of police. I should have written it down right then, because now, twenty-two years later, I can't remember a thing about it.

The next day, the twelfth, I worked all day and felt good. I cleaned bedrock all day and still came up with fair color. The Mescalero Gildardo and another Gildardo, Adán's compadre, came by at noon with El Indio and stayed all day.

Gildardo, Adán's compadre, told me Lupe, a good miner, got drunk in Mulatos, argued with another drunk called Beto, hit him on the head and broke his hand. Then he kicked him with the bare toe that stuck out of his huarache and split it open. Beto said, "You hit me and you did me nothing. You kicked me and you did me nothing. Now you are the injured one."

This was taking place in front of Gildardo's *taniche,* store, and he said, "But you are not even a Christian, Beto. You are an animal. Lupe, you should not try to hit an animal with your hand. Hit such animals with rocks."

So Lupe chose a rock from the several million in the street of

Mulatos, concealed it in his hip pocket, came back to Gildardo and said, *"Ahora sí,* I have the rock with which to strike Beto." He grabbed it inside the loose pocket of his pants, struggled to get it out and jerked himself over backward to the ground.

Gildardo said, "Get a smaller rock, Lupe."

Lupe could not seem to find a rock large enough to inflict harm yet small enough to extract from his pocket with speed. Gildardo handed him an old Boy Scout knife with a broken blade.

Beto staggered in and watched Lupe prepare himself to attack. Lupe opened the Boy Scout can opener first, but did not like that one. He took out the corkscrew and that wasn't the one he wanted, either, but the sight of the corkscrew alarmed Beto. He started looking for his own knife, another Boy Scout that he carried in a scabbard on his belt. However, in his drunkenness it had slipped around his belt to the back and he could not find it. He fell over backward looking for it and gave up. At this time Lupe sat down with his back against Gildardo's counter and found himself so comfortable he passed out beside his adversary.

Gildardo and the other Mescalero stayed in my camp that night, very *crudo.* The other Mescalero was Lorenzo Ruiz, who had worked for me in 1961 the time Abelardo Guevara and I drove the herd from Yecora to Esperanza. We reached Esperanza late at night on Christmas Eve. The crew wanted to get back to their families so I paid them and sent them home, even though the cattle were sick with tick fever. My Mayo cowboy and *compadre,* Plácido, and I spent the next two weeks doctoring them in an *equipata* rain and lost only six head.

In the morning we were up early and Lorenzo had to track his mules to bring them back from the cordón above camp. Juan Roldán came into camp with his black hair and silver neck. He drank coffee and ate chile and meat with us.

He told about the sound of a *taravilla,* the grating of a mill, he and his friends heard from time to time in the country. He and Genaro and Pedro heard it again the other day . . . "Eee . . . eee . . . eee . . . eeeeeee" while they were cutting wood. They unloaded their *leña* from the burro, each took a *trago* of mescal to dress themselves with valor, and went up there. They found holes someone had dug, and *"La gente no escarba deoquis:* The folk do not dig without a reason." But they found nothing else. *"Allí llora buen cobre.* The copper smokes out of the ground up there like the stomach belches." He believed the riches were below the smoked place, believed the Apaches stole the gold in a raid on the Jevies and hid it there.

He told about the old man Locario Anaya who worked a *matanza*, a ground for slaughtering cattle, in the mountains by Ocampo. He went into Ocampo to collect for meat they had sold and in the evening saddled a mule to go back up the mountain. A son who lived in Ocampo told him the mule was a bronc and he should wait until morning.

The old man scowled and said, "I'm not afraid of the dark or of bronc mules." He took two liters of sotol and two cans of beer and went on.

"Now be careful the mule doesn't throw you off a cliff," the son called after him.

As the old man rode through a certain *hechadero*, a bedground for livestock, he heard the rattling of chains and some phenomenon held the mule by the front feet so she could not move. He said, *"¿Que hijos de la chingada tienes?* What's the matter with you?" and dismounted. He could not see anything wrong with her front feet, so he took another big swallow of mescal, mounted again and jabbed her in the soul with his spurs. The slope of the hill ahead was steep and the mule bucked straight off with the chains rattling as though they hobbled her front feet.

He stopped the mule at the bottom of the hill, dismounted again and said, "What sons of the bad act are these?" and looked at her front feet, and no, nothing. But right there he saw a gas or a white fog rising from a round white rock and he said, "That is the end of you," put his hat on the rock and dispersed the fog. He rode to his camp and got his son and they dug under the white rock and took from there two heavy burro loads of pure silver in a natural state.

Juan said, "Thank God, I have a good patrón."

"Who?" I asked. "Anaya?"

"This river. It gives me work. It gives me the little spark of gold from time to time so I can eat lard. It gives me fish and game and provides moisture for my garden. I go to the river and pan and if I get tired it lets me turn the *batea* over and sleep. When I am refreshed I sit up and work again."

Gildardo Ruiz told the story about the Indio Rodriguez who liked to take *purgas*, purgatives, when anything in general bothered him. He heard of a *curandera*, an old witch who had a special purga concocted to purge the evil from any man. It consisted of rats, snakes, toads, worms, scorpions, tarantulas both hairy and bald, centipedes only over six inches and weighing over one hundred grams, gila monsters and a whit of coral snake. Some met the requirement of being long, others short, others white, others brown, and many for being unspeakable and unmentionable types of animals.

When the Indio took his purga, the old woman topped it off with *amól,* a member and close relative of the maguey and sotol family. The amól added a very soapy and bitter syrup which allowed the purged substances and evils to be slipped easier, almost you would say before the evils knew what was happening to them.

But the amól, like the lechuguilla, mescal and sotol, is alcoholic. The curandera told the Indio to go straight to the outhouse and sit prepared. The amól would cause the animal life inside him to become intoxicated and before he knew it a fight would start and all life would run for the door, so he must be prepared. He did as he was cautioned to do, so that was the end of the story.

Adán told us his sullen brother stole the girl Pola, Oscar's sister, the night before. She had recently been complaining of nosebleeds she did not really have. He took her to a ranch belonging to Adán's father. Her father always bragged when his sons stole other girls so he became awfully serious when his own daughter turned up missing. Adán's folks did not know about it until Adán told them this morning.

After a big noon dinner on Sunday and after we decided not to work, Adán said, "It's the sadness that comes into us from so much food we ate."

Oscar had been sick in bed with a badly dislocated hip with no hope for a cure when his sister eloped with Adán's brother. Then a prospector acquaintance of the family said that he would charter an airplane and take Oscar to see a famous curandera at Cuchibampo near Alamos. That old lady was the same one who had set my broken hand after my ten-round fight with Búfalo Hernandez. She was renowned for a string of miraculous cures and she was especially good with bones. Oscar was too poor to ever be able to pay for that trip himself and too crippled to make it any other way. But no, since Pola had been stolen and the family was in a state of mourning for her downfall, Oscar had to pass up his chance to be cured.

The old man who offered to help Oscar was Abelardo Fulano.

. . . He rented Adán's sorrel mule to ride home. When he went by my camp he spoke his greeting in a deep, hoarse voice. Then Panterita and Chapo the dog recognized the mule and followed her off, because she is their best friend. They did not come back for three days. Adán and Guillermo matter-of-factly said Abelardo was prospecting a mine, all right—a marijuana mine—but not really marijuana . . . meaning poppies.

Just after Abelardo went by I sat by the river and looked for fish. I did not hear the man who rode into my camp until he was sitting his mule only ten feet from me. I glanced up and saw him, hat over his eyes, Levi jumper and chaps, a shotgun lying on the saddle in front of him. He said he was a Federal Judicial Policeman looking for American marijuana and opium gum buyers. He wanted to see my papers. I told him I was a Mexican, because I had no passport of any kind on me. He knew Adán and if it had not been for that I'm sure he would have arrested me. He did not miss Abelardo by five minutes. As soon as he was gone, Adán hurried downstream on our side of the river to warn his friends at El Salto. Guillermo turned tail and hurried home without looking back like a guilty child. Abelardo and Oscar and his wife had all been staying with him.

I walked to the airstrip, a pleasant walk, to see if David would come in, waited there until the wind came up and I knew he could not come, then headed back to camp. I met Adán on his way home. He had stopped to cut *nopales*. Nopales are young prickly pear leaves that are very good to eat sliced up and fried. He was sending them to El Trigo with David for Don Manuel and Cucho who helped him in his adventure with the air buoy.

Adán asked me why I had not recognized the Federal officer. I said, "Should I have known him?" He said, "Sure, he was Beto Guzmán, El Coyote, don't you remember him? He worked for you on that cattle drive from Yecora. You and he got drunk in the arroyo last year the day our horse rolled on us at the bottom of the hill." I said, "Federal office changed him." "No," Adán said, "didn't change him, made his travesties legal." Adán went home and I headed for camp again.

I stopped at the corrals of the Aguileras to talk with Don Emeterio Banda. Workers were building a dipping vat for cattle there. Don Emeterio always shouted and talked *mocho,* broken Spanish, to foreigners, but not to me.

I helped him load a burro with *leña,* painstakingly holding the sling rope over the off side of the burro for him while he stacked his sticks one by one, then holding the near side while he stacked the off side. We held the bundles and tied them and balanced the sides, then stacked the center and bound the load with a diamond hitch. The old burro never moved, even though a mean dog that belonged there kept growling and prowling around me.

The next day I went to the field again and David came in. Ken the pilot and Rambo were with him. I told them about the Federal officer demanding to see my papers and of my having to convince him I was a Mexican with Adán's recommendation. Rambo gave me all his provision and got back aboard the plane. David said, "Well, they are probably watching the field so we better get the hell out of here."

Rambo said, "He probably wanted your gold."

I said, "I couldn't show him any of that nor explain my presence on the river. How could I explain a Rambo with no passport?"

Así le hice el quite. Y Adán dijo, "Aunque era la primera vez que hagas una cosa de esas, siempre la hiciste bien." Porque, todo era invento mio.

We packed up all the provision and carried it to camp and started bringing it out of the boxes. We had enough meat and vegetables for two weeks, a treat that brought a happy yell out of me. I also found a bottle of nose drops to which I was addicted, and were brought out of pure thoughtfulness by Rambo, and enough other provision to keep me a month. I gave a bottle of Rambo's good vitamins to Guillermo for the daughter who was always fainting. Rambo had brought a lot of candy, apples, oranges and salted peanuts, and that went for Adán's kids and Guillermo's grandkids. I looked again and found canned chicken, ham, bacon and sardines. I felt like a pirate unpacking the spoils. No matter what happened after that I vowed Rambo would have his share, even if I had to give up mine. I was that grateful for his provision.

The next day I gave Guillermo twenty dollars to help Oscar's trip to Cuchibampo and I gave him a letter of recommendation to Poncho and Manuelito Velderrain in San Bernardo. Guillermo said he would kill me a camp goat. Then the young Moreno they call El Molacho, the Toothless One, came into camp with Caporal the dog. He talked the same way as his brothers, mumbling quietly, a quiet, shy mumbling.

We worked a full six days. Little by little I cleaned a wide swath on the bedrock. The work was slow and required careful watchfulness for a cold, uncomfortable time underwater with my head down and my feet in the air, so to speak. The gold was now more abundant and coarser every day, though I did not feel I was getting rich. I was glad to rest Sunday, the twentieth of April. I had worked hard.

For some reason I never realized how much gold was accumulating in the jars. I had a quart Nescafé jar and Tío's medicine bottle of about a pint full by then and was starting on a gallon jar. After the gold was in a jar no one ever saw it again. The trifle of black sand that was left over with the fine gold at the bottom of the batea each time the gold was transferred to the jar always hid the gold completely. All anyone could ever see in the jar was black sand.

On Sunday four very small boys from Mulatos came by on their way to meet their mother. She was coming from Rancho la Soledad. The pert little boys chattered along every step as they made their way past my camp. About three hours later they came back chattering and pointing out my camp to their mother while I was having supper. I wondered how many American boys spent their Sundays walking ten or fifteen miles to meet their mother and escort her home.

A while later, the two Panchos from the Victor mine came by horseback drunk, shooting off their pistols. The next day Adán told me that he was in Mulatos when they arrived at the poolhall. They were still acting wild and one of the Panchos hid the other's pistol. The disarmed Pancho got mad and then Pancho the disarmer got mad and went for his pistol. Adán held the disarmer Pancho's pistol hand down in the pocket so he could not draw the pistol. When the disarmer calmed down, Adán let him go. The disarmer Pancho vomited the mescal, started crying, and rode home with the other Pancho.

Old Tomás came by that Sunday, too. I asked him to eat supper with me and to my surprise he said no. He said, *"Me hacen mucho las acedías. Ay, como sufro con las acedías. Me están dando las acedías. No puedo comer chicharrones por eso de las acedías.* I am much done by the acids. Ay, how I suffer from the acids. The acids are happening to me. I can never eat pig chitlins because of that which is the trouble of the acid stomachs."

For a week I tried to stay underwater all my waking days. I moved a lot of overburden, but the bedrock was straight up and down and could not hold gold. Even so, one day I surfaced to see Adán smiling. He said, "I lost my gold front tooth in Mulatos and here it turns up in El Desengaño." He took a piece of gold the size of a front tooth out of his mouth, a nugget weighing about half a gram, smooth and polished on one side and rough on the other.

I had been away from home six weeks. Now the gold I started saving in the first days that had looked so big, looked small. Every day the stuff I found was coarser and a new big one appeared. I calculated I had two ounces but that was very optimistic. I hoped by the time my money ran out I would be able to clean the very bottom of El Desengaño. I did not want to have to show any gold to sell around Mulatos.

On a Friday Adán and Guillermo took off work to go to El Salto to carry one of Guillermo's married daughters back to the airstrip for the route plane. She was to be taken to a doctor. I did some repairs, then dove to roll away a big white overbearing rock that had been lying in my way like an overfed pig all week. I rolled it all the way out of El Desengaño and its wake clouded the hole so bad I had to quit work.

I came out and walked to shore and a small sorrel being came up right behind me, chirping at me. He was an otter. He came out scolding me. Coward that I was, I decided there was not room enough in El Desengaño, my *queréncia,* my place, for us both. I went to the tent and got old Meat in the Pot. The little feller saw the look on my face and ran along the bank and hid in a hole where Guillermo had been panning. He didn't like that place, so he ran along the shore to a pile of rocks I had cleaned out of the bottom of the pool.

That was no hiding place. Old Meat in the Pot launched unto him his death and I immediately regretted, as always, being the agent of a firearm. That pistol always did irrevocably what she was ordered to do and I had ordered the otter hit in the head.

The otter lay on the pile of rocks with his perfect limbs twitching. In all the long months I had spent at El Desengaño I had never seen him, then his terrible luck made him present himself to me.

He was bleeding in my water so I picked him up. The blood disappeared in the water where I worked. He might have become my friend if I had thought of anything but a pistol when he came out to scold me. I felt terrible for being so selfish about the hole, and at the same time I wanted his hide. Daniel walked into camp and helped me skin him down to his webbed paws. We stretched his

hide on *amamote* wands, salted it and put it on the roof of the
ramada so it would not go to waste.

I realized I killed him only because I was jealous of the hole. I was
getting so greedy for that damned hole I killed an innocent to keep
it. I had even thought of ridding myself of old Rambo any way I
could, only I wouldn't have skinned Rambo. I had entertained
thoughts of tying rocks to his feet and hands and sending him to the
bottom of another deep hole.

Everybody else who tried to take a stand in my hole was a son of a
bitch and I could not even act human when they tried to give me
something. I should have felt privileged the otter came out and
scolded me that way. He might have been good company for me.
Now I had the sonofabitching hole all to myself again. What could
he have stolen from me? Could he have made me more poverty-
stricken than I already was? He had shown me exactly how poor a
man I was. He threatened to steal space in my hole? I stole his life
for that?

Alone in camp, my heart came apart with remorse. The otter had
probably swum by me a lot of times during the many days I spent
scratching the bedrock for gold. Since I never harmed him, he
might have thought I was a good feller. When he came out of the
hole after me he might even have been asking me to help him find
his way home. When he saw the kind of man I really was, he tried to
hurry away and not bother me. Imagine him believing any human
would understand the plight of an adolescent otter. Once he
showed himself to me he was lost. I quickly and efficiently, with
superior mind and mechanism, disturbed by him, killed him before
he could get away.

Then Juan Roldán came and visited awhile. I broke the last of the
bottles of Old Crow whiskey while swatting a fly. Then, to finish the
day in the same sorry fashion, went to bed drunk.

Part VII

On Sunday Don Toríbio came by with a new batea for Adán and sat
and visited awhile. Adán came with two armloads of chino bark for
tanning his bull hides in the tinajas beside El Desengaño. He could
not stay because Oscar had gone crazy with pain and he wanted to
help carry him to Mulatos. Adán's compadre Memo we now called
El Federal came by with Daniél Rey. We visited in good humor and

I chided him about his trying to arrest me last year and he got so embarrassed he stuttered.

The next day I left the river. Adán walked me to the strip to wait for the route plane. We met Guillermo on the way and said goodbye. When the plane came in I talked Ramón the route pilot into taking me straight to David's. He left me there and I caught David's ore truck going to the mill, met David and he took me home with him. Licha immediately fed me and David gave me a drink of Bacanora and showed me around the ranch again.

On the third day David flew Licha to Yecora and me to Sahuaripa. The taxi took us into town and David wandered down the street looking for the judge and resembled an old turkey gobbler. The route plane came in, the taxi came down the street honking for me and I got in. The *taxista* also loaded a little man and his wife and two boys. The wife was terrified about going to Hermosillo on the plane. She boarded and put her head down between her arms, braced them stiffly against the back of my seat and kept her eyes closed all the way to Hermosillo. "Ay!" she would say with each little bump of air.

In Hermosillo I caught a cab to the bus station and learned the schedule, then started walking toward the Merendero Colores to eat meat. Mike my old friend the German drove by and saw me, turned around in the middle of the street and gave me a ride to the restaurant. He said, when he first saw me, before he recognized me, he thought I was the biggest vaquero he'd ever seen. I ate meat and *tripitas de leche,* broiled marrow gut, and drank beer, then went back to the station and boarded the bus.

The bus stopped on the edge of town for gas and I got off to go to the head. While I was inside another identical bus pulled up and hid my bus. I, the dunce, boarded the new, southbound bus. A little old man was in my seat. I turned to find another place and the little man looked up at me and said, "Where do you think you're going?" And I said, "To find a seat, I thought the one you're in was it, but that's all right, I'll sit anywhere, *no hay cuidado,* no problem."

He said, "Young man. I don't know what bus you think you are on, but this is not it." I looked out the window and saw my bus. The women in the wrong bus started laughing and I got out and went back to my own bus and heard a woman on my bus say, "I wonder why the women in that bus are laughing?"

I rode to Nogales, crossed the line and went to the Montezuma

Hotel bar for a drink, then went back to the barbershop on the
Sonora side for a shave and mustache trim. When I saw myself in the
mirror for the first time in weeks I was as lean and dark from the sun
and the river as the heart of mesquite.

I went into the Cavern to start my rounds and ran into Gene
Sykes. We ran and played all day and all that night. Along in the
early morning I woke up at the bar in the Cavernita and some
bastard had stolen my 7X hat. I made a grab for the bartender when
his answer did not satisfy me and he "rajared," looked for a higher
authority to settle it, called the police.

I explained to the police what happened and they offered to jail
me. Sykes took me to the station to complain. I could take anything, except somebody fooling with my hat. A man's hat is invio-
late, especially if it is a 7X and a gift. On the way we ran into the *jefe
de transito*, the chief of traffic police. Gene told him about the deal
the Cavernita gave us and he told us to wait for him at Cerezo's
International Club. After a while the same cops from the Cavernita
who had offered me their jail brought me my hat.

Pauline came to the International Club for us early and took me
to the El Dorado. I was roaring and sleepless and sat down with
John Maher in the coffee shop. After a while he asked me how I was
doing on the river and I said, "Not one dollar, yet," and started to
bawl. I hired a room in the Coronado and slept. In the afternoon I
showered and put my torn shirt back on. I went back to the El
Dorado and threw in with Jimmy Garrett and soon we were both
roaring down the same old road again.

We went back to the Coronado holding each other up and there
was my sister and mom. I had not seen my sis in ten years. So right
then I straightened up and talked with them way into the night and
next morning I woke them up at six-thirty.

I walked out of the room while they were dressing and ran into
Bob Lockett and we sat down for a long talk. His wife Lois came to
the lobby about the same time Mom and Sharon did and we all
went for breakfast. Bob said to my mother about me, *"Es muy
hombre,"* and Mom said, "Yes, he can do anything he wants to do."

I thought, yes, he can, as long as he can get over his innate and
also natural handicaps and is willing to work longer than a mule
with a Fresno in a boghole.

We met with my *nina* Natalia Shane and went to see my Granny
Sorrells. She was in the hospital with a broken arm. She had broken

it at home and set it herself before driving herself to the hospital. I squired my mother, sister and *nina,* godmother, across the line and met Yvonne Shane Ruiz at the Cavern for lunch with the mariachis and now I had "cumplired," satisfied almost all my decent acts and respectable duties for ten years to come. I checked out of the hotel and drove to Phoenix with Mom and Sharon to meet my thenwife. My thenwife and I checked in at the Adams Hotel, the thenhaven of Arizona cowpunchers and deep, soft, shady places.

I told her about the otter and realized the otter and Rambo had represented almost the same threat to me, all 6'2" and 190 pounds of me, and knew how crazy El Desengaño had made me. The next day I put Sharon on the plane for Chico and she bawled.

When we got home to Pinetop I called Rambo and changed all the ugliness I had entertained when I was acting like a lunatic at El Desengaño. Then I thanked the otter for waking me up and that finally put an end to it.

With rest and good food I began to feel better, though I wasn't ready to go back to El Desengaño. I talked to Bill Decker my editor at the Dial Press and he said my book *Jim Kane* was great and he read the catalogue blurb to me. My condition improved some more.

Then one afternoon Bill called again and invited me to come all expenses paid to New York for a sales conference. I walked in a daze down the hill to my thenwife's shop to tell her and she started bawling with happiness, so we decided she would go too.

That night her mom put up twelve hundred dollars so she could go. The next day we went to Holbrook to buy me a new pair of drinking boots because I left my best pair in the Sierra. Everyone acted genuinely happy, even the ones who knew I was no god-dammed good and looked like they'd been slapped in the face when they heard the news. The most notable of these was the doctor who quit me three days into a trip to the Sierra one time because the Sierra turned out not to be a sanitary or sane enough place to suit him. He could not stand his look into the face of the Mother Mountains, even though the .357 magnum he carried was big and heavy on his hip. He took exception when I told him the only trouble with him was that he was seeing his mother, meaning the Sierra Madre, the Mother Mountains. He took it as a Freudian insult and demanded to be carried back to town.

On Mother's Day I called my mom at Sharon's house in Chico and told her the news. That made points for Sharon because her

mother-in-law Omah was there at a brunch she was giving. Omah
was always searching for respectability in Sharon's family.

Monday I had to go to Phoenix to buy clothes with my thenwife.
Tuesday we drank a few at the airport with a sailor, then caught the
plane to New York. Arrived in the dark. The people were not all
over ten feet tall like the buildings. The cabbie was Nathan Fried
and carried us agreeably to the Commodore. While we were regis-
tering a tall black man with a turned-down hat came in with a short
sport in a light blue suit, light blue tie, dark blue shirt, pearl blue hat
with wide band turned down over the ear, wearing powder that
made his face look blue under penciled eyebrows and eye makeup of
blue, too.

The room in the Commodore was a threadbare hole inside
twenty-one stories but to me was a palace in the sky up twenty-one
whole stories. The big paned windows started at the floor so if I got
drunk and stumbled I'd go right through the window with nothing
to grab but glass. Standing at the commode, I saw the water slosh-
ing back and forth and decided New Yorkers who lived in places
over twenty stories high must develop a strange kind of aim. We
went out to a small Irish bar to eat and drink, then to an English
pub where the drinks were so nice. I called my friend Salvatore
Fiorella at 2:30 A.M. He was my roommate at Notre Dame and now
that he was back in New York trying to go back to sleep I bet he
could not believe he had ever even known a Joe Brown.

We called room service the next morning for breakfast and ordered steak and eggs. A female Hun answered and said, "Vat iss
thiss shtek? Ve heff not shteck in the morgn. In the morgn bekn. In
the morgn hemm. Shtek in the noon. Shtek in the efeng."

We went down to the hotel's dining room for breakfast and
talked Spanish with the Puerto Rican waiter and the Cuban busboy.
We had hell catching a taxi so when we got to the meeting at the
Harvard Club we were embarrassingly late, but Bill met us at the
door so we could get in.

Another author got up in front of everybody and said, "Little
Louie has a piece of rope." I'm almost sure that is what he said.

I listened to the editors and authors tell about the books they
would put on sale. Bill made the presentation of *Jim Kane* and I
had to get up and talk. I said, "A week ago at this time of day I was
in the bottom of the Mulatos River in the Sierra Madre of the west
in Mexico." I told them what placer gold looked like when it was

uncovered and streaming into the nozzle of the sucker down in the clear sunny water, but not one dollar, yet, lots of hopes, though.

I said I was a cowpuncher, but had been a whiskey smuggler and didn't like scotch since then, told about my last fight in the ring boxing ten rounds with a broken hand at thirty-four, and how long a time that was to think . . . writing was the last thing I tried. An American in Mexico has to try a lot of ways, any talent he might have to get along, and writing was the last kind of work I tried. Now I was stuck on it, or it had me, because I would always be trying to get it right. I told about cowboying in Nevada, about mechanics on motorcycles with little leather caps and goggles trying to move cattle, and about having to explain to the Hollywood owner what a husbandman was. His Hollywood culture would prefer cowboys that became extinct, more drama that way, and it would keep cowboys out of sight while better ways were implemented. I told about having to go back to the Sierra for my six-shooter that had been my father's and grandfather's, but I was not sure I had any better reason, was not sure that was even a good reason.

The people seemed to like it and understand what I was trying to tell them. After the girl author of the child's book convinced everyone about the truth of her book, the meeting was over. Various men came up and shook my hand and the women shook my thenwife's hand and seemed to like it when I thought I'd blown it. My thenwife said, "I was so proud of you I don't care what you do the rest of the trip."

We walked down with Bob Cornfield, Miss Donna Shrader the Dial's publicist, and Bill to the Algonquin where they told what Miss Bacall said to somebody who was bothering her and everybody was very literate and sophisticated and we would be part of it for a little while. Bill said he was going to float out of there on martinis he was that glad to be through with the sales conference. I drank about ten gin and tonics and they disappeared like one drop of sweat in hell.

We ate a lunch of clams, then went down to the office of the Dial Press. I showed them the new outline of *The Outfit* and talked all afternoon about *Jim Kane,* met everybody, then got on the subway with Bill. A gimlet-eyed son of a bitch stood with his nose on my shoulder and stared at my ear the whole forty-five minutes on the subway. About the time we reached the wire of the finish line at

Brooklyn Heights where Bill lived I was ready to have a runaway. It was a dead heat between me and gimlet eyes right until we stepped away from the car.

My thenwife and I and Bill walked to his house and met his wife Ann who was shiny and smart and looked to be the best kind of New York dame through and through. She was on her way to the opera and out she went. Bill started pouring bourbon and water and talked about when he cowboyed and I could see he really did cowboy. We ate steaks about eleven and then Ann came home and we took off in a cab to the Commodore, getting to bed the second night about three-thirty.

The next day, Thursday, thenwife and I ate broiled beef at Dawson's English Pub, very good with Guinness and ale, and then she went to see her publisher and I went up to Dial in the Schrafft Building. I'd been led up to the office full of gin and tonics the day before, so I did not know the way too well. I stopped at the directory by the elevator, searching for the way. A curly-headed man with a ferocious mustache whisked by me, grinned big and said, "Go get 'em, cowboy," and made me feel welcome in that place. I liked the way he looked me in the eye and the electricity with which he livened that mostly inhospitable place.

When I got up to the Dial office I saw his picture on the jacket of a Delacorte book. He was Kurt Vonnegut. I sat and talked with Bill all afternoon. We went to the Harvard Club banquet room at five for the sales representatives' cocktail party and met a lot more people from the Dials.

Everybody was just naturally nice and handled well the unlimited splashings of cocktails that disappeared inside them. An old man from Canada had to know all about how I started writing and that made me feel a lot more important than I'd felt on the Mulatos River. On the Mulatos River nobody wanted to know how writers got started or what it was like to be nice with cocktails.

By six thenwife was still not there, so I went downstairs and waited by the door. After a while the doorman came up to me with his white hair, redcoated uniform, white grenadier's mustache bristling, and said, "Young man, are you a member?"

"No, sir, I'm waiting for my wife."

"Why in here?"

"Because she'll be afraid to come up to the party by herself, have a runaway, and I'll never find her in this town."

"Are you one of the authors of the Dial party?"

"Yes, sir."

"Go right up, then. The party is for you. I'll make sure your wife finds you."

Right then the lady appeared, so we went back up together. Bill asked if Louie of "Louie has a piece of rope" could wear my hat and I said yes, so Louie pranced around for a while under my hat. When the party was over I was dead level full of cocktails and laid back on the banister and spurred it all the way to the ground floor without falling off. Then, sedately, respectfully walking along the edge of the room where all the distinguished fellers were sitting in chairs by themselves contemplating and smoking quietly, I slipped on the wax and took my thenwife to the floor with me like falling timber takes bark. She said, "I bet that's the first time anyone took a spill in the Harvard Club."

Bill said, "Oliver Wendell Holmes did once."

We went down to a lobster place and after a while Salvatore Fiorella came in wearing a dark suit, dark shirt, red tie, and his hair combed down over his forehead. Otherwise he was the same as ever. We laughed a lot with awful good lobster and clams. Walking down the street Sal struggled and kicked to get away while I laughed and carried him under one arm. Bill and the wives came along laughing.

Bill said, "I hope the New York cops will understand cowboy exuberance."

The next morning I closed up the bathroom and got it to steaming while thenwife ordered breakfast. But first she had to order steak and eggs from the Hun again just so she could hear her say, "Shtek? Ve dun't heff shtek in the morgn. Ve heff shtek in the efeng. In the morgn eks. In the morgn bekn. In the morgn no shtek."

Thenwife went on to her appointment at Doubleday. I went down to have my new boots shined by the Italians in the basement, then into the stand-up bar of the Commodore for two tequilas to start the day.

The Dials were still nice and men were painting their walls. All the desks were covered with sheets and the books stacked up, the girls in jeans except Miss Donna. I glommed Bob Cornfield and took him down to the Schrafft Bar for tequila and he read parts of the *Jim Kane* galleys and enjoyed them, then left for a lunch date. I read parts of *Jim Kane* too and couldn't believe how much better it was in print, or that I wrote it.

Miss Donna and Bill came down and visited and after a while Bob Cornfield came back with a nice lady and invited me to lunch. We lunched on a balcony and I threatened to spit off it, because isn't that what balconys are for?

I was getting so wild I felt obligated to calm down, be a gentleman, and even paid for the lunch. Went back to Schrafft's again and Donna and Bill joined me and I looked up and there was my lovely thenwife with a brand-new copy of a biography of Ernest Hemingway as a present for me. By then I was roaring and we took a cab back to the Commodore. Thenwife was disgusted with me, so I went to bed. After a while she awakened me and I was rummy as hell. She stared at me bug-eyed like an old cow on the prod because we had eleven-dollar tickets to *Man of La Mancha* and Bill had told her I would never make it.

Thenwife said, "By God, we ain't going with you drunk and if you don't straighten up I'm going home and maybe, by God, I'll divorce you."

So I had to straighten up. I took a sweat bath and put on my suit of clothes and went downstairs in good shape, but it took an hour and a half to catch a cab and another hour of wandering to find the theater. We were an hour late for the show. I was disappointed because Sancho the great Everyman was packing sixty pounds of baby fat, had a New York accent, 1970s big-city mannerisms, and that was all supposed to be funny. After the show thenwife acted funny and looked at me like she wanted to hook me over the fence and out of her life. I ate two steaks in the Irish bar and went to bed.

Thenwife allowed me two gin and tonics Saturday noon and we met her cousin Marian and Marian's husband Bob Martin at the Brasserie. They were stouthearted and gentle. Bob was quiet and a gentleman and Marian beautiful and a lady. We had more gin and tonics and then walked to Rockefeller Center for more drinks in the bar on the plaza. When a young French headwaiter said I must be from Texas I said you must be from France.

We were there two hours and Marian suggested the Caliban, maybe so I'd feel more at home. That was a swell place with fine German bock beer and high, old-fashioned ceilings. We discussed Cassius Clay and Norman Mailer with an English teacher who wanted to write named Tom Boyle and a young black teacher down to earth named Charley Afternoon. Marian got tight, but with a quiet show of great, gentle character.

THE MULATOS RIVER JOURNAL

About seven Sal came to take thenwife and I to dinner. He accompanied himself with a gal who was put together so carefully I was afraid she would start falling apart any minute beginning with the eyelashes. Thenwife asked her what she did for a living. In answer she turned up her nose and turned her profile for us and said, "I'm a model." As if to say, "Can't you tell?" I laughed like hell and the rest of the night she gave me and Sal dazzling smiles and ignored thenwife.

At Le Boeuf, a supposed French restaurant, at first they did not want to let me in because I was wearing a suede jacket Western style, but they finally relented down their bony noses. Later I got even by telling the same headwaiter to keep his goddam hands off my potato. He was about as French as I was Puerto Rican because he sarcastically said, *"Perdón, perdón,"* in Spanish.

Seated at our table were other guests of Salvatore Fiorella. Sal was really putting on the dog for his model, whose name was never given. The guests were a young feller who, when thenwife asked what he did, said he had gone to a school where Sal was known. He was mine and Sal's age and that's what he'd done. I looked at him closely then and I swear he must have worn a size 44 jacket and a number 6 hat. Sal asked him to order the wine and thenwife asked him if he was a connoisseur. He told her he always bought the wine that cost the most. He always chose the fourteen-dollar bottle over the ten-dollar bottle. He didn't really know wine, but French had the status.

Size 6 hat, 44 jacket was accompanied by someone thenwife said had been an airline hostess. I never got to say a word to her myself. She had been married to sizes 6 and 44 a month and didn't speak to him or to anyone else all night except Miss Might Fall Apart Any Minute. We enjoyed all this lack of communication even though the table around which the six of us were sitting was only a little bigger around than my hat.

I was leaning toward Sal talking and the waiter came by and set my salad by my elbow and said, "Sir." I turned to him and knocked the salad onto the floor with my elbow. I apologized, but he got huffy so I got good and mad finally and cussed him out, but just to him quietly in Spanish. He went away and when he came back he was swollen twice his size and went about shoving everybody and everything aside while he picked up a few little old green leaves.

There couldn't have been over a nickel's worth of salad in the portion allowed, anyway.

I then asked him quietly and as seriously as I could, so that his face went white, to sing, or dance, smile, or deflate and act happy in some way, or I was going to carry him out and flush him down the toilet.

By this time Sal had turned his back on me, but that was O.K. because thenwife was happy and finally enjoying herself again. After supper I talked Sal into taking us to Greenwich Village and when we got in the cab and started out I went to sleep, so he turned the cab around and deposited us at the Commodore.

Me and thenwife got out of town early and went to the airport for breakfast. We enjoyed each other on our flight home, laughing a lot over the good time we had. We flew right square over Pinetop and saw our house. We registered at the Adams in Phoenix, met Mom for drinks and took her to see *Sweet Charity,* then slept late the next day.

At lunch Mom gave me a quiet bawling out about drinking too much and saying bad words when drunk and I realized I sure deserved it. Thenwife and I were glad to get home. Everything was fine with the kids, too. This was Monday and I rested the remainder of the week.

Part VIII

I left home again at 3 A.M. the next Friday and met Rambo and his dad in Nogales. We drove all the way to Sahuaripa that day and slept in the hotel. We arrived at Mulatos the next day at dark. Emeterio and the old son of a bitch who denied me the use of a mule that day last year in the hot sun at the viejas' corral came out to snoop around Rambo's truck. Exactly one week ago my thenwife and I had enjoyed our fine time in the French restaurant.

Adán's face was flushed, his eyes bright, when he welcomed us and took us to his house. Rambo drove the four-wheel drive pickup off the road with the wheels on one side rolling along a *trinchera,* rock wall. I think the Chevrolets would have given a lot to see their thing walk up a bank along a wall of loose river rock like that.

Lucrecia gave us supper and I told the Martínizes about New York and gave them their presents. New York was pale in the telling because I could see they could not picture the canyons of buildings, crowds, machines and noise. They could not understand the language and terms I used to describe the place the way I wouldn't understand a geologist's language of the landscape on Mars.

In the morning the whole town turned out to watch us pack for the river. Rambo took a picture of Adán and his family and Indio Adán's brother said, *"Para que se ríen despues.* So they can have a laugh later." I said, *"No crees que son así.* Don't believe these people are like that."

I tied on my bandana under my hat and walked with Rambo as he took pictures of the white buildings at sunup under the dark old shake roofs. The community was enclosed by the purple blue mountains looming in the sky overhead. The abodes were in a small cluster on shelves tiered on the mountainside. The buildings seemed to have become more a part of the mountain than of the people's community. Rambo took some good pictures from the high trail, the only foot exit from the town.

Then we made the gradual, winding descent down the trail to the bottom of the arroyo. I enjoyed sweating with the morning walk again. We stopped at Don Toríbio's and kidded the women about how lazy he was. We had a drink of mescal at Adán's ranch and went on.

When I saw Don Toríbio washing new leather in the river where I bathed last year I let Adán and Rambo go on and went down to talk to him. Two of his sons were helping him wash and scrape hides. The wet hides were so clear and transparent the sun shone through them. The brown feet of the men were sure foundations in the fast, ankle-deep water, their soles washed and rewashed until the tough skin was transparent like the hides. They draped the hides over lean-to poles and scraped them with knives that were tarnished black with the work.

Toríbio's dark, mesquite-heart, leather face was glad to see me. He said, "I couldn't tell it was you, but Manuel my son said it was you." He had just splashed his face to cool the sweat off and the reflection of the sun on the river was glisten-drying it quickly. I paid him for the batea he'd made for Adán and talked awhile and went on.

Adán and the Rambos waited for me at the first crossing. Oscar and his wife and baby had come down with Oscar's father and others to greet us, so we stayed to talk. When we were back on the trail, Adán moved up close and told me Guillermo had been plan-

ning, threatening, to charge me for the food he bought for himself
after mine ran out. He also wanted to charge for the nights he spent
guarding the camp. He had fallen into the habit of remarking, *"Que
hombre tan jodido.* What a screwed-up man," when referring to me,
because I had not returned to the Sierra quick enough to suit him.

Adán said that Guillermo showed the rifle and the pistol to everyone who visited him and told them he was going to take the fire-
arms in payment for wages the gringo owed him. One day Adán hid
the pistol under the tent. He laughed when he told me, "The next
time he started to go through his ritual, he skulked around the tent
for the pistol, straightened, skulked some more, but did not find it.
He returned to the visitor with a long, serious face, but said no
more about the pistol, or the rifle."

Guillermo told Adán that I had given him Rambo's tennis shoes.
When Rambo returned to work and started using the shoes again,
Guillermo told Adán, "Eh, I guess now Joe's going to *rajar,* go
back on his word, about the tennis shoes, because *falta que ni son de
el,* they probably aren't even his to give away."

Guillermo also told everyone that I was making a fool of myself,
sacrificing myself for nothing, because I would never find any gold
in that place. I figured he did me a good turn by saying that, because I didn't want anyone to know the kind of gold we were finding. Later, one day before Rambo left, Guillermo panned good
color off the sluice and remarked that it was *"muy buen asiento,"*
and showed us a good, heavy settlement of gold in the bottom of
his batea.

When I reached the camp and after we had visited awhile, I paid
Guillermo what I owed him to the last dime. He did not say anything about me owing him more, but for the next two days he
would not look me in the eye and I swear his nose seemed to grow
longer. He would come to camp and squat away by himself and
stare at me like a hungry dog. Finally one morning he came closer,
squatted under the ramada and said, "How are you going to settle
that which is *pendiente,* pending?"

"What is *pendiente?"*

"You still owe me for the food I had to buy after yours ran out
when you were gone."

"I did not have an obligation to furnish your food."

"You said twenty pesos and my food when I came to work."

"No, señor. I said twenty pesos a day, the same as I have been paying you for panning. I have done you a favor when I invited you to eat here with me. Tell me of anyone in this region who would pay you twenty pesos and your food. The wages common to this region are fifteen and food and only one meal is provided. Here you have often eaten three meals a day, an amount that equaled your salary. I have no obligation to feed you."

"That is what Adán said, but I thought you told me you would furnish food. I think you told me, but now you don't remember, and are mistakenly refusing to pay."

"No, señor. I'm not mistaken. You are mistaken."

"I am mistaken then, but not mistaken about the other."

"What other? What else?"

"You need to pay me extra for the nights I spent here alone."

"No, I do not."

"How not? I had no obligation to stay here at night."

"When I left I told you that your salary would continue while I was gone. I said that you and Adán could take turns watching the camp. You could be on a day and a night and off a day and a night. Remember that?"

"Yes, but you didn't come back. I did not think you were coming back."

"I paid you for each shift that you stayed in camp, did I not?"

"Yes, if you put it that way."

"You didn't expect me to pay you for the time you were at home, did you?"

"No."

"Then I don't owe you for anything."

"I guess I am mistaken, then."

"I guess you are."

All that day I caught him staring at me out of his yellow eyes, half worship, half hate, predatory. He was like an old coyote watching a fat bull, loving the abundance of meat, longing to be big enough to make the kill, knowing that waiting was his only, though very slim, chance.

I could imagine what he was thinking. What if by the greatest good fortune the bull should lie down and bare his throat to the coyote's teeth? No, that would not be good enough, the monster might wake up with the first bite. But what if he had a seizure, or fainted, drowned in El Desengaño, or got drunk and passed out? But no, the hot day went by and nothing happened to incapacitate me, so he picked up his batea, came to the ramada and said, "I guess I won't be able to come tomorrow."

"Why not? Do you have something else to do?"

"No, but you say I have to provide my own meals. I'm all by myself at the house right now and have no one to prepare them for me."

"I didn't say you had to provide your own meals. Have you ever brought meals before?"

"No. But you said you weren't going to furnish my meals."

"No, I did not. I'm not that way, Guillermo. You can eat here anytime we eat, anytime we have food. I just said I had no obligation to provide food."

"Then, shall I come tomorrow?"

"Do as you like."

"Then, until tomorrow." He left.

Later he told Adán he couldn't understand me. "The gringo says one thing and means another."

When he had been talking about how he was going to pay himself his salary he said, *"Como el gringo no viene, ya ves como son. Dejan a uno prendido y no vienen.* Since the gringo doesn't come, now you can see how gringos are. They leave a man stuck to his job and don't come. I say let's fold up the camp, put the gear under lock and key and hold it for our wages."

Adán told him, "If you want to quit I'll sell a heifer and pay you so you can quit."

Through the week that Rambo and his dad helped me Guillermo loafed around and slept while everyone else worked, but watched me and our fresh provision with his yellow look. Rambo had brought a carton of Hershey bars. He and I ate one apiece and Guillermo ate about five or six. My son Billy got out of school and came down to help me and ate what was left. Guillermo complained to Adán that Billy ate too much and there was the proof, he ate all the chocolate.

Rambo was not bothered much about the chocolate. His pet treats were the salted peanuts and dried fruit. I was bothered even less, mine was the soyate. As soon as Guillermo discovered the peanuts and dried fruit he made such a dent in them that Rambo hid what was left down in his duffel bag. The last night before he went home he ate half the peanuts and some of the fruit and went to bed.

The next morning David was bringing my son to the river and

taking Rambo home. I took Rambo to the strip and when Billy and I got back to camp Guillermo had finished off the peanuts and fruit plus the remaining half of a canned ham. *"Lo poco que quedaba me lo comi yo.* I ate the small amount that was left," he said.

Rambo and I were able to work El Desengaño ten days. Before I went to New York I had put off a lot of the heavy cleaning that needed to be done, so Rambo and I spent a lot of time moving big rock and overburden. At first, every time he came up out of the water he'd say, "I don't know, Joe." And then make a complaint about the hole. Finally, so as not to get all obsessed again with El Desengaño, or at least not to let it show, I said, "Let's prospect for a new hole, then."

He had been taking every spare moment to go downriver and look for new prospects anyway. So one day he and Adán and Guillermo took the little goldsucker downriver and worked all day. The next day he went back and worked some more and at noon said he had found good color.

That evening he and I went down and tried to work, but the natural riffles in the rock he found were too washed to hold much gold except down on the bottom underneath boulders that we could not move. The next two days we spent cleaning out a crack that washed clean every year, and nothing. So we proved two facts about the river that I had already learned. Where the bottom will hold gold we would likely be forced to contend with monstrous boulders and where the bottom was readily accessible it was washed too much with fast water to hold gold.

We went back to El Desengaño and worked the next four days and every day Rambo would come up with an "I don't know, Joe," even though we were getting better color every hour. Then one day Rambo worked under the big rock on the south side of the pool and after a while he came out and he didn't say, "I don't know, Joe." Guillermo and Adán panned everything on the sluice and got three times more than ever before. After that Rambo had the fever and acted as though he had discovered gold in El Desengaño. He kept saying to me there was no need to try to go on down to find the bottom now, it would only be necessary to clean out under the big rock.

I kept wondering why he always stuck to the same theme and that is, don't keep trying for the bottom, it might not be there. I always said, keep driving for the bottom, it had to be down there thicker than anyone could imagine. We found gold everywhere along the bedrock near the surface, so the bottom must be paved with gold.

Adán was to be gone a few days to move his family down to the ranch from Mulatos. During that time I showed Billy how to use the air buoy and work the venturi sucker and he started helping me. We worked straight down the middle of El Desengaño and the day before Adán was to come back we uncovered three big red rocks that surrounded a square yard of hardpacked stucco on the bedrock. These rocks served to shore the hole on all sides, but completely barricaded the bottom, except for the yard of stucco in the middle.

I surfaced at dark and decided to wait until Adán came in the morning to help me before I started sluicing out that level yard on the bedrock. The stucco was the stuff of placer gold and I was sure it would be rich.

That night I lay in bed and thought about it all. The rains would come soon. I was not sure I would be able to get past those boulders and follow the bedrock any farther down. If I could not go any farther, I still had been favored by God in this work. If I did not go home with a lot of gold, I could say I had enjoyed the best values of the endeavor. They were the warm days and the hours of cramped, cold self-denial; the fine alert sleeps on the hard bed; the sun on the body, meager food, the indulgences of mescal, when they were small; bare feet over hot rocks and sand before the blessed cool in the deep, sunshiny water; the San Nicolás Mountain and all the country in the Sierra's purple haze; the walks on the hot track with the clean sweat on my back; the traffic on the Camino Real by the river.

I would be taking out the friendship of Juan Roldán, who cooked maguey last week, took it on his burro to Mulatos riding his brown stud, wearing his one spur on his completely unsewn *tegua,* and came back drunk singing at the top of his voice. I would remember the friendly company of the Rey brothers, who came to take the hides out of the silo in the boulder on the south side of El Desengaño and awakened my son and I with the stench. I would always admire the dignity, honor and great heart in Adán Martínez and the complete and dignified untrustworthiness of Guillermo.

I would remember the hen that Adán brought me once when I had been alone and out of meat two weeks. I fed and watered her and left her tied by one leg in the shade of a rock. I went to kill her that evening and she sang to me and raised up and showed me the egg she had laid and kept singing to me while I examined it and picked it up. I spared her ten days and she gave me ten eggs. I did not want to believe she would give me another, so I killed her to eat her. I found three or four more eggs in various stages of development inside her and remembered how she sang to me every morning and every evening when we were alone.

We worked with great success for two more weeks before I found that I could not get any farther below the boulders. Every inch of the stucco was gold-bearing. I would come up out of the hole and Adán would show me the bottom of his batea rich with coarse gold. Guillermo's batea never showed the chunky gold that Adán's did.

When I was no longer bringing up a volume that necessitated two panners I took that as an excuse to let Guillermo go, because I did not trust him. I could not do anything else about him. After all, we were on his river.

It rained, the river swelled and we telegraphed David that we were ready to go out. Adán and his family saw us off at the airstrip and cried, but Guillermo did not come. As we lifted off the field I saw Guillermo hurrying downriver toward El Desengaño with his batea and I remembered the hole he always kept under the water between his feet when he was panning, the hole the otter had shown me.

We spent one day at David's ranch. Cucho weighed and evaluated our gold. He said it was the prettiest gold he had ever seen and, discounting the trace of black sand, it weighed 7 kilos 200 grams. At that time it was worth about thirty dollars an ounce. I left it at David's for his and Rambo's contributions to the venture, except for a pinch I kept for a souvenir. I figured on going back next season with a means of blasting the boulders out of my way and reaching the bottom.

I remembered the day I was alone on the river and made the discovery of *pedeoS*. I was sitting under the tepeguaje tree having a bowl of dried soup. Almost all my food and money were gone. Adán was gone to Tarachi after gas. I looked down, and there in the trace of light under a boulder I saw that word *pedeoS* engraved on a slab of bedrock. My heart fell to running as though I had just finished a long race. I stared at the word. Was it a sign someone left there to point to a treasure? How did it translate? Did "ped" mean foot, or walk, or afoot? Did "deos" mean God? Was it Portuguese, or a misspelling of a word that meant "walkwithgod" or

"godwalkedhere" carved there by conquistadors, maybe even
Coronado himself? I crossed the three yards and fell to my knees so
I could look at the engraving closely and saw that *Soapad* upside
down on a cardboard box spelled *pedeoS*.

ABOUT THE AUTHOR

A native of Nogales, Arizona, J. P. S. Brown is a fifth-generation cattleman. He was the middleweight and light heavyweight boxing champion at Notre Dame University in 1951 and 1952.

His first novel was *Jim Kane*, published to critical acclaim in 1965; it became the movie *Pocket Money* with Paul Newman and Lee Marvin in 1971. His second novel, *The Outfit*, is considered a Southwestern classic. In 1974, his third novel, *The Forests of the Night*, was published, and 1986 saw the publication of *Steeldust*. In 1989, Bantam Books began publishing his original series, the Arizona Saga.

The author and his wife, Patsy, currently make their home in Tucson, Arizona.